Al

I put the

surprise,

fell into the foyer.

"Dolce?" I called so as not to startle her into calling the security people. "It's me."

No sound. Nothing. Of course she would be upstairs and not have heard me. Maybe I should just leave the dress and respect her privacy. I gathered up my stuff and took a few steps inside, closing the door behind me. The ridged rubber soles of my slip-ons made no sound as I walked in. That's when I saw her.

It was Vienna. She was lying facedown in the entry to the great room. I knew it was her by the huge pink bow on the back of her dress.

"Vienna," I said, stopping abruptly just a few feet away. "What are you doing here? Are you okay?"

What a dumb thing to say. If she was okay, why was she lying there like that? She was not okay. I knelt down next to her and realized she was not breathing. My heart started hammering. She must have fallen and hurt herself. Badly. I put my hands on her bare shoulders and turned her face to one side. She felt cold. There were ugly red marks on her neck. I stood up and screamed . . .

Berkley Prime Crime titles by Grace Carroll

SHOE DONE IT
DIED WITH A BOW

Died with a Bow

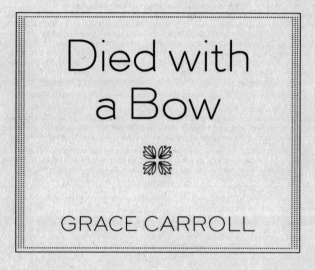

GRACE CARROLL

BERKLEY PRIME CRIME, NEW YORK

THE BERKLEY PUBLISHING GROUP
Published by the Penguin Group
Penguin Group (USA) Inc.
375 Hudson Street, New York, New York 10014, USA

Penguin Group (Canada), 90 Eglinton Avenue East, Suite 700, Toronto, Ontario M4P 2Y3, Canada (a division of Pearson Penguin Canada Inc.) • Penguin Books Ltd., 80 Strand, London WC2R 0RL, England • Penguin Group Ireland, 25 St. Stephen's Green, Dublin 2, Ireland (a division of Penguin Books Ltd.) • Penguin Group (Australia), 250 Camberwell Road, Camberwell, Victoria 3124, Australia (a division of Pearson Australia Group Pty. Ltd.) • Penguin Books India Pvt. Ltd., 11 Community Centre, Panchsheel Park, New Delhi—110 017, India • Penguin Group (NZ), 67 Apollo Drive, Rosedale, Auckland 0632, New Zealand (a division of Pearson New Zealand Ltd.) • Penguin Books (South Africa) (Pty.) Ltd., 24 Sturdee Avenue, Rosebank, Johannesburg 2196, South Africa

Penguin Books Ltd., Registered Offices: 80 Strand, London WC2R 0RL, England

This is a work of fiction. Names, characters, places, and incidents either are the product of the author's imagination or are used fictitiously, and any resemblance to actual persons, living or dead, business establishments, events, or locales is entirely coincidental. The publisher does not have any control over and does not assume any responsibility for author or third-party websites or their content.

PUBLISHER'S NOTE: The recipes contained in this book are to be followed exactly as written. The publisher is not responsible for your specific health or allergy needs that may require medical supervision. The publisher is not responsible for any adverse reactions to the recipes contained in this book.

DIED WITH A BOW

A Berkley Prime Crime Book / published by arrangement with the author

PUBLISHING HISTORY
Berkley Prime Crime mass-market edition / September 2012

Copyright © 2012 by Penguin Group (USA) Inc.
Cover illustration by Jennifer Taylor/Paperdog Studio.
Cover design by Rita Frangie.
Interior text design by Tiffany Estreicher.

ISBN: 978-0-425-25156-0

BERKLEY® PRIME CRIME
Berkley Prime Crime Books are published by The Berkley Publishing Group,
a division of Penguin Group (USA) Inc.,
375 Hudson Street, New York, New York 10014.
BERKLEY® PRIME CRIME and the PRIME CRIME logo are trademarks of
Penguin Group (USA) Inc.

PRINTED IN THE UNITED STATES OF AMERICA

10 9 8 7 6 5 4 3 2 1

ALWAYS LEARNING   PEARSON

This book is for everyone who loves San Francisco as much as I do. I hope I've done the city justice with its well-dressed citizens, its beautiful views and its gourmet dining experiences. Come and see for yourself. But whatever you do, don't call it Frisco!

One

April in San Francisco is all about layers. Not the layers of fog that blanket the ocean beaches; not the layers of cake that tempt passersby at bakeries like Miette or Tartine. I mean layers of clothing: a sleeveless tunic worn over a polo neck, for example, and paired with leggings and ballerina flats or plain pumps. Under no circumstances should you wear a tight shirt or sweater with your leggings. The overall look must be balanced; the top should be roomy, and the leggings must be fitted. It's simple really.

That's what I'd been telling the customers at Dolce's, the boutique where I've worked for the past year. Because in our city surrounded on three sides by water, chilly fog and a brisk wind can sweep over the town without notice in any month and you have to be prepared for them. Sometimes a burst of brilliant warm sunshine gives way to damp mist or, in winter, a heavy downpour. If you ask me, and many customers do, I would recommend wearing a narrow fitted top under a classic belted trench coat, along with dangling earrings and, in this case, knee-high socks over tights.

Today I was wearing all gray, which looks softer next to the skin than black or navy and is not as boring as it sounds. With a boyfriend blazer smartly layered over a tank top and thin Alexander Wang sweater I love, I headed out the door, confidently carrying my striped canvas tote. Wide-legged pants and strapped loafers made me feel ready to take on the world, or at least Dolce's regular customers, the rich and well connected to the city's social scene.

One thing I was not ready for was to be greeted by a stranger at the door of the Victorian mansion Dolce Loren, my boss, had converted into an exclusive shop.

"Hello!" The young woman in satin shorts so full I thought they were bloomers, along with tights, a ribbed long-sleeved T-shirt and patent-leather wedge sling backs invited me inside as if I were a customer and she worked at the boutique. It turned out she *did* work there.

"I'm Vienna Fairchild and welcome to Dolce's," she said with a dazzling smile. So dazzling her teeth must have recently been laser whitened.

"Hi, Vienna, I'm Rita. I work here."

"Rita," she said, looking puzzled for a moment while she scratched her head. "Where have I heard that name before?" Which made me wonder, was she kidding or was I not in the right place? Had I landed in an alternate universe? "Oh, I know. Dolce mentioned you."

Mentioned me? Me, her right-hand girl? That's funny, I thought, because she hasn't mentioned you to me.

Right away I could tell things were different and I'd only been gone for two days. I'd taken Saturday off to move into a smaller, more affordable apartment, and Sunday the shop was closed. While I was gone, the Accessory section had been moved from the foyer with the jewelry. Racks of new clothes were pushed against the far wall of the great room, and our mannequins wore bright, bold spring outfits that I'd never seen before, and if I had, I would never have worn them or dressed anyone, even a fiberglass model, in them. I knew the theme was citrus colors, but someone had gone way too far. I mean, who wants to look like a grapefruit?

I surveyed the shop, feeling a chill of apprehension. Vienna was rubbing her slender ringed fingers together and staring at me as I looked around. Was she thinking, why is Rita wearing so much gray today when clearly spring is in the air?

"How do you like it?" she said. "Don't you just love, love what I've done?"

"You did this?" I asked.

She nodded, waiting for me to go off into ecstasy.

"It's stunning," I said. It was. I was stunned. But not in a good way. "So, Vienna, are you . . ."

"Working here? Yes, I am. Isn't it amazing? Last week I was wondering what to do with myself, just out of school with a degree in marketing and nothing to market. I thought I'd be perfect as a personal shopper for celebrities who don't have time to shop for themselves. Or should I be a buyer for a store like Saks or Nordstrom's? Then my stepmother—I believe you know Bobbi—suggested I move to the city. Next I land a job here at her favorite boutique. How perfect is that? Works for them and it works for me. I mean the suburbs where my parents and their significant others live are way too quiet for me. *Borrring.* So I came in for an interview on Friday night, got hired, and Saturday was my first day." She sighed, no doubt exhausted from this long speech, and spread her well-toned arms out wide. She beamed at me and said, "And here I am."

I tried to beam back, but all I could come up with was a weak smile. How on earth was there going to be room for both of us and my boss Dolce in this chic little store? I got my answer before I could say "Diane von Furstenberg" when Dolce came down the stairs from her apartment above the store.

"Rita, I see you've met Vienna." More beaming, this time from Dolce, who was wearing business casual—a magenta ruffled top with a tweed jacket and some sleek straight pants. "I knew you two girls would get along. And having Vienna here will free you up for some important work I need you to help me with," she said to me.

The work she had in mind was unpacking boxes of clothes, pressing them and hanging them on racks. The kind of thing you would ask the new girl to do, I thought. But no, Dolce, ever tactful, said she trusted only me to handle the new merchandise. Which made me feel good for about ten minutes. Then I missed my old job of being out front. The question was, didn't the customers miss me too?

As I worked by myself in the back room sorting endless boxes of new clothes and accessories, I could hear the sound of voices out in front. There was laughter and gossip, but I wasn't part of it anymore. That hurt. How long was I going to have to play the role of the backstage understudy? Once I overheard a customer saying, "Where's Rita?" I stopped and straightened my shoulders, ready to pop out and say, "Here I am," but then I heard Vienna say I was busy today and could she help her?

Of course it was her first day and she was excited and eager to prove herself without me around to show her up. I could understand that. Tomorrow would be different. How,

I wasn't sure. Would Vienna be willing to do this kind of work when the fun of the job was finding the right outfit for the right customer for the right occasion? I suspected the answer was no, she wouldn't.

After we'd closed that evening and Vienna had left with her boyfriend Geoffrey, a tall, lanky guy she pointed out to us when he stopped in the street to pick her up on his BMW motorcycle, Dolce explained that Vienna was working on commission only.

"It's the only way I could afford to hire her," Dolce told me. "And why she has to work up front with the customers she promised to bring in. If she isn't selling anything, she isn't earning any money. Whereas you . . ."

She didn't have to say more. I had a salary. It wasn't very much, but it was enough to live on as long as I got a big discount on my designer clothes and didn't go out to eat unless someone took me. Which hadn't happened lately. And which used to happen more frequently when I was the new girl in town. There was no guy on an expensive motorcycle waiting outside for me today. No guy at all.

Only a few months ago I'd been juggling dates with Nick, an athletic Romanian gymnastics instructor; Jonathan, a gorgeous ER doctor; and Detective Jack Wall of the San Francisco Police Department, but my phone had stopped ringing after I helped Jack solve a murder. It seemed to be a case of No Good Deed Goes Unpunished.

Maybe Dr. Jonathan Rhodes was dating one of those attractive nurses I'd seen the last time I was at the hospital to have my sprained ankle examined. They'd have more in common with him than I ever would. I couldn't discuss sprains or infections in a meaningful way if that's what he was looking for in a date.

Maybe Nick the gymnast was busy giving classes in Competitive Trampoline, Introduction to the Balance Beam and so forth. He'd wanted me to sign up for one of his classes, but instead I joined Alto Aquatics, a swim club where I got my exercise swimming laps and learning flotation and water safety techniques from the swim coach. Maybe it's because I was born under the sign of Aquarius, the water bearer, that I'm more at home in the water than at a gym. What I do know is that I'm a typical Aquarius in that I look good in turquoise and I'm tolerant of others' viewpoints. To a certain degree.

It might be time to check up on my favorite police detective, though I knew my aunt Grace strongly disapproved of women chasing men. At age eighty, she's so with-it, she even has a Facebook page. At the same time, she has such strict rules, she doesn't approve of calling or texting men unless they contact her first. She definitely wouldn't approve of going to the neighborhood where a certain man worked and having dinner at his favorite Vietnamese restaurant just in case he dropped in. I could just see her shaking her head, the curls in her bold, blond updo quivering at the very idea.

It was possible the sexiest cop in the city had been transferred out of town, or he'd gotten disillusioned with law enforcement and quit, or he was wounded in the line of duty or . . . It was only common courtesy for me to find out if he was okay.

"Date night?" Dolce asked me hopefully before I left. She'd probably noticed there'd been a drop in the number of men in my life from three to zero, and maybe she guessed I was eager to leave the shop where I didn't exactly feel important today.

"Not tonight," I said brightly, as if every other night was booked. She knew better. She knew I'd tell her if I was going somewhere and that she'd get a kick out of dressing me up for whatever the occasion.

"You know there's the Annual Bay to Breakers Bachelor Auction coming up," she said. "I bought tickets today from Patti for you and me and Vienna. All the money goes to support the San Francisco Art Museum. It's a black-tie gala at the Palace Hotel. Every eligible bachelor in town will be on stage. We'll all get dressed up and go ogle the beefsteak," she said with a youthful gleam in her eye, though she always said she was too old to lust after men.

I wasn't too old to lust, but I was too poor to have fun bidding on men I didn't know. It would be no fun losing out on the good ones because I'd been outbid by women with more money than I had. But it was kind of Dolce to get me a ticket and help me dress up for it.

I thanked her, said good night and walked outside. Now what? I couldn't stand the thought of facing an empty flat even though it had a deck and a sliver of a view of the Bay Bridge. After a day of unpacking boxes at work, I wasn't in the mood to unpack my own belongings. I also didn't feel like facing an empty refrigerator in my empty flat. The police district where Jack Wall worked was only a bus ride away. Or I could hop a different bus and drop into the gym where Nick taught classes. But what would be my excuse this time? I'd already observed his class, signed up for lessons that I never took and stopped in for a smoothie at the snack bar. It was his turn to call me.

There was that voice inside my head that kept repeating, "Don't pursue men. If they want to see you, they know where to find you." So I took the bus straight home and called Azerbyjohnnie's, a gourmet pizzeria recommended by one of our customers.

The woman who took my phone order had a distinct foreign accent, one that was vaguely familiar. When I gave my name, she said "How are you, Miss Rita? I haven't seen you since the funeral of that woman who was murdered."

"Meera?" I said, recognizing the voice of Nick's Romanian aunt whom I hadn't seen since she crashed a "celebration of life" party at a tavern across from the cemetery. Shy she was not. "What are you doing there?"

"Filling out for a Romanian friend," she said in her distinctive Eastern European accent. "Who had to return to our country on family business. I didn't want him to lose his job here. I help out and I get free pizza. And some vodka he promised to bring when he returns."

I was surprised that mattered to Meera, a self-proclaimed vampire. Romanian vodka was not a delicacy according to my Romanian professor at college. He called it rot-gut. As for pizza, I thought Meera only ate traditional Romanian specialties like *sarmale*, *salata boeuf* and *papanasi*. "What about your job leading tours?" I'd taken her vampire tour of San Francisco with Nick a few months back, which was interesting as long as you didn't take seriously Meera's claims that she was a one-hundred-twenty-seven-year-old vampire herself.

"Friday and Saturdays only. You must come again. I have some new sites and information to share with you. Bring a friend. Half price because I like you," she said. I noticed she said nothing at all about her nephew Nick. Did that mean he, like Dr. Rhodes, had another girlfriend? Someone who was in his adult gymnastics class who was more flexible than I was? If he did, I didn't want to hear about it and I was glad I hadn't pursued him. But a minute later I heard myself say, "How is your nephew Nick?"

"Not so fine. He had an accident on the high bar and tore his ligament."

"I'm sorry to hear that," I said. Though I was glad to hear he had an excuse for ignoring me.

"He was doing a demonstration when he had a miscalculation, and now he has to stay off the leg, so I bring him food after work. I am sure he would like to see you at his flat on Green Street, number seventeen-forty-two," she said pointedly.

Actually I owed her nephew because he had shown up with food for me when I fell off a ladder a few months ago. "I'll go see him," I promised. And I would, but not tonight. I was in no mood to cheer up anyone but myself.

"What about your pizza?" she asked.

"I'll have the daily special," I said, looking at my takeout menu. "Rainbow chard, red onions, feta cheese . . ."

"Why not try the Romanian special instead?" she asked. "My personal favorite, which I am making myself when not taking telephone orders. It comes with cabbage, tomato sauce and grilled carp."

"I'll stick with the pizza of the day," I said firmly. Grilled carp might be delicious, but on pizza?

She sounded disappointed, but she confirmed my order, and I said, *"La revedere,"* and hung up.

The pizza arrived an hour later—it was delicious with a glass of two-buck-Chuck Merlot, which I sipped while congratulating myself on being sensible and frugal. Tomorrow would be better. Tomorrow I would sign up for cooking classes somewhere. If Meera could make pizza, why couldn't I learn to cook too? Maybe the California Culinary Academy or a small, more intimate place like Tante Marie's Cooking School where I'd learn basic French techniques. I would unpack my dishes, buy a set of pots and give little dinner parties instead of sitting around waiting for men to call and invite me out. Yes, tomorrow had to be better.

But it wasn't.

It was actually worse. Not only did I spend the day doing routine jobs like taking inventory of our winter hats, separating the cloches from the knitted caps and wool berets and packing them away to make room for spring, but I also had office duty and sat in Dolce's office, which was once a coat closet, answering the phone. Talk about boring and feeling useless. There I was, forced to take multiple messages for Vienna because she'd turned off her cell phone after announcing she was not taking any personal calls at work. So when her father phoned to see how she was doing, I assured him she was a crackerjack saleswoman, which I didn't know for sure until Dolce confirmed I was right. Good news for her, bad news for me. I started to wonder if I'd ever get out of the back room.

Her boyfriend called and asked me to give her a message. He had a conflict and wouldn't be able to pick her up tonight. I hoped she wouldn't be too upset. Then her roommate, Danielle, called to tell her the rent was due.

"Already?" I blurted. Though it was none of my business, my understanding was she'd just moved in this weekend.

"The deposit," she snapped. "Ever hear of it?"

Just when I was about to do some online research on cooking schools, the phone rang again. It was Vienna's stepmother, Bobbi, who asked me to have Vienna call her when she had a break.

"Or maybe you'd know," she said. "What is your employee discount there at Dolce's?"

"I'm afraid I can't say," I said. Mine was thirty percent, but I wasn't about to share that information with her.

"Of course you can," she said. Note that I had never met this woman, though Dolce said she was a good customer.

"I'll have Vienna call you," I said politely.

"What time does she get off work?" she asked.

"It depends. We close at five, but sometimes there's work to be done later or there's a customer who needs something."

"I see," she said. "I'm looking for a moto jacket, something in black leather. What have you got?" she asked.

"We have a whole rack of them. My favorite is a vegetable-dyed lambskin with an asymmetrical zipper."

"Hmm," she said. "What would I wear under it?"

"I'd go totally girly," I said. "To offset the biker image, if you know what I mean. A leather jacket would be fabulous over lace with a skirt just below the knees. Boots, of course."

"Of course," she said. There was a long silence during which I supposed she was thinking it over. I heard a voice in the background, and then a door slammed.

"One more thing," she said so softly I could barely hear her. "Has she been driving a new car lately?"

"I don't know," I said. "I haven't seen her driving a car at all."

"She'd better not," she muttered and hung up.

I went out to the great room where Vienna was artfully tying scarves around the necks of our latest black-and-white striped sweaters. I gave her her messages, which I'd scrawled on a notepad. I didn't mention the odd question about the new car.

After she scanned the messages, she said, "Next time tell Bobbi I can only take business calls at work. She thinks I'm her personal shopper and gofer. Well, not anymore. That's why I had to move out of the house. My poor father. He has to put up with her whining. What did she want?"

"Advice about a leather moto jacket."

She winced. "As if she doesn't already have a closet full of leather. Now she'll be begging my father to get her a new jacket. She thinks he's made of money."

I didn't point out that that's what everyone thought, since Lex Fairchild, who owned a whole string of car dealerships around the state, was pretty well set up, moneywise. Why would Bobbi resent his giving his daughter a new car when he probably had some models just sitting around the lot and could well afford it?

"I hope you didn't encourage her," Vienna said sternly.

"Sorry, I did give her a suggestion for a jacket. She asked me, and after all, I'm a saleswoman first and foremost," I reminded her in case she thought of me as a drone, which was quite possible. I was in danger of thinking that myself. "Maybe I should have kept quiet."

Vienna nodded. "Maybe you should. Now you get the picture of how she's always trying to turn my father against me."

A customer came in, and Vienna positively leaped to attention. My own way of interacting with customers was more subtle, which I thought had worked pretty well, but maybe it was too subtle. Vienna's eager approach was possibly the wave of the future and I was hopelessly out of date. I sighed and went back to the office, my shoulders drooping. After a dozen or more calls asking if we had a certain Kate Spade bag or a pair of Nina animal-print wedge heels or a Vera Wang beaded necklace or a pair of Ferragamo bow flats, all of which kept me running out to check and hurrying back before the customer hung up, I was exhausted.

I was just about to take my lunch break when Dolce came to ask if I'd mind staying in while she took Vienna to lunch at Gioccamo's where they had homemade potato chips to die for and delicious pastries.

What could I say besides, "Of course. I'll be glad to." At least I'd get a chance to get out of the office and into the showroom. For an hour it was almost like old times. The good old days before Vienna. I felt liberated, lighthearted and full of energy. Customers like Patti French, whose sister-in-law—whom Patti never really liked—had been murdered some months ago, came in to look for a little black dress. I refrained from saying, "Another black dress?" because really, who can have too many? I helped her find a gorgeous Versace full-length dress she said would be perfect for the Bachelor Auction, for which, as cochair, she was selling tickets.

"I'm glad to hear you and Dolce will be there."

"And our new employee. Have you met Vienna?"

"No, but I know her stepmother, Bobbi."

I studied Patti's face and I thought I detected a whiff of disapproval. I waited, hoping she'd spill some dirt, but she didn't.

I said I hadn't met Bobbi, although she was a good customer.

"There are going to be some real prizes on the auction block, Rita," Patti said. "Some fit-looking dudes, and not just ordinary run-of-the-mill single bachelors. These guys are big-time eligible, if you know what I mean."

I thought I knew what she meant: she was talking about men with money.

"There's Steve Gray, the founder of Internet Solutions; that police detective, Jack Wall; Rick Fellows, venture capitalist; and a professional athlete or two. Oh, even an ER doctor from SF General. I've seen his picture, and he is to die for, if you'll excuse the expression."

I gulped. I thought I knew who that doctor was and agreed he was to die for. I was just glad I hadn't died before I had a chance to date him, if only once or twice.

"Each one of these men comes with a fabulous prize package like cocktails, dinner, dancing, a tour, a ball game, a show, whatever. You can't miss this." She paused as she fingered a wool cape we'd just gotten in. "So bid early and often. It's for a good cause."

I smiled, though I didn't see how I could bid on anyone, no matter how fit, on my salary. Did Patti think I was independently wealthy and just worked here for fun? She didn't say, and I took her credit card and carefully wrapped up her gorgeous dress for her in a long plastic bag.

Next I convinced Miranda McClone, one of Dolce's oldest customers, and by oldest I mean the woman was at least eighty-something, to buy several casual pieces to layer. I hoped when I was her age I'd still be in the market for the latest, trendiest styles as she was. Her dapper husband, who was wearing a classic, two-button navy blazer, a maroon bow tie and Ralph Lauren tasseled loafers, sat in one of Dolce's upholstered chairs and smiled benevolently while Miranda tried on a superb outfit: a sweater, a scarf, a faux fur vest and a pair of cropped pants, ankle socks and Marc Jacobs shoes. Worn one on top of the other as I'd suggested.

"So this is what the style is?" Miranda asked, staring at herself in Dolce's full-length mirror. "Are you sure?"

"Absolutely," I said, stepping back to take in the whole picture. "What do you think, Mr. McClone?"

"Cute as a bug," he said. And he was right. Some might

say the outfit was totally inappropriate for someone her age, but she pulled it off. I knew she would.

She bought every single thing I'd shown her. I was feeling like my old, successful salesgirl self until Dolce and Vienna came back from lunch. They barely said hello, though I was dying to tell them what I'd done. They just kept talking about who they'd seen at lunch. About who was married to whom and who wasn't. Without missing a beat or a nugget of juicy gossip, Dolce handed me a take-out box of food. I guess I should have been grateful they hadn't forgotten completely about me. I went back to the office to eat without having a chance to tell them about my big sale. And it was big.

Just as I was digging into my Caesar salad topped with grilled shrimp, the phone rang. I was chewing on a spear of romaine lettuce, but I was glad I'd picked up instead of letting the machine answer because it was Dr. Jonathan Rhodes, ER doctor.

"Rita, it's been a long time," he said.

"How are you?" I said as if I hadn't noticed he'd been AWOL from my life.

"Tired," he said. "I've been covering for another doctor as well as taking my usual shift in the ER. I haven't been home for days. But you don't want to hear about all the gunshot wounds, emergency appendectomies, cardiac arrests, broken arms, irritable bowel syndrome . . ."

What could I say? "I'd love to hear all about your cases, perhaps over dinner sometime? And by the way, are you really being sold off on Saturday night?" Fortunately I didn't have to say much of anything. I just murmured something sympathetic and he continued.

"I'm calling to see if you're coming to the Bachelor Auction Saturday night."

Ah-hah, so it *was* him. "As a matter of fact, Dolce bought tickets for us. I understand it's for a worthy cause."

"I hope so because I'm going to feel like a fool up there on the stage like a prize heifer. Especially when no one bids on me."

That's what I liked about Jonathan: he was drop-dead gorgeous, but he didn't seem to have a clue.

"Oh, I'm sure someone—"

"That's why I'm calling. I was hoping you'd be that someone who will bid on me. Can you imagine how deadly it'd be to be stuck going out with a stranger for dinner and dancing at the Starlight Room on my one night off?"

I could almost hear him shudder at the thought.

"I'll be glad to bid on you," I said, though considering my modest means and his outstanding looks, I wouldn't have a chance.

"Thanks, Rita. I knew I could count on you. Uh-oh, they're paging me. See you Saturday."

I hung up and finished my salad feeling better about my dismal social situation. Unless Jonathan was on the phone again calling every woman he knew to get a bidding war going. But now that I knew he'd been working overtime, maybe that's why he hadn't called me for weeks. Maybe he wasn't dating a nurse or two or three. If he was, he would have asked them to bid on him. But he'd asked me. As long as I didn't win, I'd do what I could to help him out. That's the way I am.

Two

The next few days went just as I expected. Dolce raved about Vienna's sales ability but said nothing about how beautifully I unpacked and pressed the new clothes. I felt like Cinderella sweeping up the ashes in the back room, while Vienna was my stepsister who got to go to the ball.

Actually we all got to go to the ball, so Dolce offered to let us wear anything we wanted from the shop. I waited until we closed to try on dresses for the auction, but Vienna said she had an outfit already and dashed out at five o'clock. I glanced out the window to see if she was driving a new car or meeting her motorcycle-riding boyfriend. Neither turned out to be the case. She got into a yellow Lotus, a low-slung British racing car, driven by someone else.

I was just about to ask if Dolce knew who the owner of the sports car was, but she locked the front door and seemed to have forgotten all about her new favorite salesgirl. Instead, she'd gone into her fairy-godmother mode, which was fine with me. It was worth being Cinderella if I got transformed and my story had a happy ending. But I didn't see it happening. For now it was good to be on the receiving end of my boss's attention. It reminded me of the good old days, before Vienna.

"I say we pull out all the stops," Dolce said as she rolled out a rack of dresses into the high-ceilinged great room, which once had been some rich Victorian family's salon.

"You mean strapless?" I said, thinking of the gorgeous dresses worn to the opera by Julia Roberts in *Pretty Woman* and Cher in *Moonstruck*. But I'm not a movie star and I pictured myself tugging on my gown all evening to keep it from falling down.

"I mean elegant," she said, taking a long, sleek black dress by Elie Tahari off the rack and removing it from its flexible hanger. "It may be a bit wintry for April, but I truly think you'd look terrific in it."

I went into the tiny dressing room and slipped into the high-necked dress with sheer long sleeves. When I came out, Dolce didn't say a word, she just fluttered her eyelashes and sat down in her favorite chair as if her legs wouldn't hold her upright another moment.

"I love it, but what do you think?" she asked me.

I looked in the three-way mirror and realized that the back was open to the waist with a low-cut V-shaped embellishment. It was chaste in the front and daring in back. And quite elegant. It made me feel glamorous.

"It's a beautiful dress," I said. For some reason, I'd never seen it on the rack, never showed it to any customer.

"It fits you perfectly. I wouldn't be surprised if the men started bidding on *you*," she said with a chuckle. I smiled, but I was reminded it didn't matter how glamorous I looked, I would not be leaving with a date because I couldn't afford one.

"It will be fun to go and see who's who and what they're wearing," I said. Dolce had provided my dress and the ticket to the event. Just because I'd be forced to watch two men I was interested in being auctioned off to rich society women was no reason to act ungrateful. I would smile my way through this evening, confident I looked my best. So I hung the dress I'd wear on Saturday back on the rack, and after thanking her again, I said good night to Dolce.

Making my way down the street, I thought of poor Nick the gymnast, who'd not only picked me up from the hospital when I'd had my concussion but who'd also supplied me with Romanian food he'd made himself. Now he was lying helpless in his apartment on Green Street, and where was I? On my way home alone, and of course I was hungry.

I decided to pick up some food at one of the restaurants in his neighborhood and take it to his house. After all he'd done for me, it was the least I could do. I pictured Nick's face when I knocked on his door, his mouth falling open when he saw me, then a huge warm, welcoming smile when he noticed the boxes of food in my hand. It wouldn't be Romanian food, but I'd find something reasonable and tasty in the trendy Cow Hollow neighborhood where he lived. If I was totally honest, I'd admit I hated to eat alone. I never used to mind so much before Vienna. Now when I saw her being whisked off on a motorcycle or in a sports car, I felt a pang of jealousy and curiosity. Who was she going out with? Where were they going? Not that it was any of my business. Still . . .

When I got off the bus on Union Street and walked to

Green Street, I remembered hearing that Cow Hollow was
named for the cows who'd lived on the dairy farms here in
the mid-1800s. Not a cow or a farm to be seen these days.
Just ornate three-story Victorian houses with turrets and
gingerbread trim built after the gold rush in 1849 when the
neighborhood became fashionable. Fortunately the area
hadn't been heavily damaged by the 1906 earthquake and
fire that leveled so much of this city, so these converted
barns, carriage houses and mansions were still standing,
still looking good as I walked down the street, wondering
how Nick could afford to live here on the salary of a gymnastics teacher. Maybe the same way I managed to live on
upscale Telegraph Hill: by taking the smallest apartment on
the top floor with no elevator and scarcely room to turn
around inside.

   I was tempted to stop several times at restaurants filled
with yuppies wearing what I call boho chic, both men and
women in tight denims, boots and—what else—layers of
shirts, sweaters and jackets. What would happen if I stopped
in for a drink with all these other professional, well-heeled
men and women in my age bracket? Would I find the love
of my life at the bar? Would we look across the packed room
and make an instant connection? Or would I stand there by
myself, surrounded by throngs of the beautiful people, alone
in a crowd, while all around me the young and the restless
flirted and fawned. The worst kind of alone possible.

   So I hurried on by, until I saw what I was looking for,
only I didn't know I was looking for it until I saw it: Ye Olde
Bonne Creperie Bretonne, where in the window a guy was
flipping paper-thin crepes in the air. The menu was written
on a blackboard in chalk and it made my mouth water. One
side listed the savory crepes—Mediterranean, New Orleans,

Miami Heat and so many more I just stood there and stared at the dizzying number of choices. Finally I decided to get an eggplant crepe with jack cheese, tomatoes, onion, roasted red pepper and, of course, eggplant, and one called The Sopranos, with Italian sausage, mozzarella, black olives, mushrooms, spinach and pesto sauce. Then, after a quick perusal of the dessert options on the other side of the board, I ordered a bananas Foster crepe, with bananas, brown sugar, walnuts and cinnamon.

According to his aunt, Nick would enjoy the food and my company, and I'd leave with a good feeling that I'd brightened an invalid's day. I suspected that after sitting alone day after day with only his vampire aunt for company, he would be desperate for someone like me to talk to.

I found number 1742 and was impressed by the well-cared-for Victorian house painted blue, its flower boxes filled with daffodils, tulips and trailing verbena. I saw "Petrescu" listed next to the mailbox and was about to ring the bell next to his name when someone came out the front door, so I hurried in. Why announce myself over the intercom when I could surprise Nick with a friendly knock on his apartment door?

I climbed the three flights of narrow stairs and finally reached his apartment. I knew it was his because there was a sign on the door saying *Bun Venit*, "Welcome." Also, I heard his voice. I pressed my ear to the door and heard him speaking to someone in his language. Although I had minored in Romanian, I had a hard time understanding it when spoken rapidly by two native speakers, especially when those speakers were on the other side of a closed door.

What I did understand was that he wasn't alone. The other voice I heard belonged to a woman. I didn't know who she was, but I did know it wasn't his aunt. Unlike the vampiric Meera, this woman made a light tinkling sound when she laughed. So much for poor Nick being sick, sad and alone. Not only was he not alone, he also wasn't hungry, because I smelled food. Romanian food. I could tell by the scent of cabbage, onions and paprika in the air. I looked at the box of crepes I'd brought and I felt foolish. The least I could have done was to cook up something myself, as he'd done for me. But no, I'd bought some trendy French food. I stood there for another few minutes, one hand poised to knock on the door. After all, maybe it was not his girlfriend. Maybe it was his cousin who had flown in from Bucharest to take care of him while he was laid up. But why hadn't Meera told me instead of asking me to drop in?

Finally, after standing there for several minutes listening to the lighthearted laughter and what sounded like flirtatious conversation, I turned around and walked back down the three flights of stairs. I went back the way I'd come to the bus stop, still carrying the boxes of crepes while my stomach grumbled and my head ached. My aunt Grace was right: Don't drop in on men without an invitation. Don't call them unless they've called you first.

Back in my own tiny flat, I finally opened the boxes, heated the Mediterranean crepe and ate it by myself. It was delicious. The other crepes I saved for another day.

The days dragged by until Saturday. Vienna continued to rack up sales until I was sure she was making more money in commissions than I was making in salary. The customers seemed to like her from what I could hear from the back room, where I continued to do inventory when I wasn't answering the phone in Dolce's office.

I followed Vienna's orders and told anyone who asked

for her that I would take a message. She got lots of calls, so scribbling messages for her kept me quite busy. I didn't know what she did with them when I gave them to her. I did know that each day, instead of her boyfriend on his motorcycle, a car picked her up after work, sometimes right at five, sometimes later. I'm not good at identifying cars, but this one was long and low and looked expensive. I didn't ask her who it was. After all, I didn't want her asking me questions about my private life, like why no one ever picked *me* up.

On Saturday after work Dolce suggested the three of us get dressed at the shop and go to the Palace Hotel together. But Vienna said she would meet us there. She mumbled something about family obligations. Dolce looked disappointed, but surely she understood. Not only did Vienna have parents, she had stepparents too. It was clear Dolce really liked Vienna, and treated her the way she used to treat me, like a favorite daughter. Only Vienna had two other mothers. If it were me, I'd choose Dolce, but I didn't have a choice.

I didn't mean to complain. Dolce had given me a dress to wear and a ticket to the gala fund-raiser. On the other hand, it was a ticket to an affair I didn't belong at. Where I couldn't participate in the bidding if I'd wanted to, which I did. What would Jonathan say when no one bid on him? Hah, that wasn't going to happen. Both he and Detective Wall would be snapped up by some gorgeous socialites and they'd forget about me—as if they hadn't already.

But I put on my happy face along with the gorgeous slinky black dress I liked so much. Dolce helped me iron my hair so that it looked long and slinky too. As for my boss, she wore an elegant satin coat over a simple long dress in a teal color. Next to Dolce in teal I suddenly felt like I was going to a funeral; my long black gown now seemed entirely inappropriate. I couldn't say a word, since she'd picked it out for me, but it was spring and I looked like winter.

"What's Vienna wearing?" I asked Dolce when we were on our way to the auction in a cab.

"I don't know. I asked her, but she said she hadn't decided."

There were so many questions I wanted to ask about Vienna, I didn't know where to start or even if I should start. I had to be careful not to show any signs of jealousy or resentment. Both unbecoming traits in anyone.

I'd never been to the famous Garden Court of the Palace Hotel. The original was destroyed during the big 1906 quake, but they say that when it reopened in 1909, it was more beautiful and splendid than ever before. The cab let us off at the side entrance, and when we walked into the hotel, I could tell by the expression on Dolce's face it held memories for her. We stood together in the middle of the court with its towering Italian marble columns, gazing up at the Austrian crystal chandeliers hanging from the stained-glass dome. I was awestruck. Dolce had tears in her eyes.

"So much history made at this hotel," I said. "Didn't one of those Hawaiian kings die here?"

"King Kalakaua. They called him the Merrie Monarch, the one who restored the hula to the islands," she said. "He died here at the old hotel. Years later, after it was rebuilt, Woodrow Wilson gave a speech here, and Warren Harding died here," Dolce said, looking around as if there might be a ghost or two lurking behind a pillar.

"You've been here before, of course," I suggested, wondering what would happen to those chandeliers in an earthquake. Seeing as we were in a Seismic Zone Four, I could imagine the room shaking and the glass raining down on us.

"Not for many years," she said with a sigh. "It was an engagement party."

I wondered if it was *her* engagement party, but I was afraid to ask. I always wondered why she'd never married, but I thought if she wanted me to know, she'd tell me. Then she seemed to pull herself together and waved to someone across the room.

"Who's that?" I asked, thinking I should recognize her if she was a customer.

"Muffy Spangler," Dolce said out of the corner of her mouth. "Don't look over at her. I haven't seen her since I had to ban her from the store."

"What?" I was shocked. Dolce banning a customer?

Dolce leaned forward and spoke in a half whisper. "She got into a fight with a customer over a dress they both wanted, and Muffy actually punched the poor woman in the face. Someone called the police, and we all had to go down to the station. It was horrible. That was a few years ago, and she hasn't dared come been back since, though I've heard she wants to. I hope she stays away."

I could empathize. I'd spent enough time with the police when MarySue Jensen was murdered some time ago. Not that I minded having contact with Detective Wall; what I did mind was being hauled down to the station, which was inconvenient to say the least, and where I'd had to worry about saying the wrong thing and incriminating myself or someone close to me, like Dolce.

"Could that tall, glamorous woman with the short bald man be Vienna's mother and stepfather?" I asked Dolce. I'd seen their pictures in the society pages of the newspaper, and the resemblance between this woman and Vienna was striking even from across the room. The same blond hair, the tall, willowy body and the angular face.

"Yes, that's Noreen Fortner and her husband Hugh."

"She looks too young to be Vienna's mother."

"She'd love to hear you say that," Dolce said. "She likes to be told they look like sisters. She used to be a good customer until they moved across the Bay and now she shops . . . well, I don't know where she shops. I would be surprised if Vienna was with them. After what she said about Hugh."

I waited but Dolce didn't elaborate, and it was none of my business what Vienna had said about her stepfather. If it was anything like her feelings for her stepmother, I didn't want to hear her ranting.

Dolce looked around, keeping her eye on the door. She wanted us to sit together, her and "her girls." But maybe Vienna preferred to sit with either her mother or her father despite what she thought of their current mates. According to Vienna, the two families did not mingle. Ever. Which, from what I understood, forced Vienna to make some hard choices.

Suddenly Dolce's face lit up. "There she is."

I turned and watched Vienna enter the room in a gorgeous black strapless dress with a hot pink satin bodice tied in back with a huge pink bow. Around her neck was a sparkling diamond necklace with a huge pink stone. It stood out even in a room full of beautiful people dressed in everything from Versace to Nika to Stella McCartney. There were all kinds of gorgeous jewelry and designer dresses, some strapless, others one-shoulder or Grecian.

Dolce waved to her. But Vienna hardly noticed us. After

the barest hint of a cool smile in our direction, she headed across the room toward . . . someone. But who? Which family? Would they fight over her or try to avoid her altogether?

Dolce's face fell when Vienna passed us over for someone more important. At that moment I could have smacked Vienna for her rudeness. I could understand how she'd have to sit with her family, but couldn't she have spared a moment to greet the woman who'd hired her, who'd done everything she could to help her succeed in her new job? As if Dolce just wasn't important enough or rich enough or young enough to deserve more than that.

Would Vienna sit with Noreen and Hugh or her stepmother and her father, Lex? I stood on tiptoes and craned my neck, but I couldn't see.

I wanted to ask Dolce about the necklace and the dress, but I felt it was out of place for me to bring it up. If either had come from the shop, why hadn't I seen them? Instead, I tried to distract her by pointing out several women I thought were either well dressed or not.

"What do you think of the organza and tulle dress over there?" I asked with a nod toward a woman hanging on the arm of a tall man.

"It looks like Jason Wu, and I think it's too frilly for the occasion and for someone her age."

"What about that flirty Oscar de la Renta number?"

Dolce squinted and shook her head. "Terrible. And the shoes."

"Miu Miu platform sandals if I'm not mistaken."

"All the money in the world doesn't make up for poor taste," Dolce said.

We laughed at a striped Missoni maxi dress, and I was hoping she'd forgotten that Vienna had snubbed us.

I scanned the room to find something to applaud and finally found it: an off-the-shoulder goddess dress. If the woman didn't have a gorgeous shape to begin with, she had one in that dress with its gathered knee-length skirt. When I pointed her out to Dolce, she agreed with my assessment but told me I looked even better.

Finally some other people Dolce knew joined us at our round table, and we all sat down to eat dinner. Next to Dolce was a suave gray-haired man in formal wear with a red bow tie who seemed unaccompanied by a date. I'd never seen him before, but he and Dolce appeared to be getting along splendidly.

I'd never seen her flirt before, maybe because we saw so few men at the shop to flirt with. But in between the shrimp cocktail and the crab bisque, she was smiling, gazing into his eyes, listening intently to everything he said and laughing appreciatively as if he were a combination of a guru and a stand-up comedian. I wished I knew who he was. I certainly didn't want her falling for some guy who wasn't suitable after all her years of abstinence.

Over steak Diane in a velvety rich sauce laced with Cognac and served with creamy mashed potatoes and sautéed mushrooms, Dolce finally introduced him to me as William Hemlock. I was happy to hear he was a retired airline pilot. Immediately I pictured Dolce flying off to exotic locales with him on his airline discount. Leaving me in charge of the shop, of course. To add to his appeal, William mentioned that when he made steak Diane he always served it flambéed. I wanted to give Dolce a thumbs-up sign, but since that would be a little obvious, I nudged her instead to indicate my approval. A man who looked like that, flew airplanes and cooked too? How unusual was that.

After a dessert course of tiny little frosted cakes and coffee, I was ready to leave. But of course I couldn't. The fun hadn't started yet. Where were the men to be auctioned off, I asked myself, wishing I could slip away so I didn't have to sit there watching while gorgeous hunks paraded across the stage and every woman under fifty but me held up banners supplied by the waitstaff indicating how much they would bid.

I looked around the room. Nothing but beautiful people. And no escape without looking like a bad sport or a wimp. Suddenly a blast of music. A fanfare. An emcee in a tux stood up and told us it was time to start what we'd all been waiting for—the Bachelor Auction.

I could hardly wait. Not.

Three

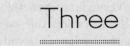

The bidding went beyond all expectations. The men were snapped up for astronomical amounts so fast I had no idea who were the lucky winners. I didn't even have time to raise my hand. So much for my promise to Dr. Jonathan. How could he blame me when he didn't need me at all? By now he'd forgotten all about me and his desperate call for my help. Not all the men on the stage were gorgeous, I could see that. Not all were millionaires either. Some were billionaires. But they all acted like they were both gorgeous and rich. Except for Dr. Jonathan and, of course, Detective Jack Wall. Even from the back of the room I could tell those two both looked uncomfortable, like they wished they were somewhere else.

I wanted to leave before I saw them being claimed by the high bidders, leaving me conspicuously dateless, and I almost made it. I left the table thinking I'd sneak out and make up an excuse later, but I got stuck at the door and couldn't leave. It wasn't so much that the doors were closed, it was that I was frozen in place. My legs wouldn't move. Some otherworldly force kept me glued to the spot and compelled me to watch the men on stage being claimed by their dates.

That's when I saw Vienna in her dress with the giant bow, her blond hair pulled back in a sleek chignon, hold the winning bid of a few thousand dollars for Jonathan. I couldn't believe it. With all those men up there, she had to choose the one I knew. I didn't blame her for bidding on him. The emcee made him sound like a cross between a young George Clooney on *ER* and a surfer dude. Which was actually pretty accurate.

To cap off the evening, Detective Wall was auctioned off to a woman who looked like a runway model in a wild print chiffon ball gown with a ruched strapless bodice. Her short white-blond hair was swept behind her ear. Did she know Jack in his professional capacity as I did? Or was she just a rich woman who wanted to contribute to a good cause? Or was this the beginning of a beautiful friendship? I didn't want to know. I just wanted to disappear.

I made it as far as the bathroom, where I ran into Vienna, who else? She was standing over the sink applying a fresh coat of makeup, as if she needed it. Her skin was flawless, and her eyes sparkled brightly. Almost as brightly as the diamonds that surrounded the hot pink tourmaline in her necklace. When I'd seen it from across the room, I hadn't really appreciated how stunning it was, but up close I couldn't take my eyes off of it. It was so perfect with the dress.

"I love your dress," I said. "And the necklace."

"Thanks. You look terrific, Rita. Very Hollywood." So she wasn't ignoring us after all. She was her usual self.

By Hollywood I hoped she meant Sandra Bullock and not Joan Rivers. "So you won a date with my doctor, I see."

"Your doctor? No kidding. Doesn't matter. I got carried away. I can't go. My boyfriend would kill me."

"Geoffrey?" I said.

She laughed. Her perfect white teeth gleamed in the softly lit ladies' lounge. "Yeah, yeah, Geoffrey." She reached into her hot pink satin clutch and pulled out her winning bid. "Here, you take it."

I stood there openmouthed while she pressed the ticket in my hand. Then she smiled briefly, said, "Have fun," and walked out.

"Wait," I said, "I can't take this." But she was gone.

I put the ticket down and splashed cold water on my face. Did Vienna just give me her winning bid for a date with my doctor? Because her boyfriend would "kill" her if she went? Or had those two glasses of champagne I'd drunk during dinner affected my brain? I picked up the ticket and stood there staring at it, feeling numb all over. I should have left, but who knew there was someone in the other stall who'd heard the whole bizarre exchange? The door opened and out walked Frances Martin, a customer I knew from the store.

"Was that Vienna Fairchild just now?" she said, her eyes wide with disbelief.

I nodded.

Frances looked at the ticket I held in my hand and said, "I can't believe she gave you her date. Didn't she just spend thousands on it?"

I didn't say anything. I couldn't. I was lucky to manage a smile, as if I couldn't believe it either, then I walked out.

And almost bumped into Dolce. I wondered if she'd seen Vienna or just missed her.

"Are you all right?" she asked, putting her hand on my arm. I didn't know how I looked, probably dazed and disoriented.

"Fine, but I think I'll head out. It was a wonderful evening," I lied. "I had a fabulous time. Thank you so much for inviting me." I wanted to say something about the pilot, but I didn't want to jinx it, so I said nothing except, "Enjoy the rest of the evening."

She nodded and before I could escape out the front door of the hotel, she said, "I meant to ask you. What did you think of Vienna's dress?"

I hesitated. Had Dolce seen Vienna when she exited the ladies' room or not? I almost mentioned the necklace but decided to pretend I hadn't had that close-up exchange with Vienna just now.

"Sensational. Where did she get it?"

"I don't know."

I could tell Dolce was hurt she hadn't worn something from the boutique, but I pretended I wasn't aware of the slight.

"Who was the man she bid on?" Dolce asked.

What could I say? "He's my doctor and she just handed over her date to me"? Or, "He's the man who asked me to bid on him but I didn't, and anyway she just gave me her ticket"? Or, "Isn't it nice she has enough money to contribute to the cause?" Instead, I just shrugged, gave her a hug and walked out into the cool night air where I caught a taxi.

When I got home, I carefully hung my dress on the flexible hanger it came on. Dolce had ordered the hangers in assorted colors because you could bend them up to hold

strappy dresses in place or bend them down for sweaters or
knits so they'd hold their shape and you didn't end up with
bulging shoulders. They were strong but flexible, which
reminded me of Nick Petrescu, the only man I knew who
hadn't been at the auction tonight. He was probably at home
eating *ciorba de burta* with the tinkling-laugh woman. He
didn't need me. Nobody needed me. It sounded pathetic, but
it was true. Dolce used to need me, then Vienna showed up,
and now my boss had a potential former-pilot boyfriend. I
couldn't be happier for her.

   It was time for me to face the future. A future on my own.
From now on I would devote myself to self-improvement.
Instead of depending on men to take me places and supply
me with food and entertainment, I would become self-
sufficient. I didn't need a date to have cultural, body-building
or gourmet experiences. I would volunteer to usher at the
opera and save hundreds on expensive tickets. Not that I'd
ever bought an expensive ticket to the opera, but now I'd go
for free. I'd meet a different crowd. I wouldn't limit myself
to self-centered women.

   I'd meet new people. Those who were not only fashionable but into culture and well-heeled as well. Then I'd step
up my exercise program. I'd move beyond workouts at the
pool, perhaps graduate to doing an open-water swim across
the Bay to Alcatraz. Besides the cooking classes I was going
to take, I'd watch cooking shows on the Food Network for
inspiration.

   Speaking of being inspired, right in front of me every
single day was a woman who'd created a life for herself
without depending on anyone. Dolce had taken an old Victorian house, remodeled it and turned it into a shop and a
home above the shop. She'd turned a lifelong interest in

fashion into a full-time job. She was her own boss. She'd never been married, and she didn't have any regrets that I knew of. She may have had lovers in the past. If so, she never talked about them. She knew everyone in town, and everyone knew her. I'd just found out that the one and only person she was on the outs with had been banished from the store and most probably had regretted it every day, since everyone who was anyone shopped at Dolce's.

By going through three boxes of clothes in my bedroom that I hadn't yet unpacked since moving in, I finally found a long-sleeved T-shirt and a pair of flannel drawstring pants to wear and made myself a steaming cup of instant Mexican hot chocolate. I'd been given a box of ready-mix with a set of cups as a housewarming gift.

I promised myself that tomorrow I would definitely unpack and start my new life as an independent woman. I would make my own hot chocolate mix with homemade marshmallows. Sipping a comforting hot beverage at my kitchen counter, I tried to forget the sight of my doctor on the auction block.

I was just lucky I hadn't had to confront the woman who'd bid on Jack and hear her go on about how much she'd paid for a date with a hot cop. If I ever saw him again, I would definitely tweak him about dating a socialite. But I doubted I'd ever see him again unless I ate every meal at the Vietnamese restaurant from now until he realized I was stalking him and he found a new hangout.

Before I went to bed, I stuck the winning ticket Vienna had given me to the mirror. I wasn't sure what my next move would be or what it was supposed to be. I didn't want any men in my life to accuse me of chasing them, so I'd have to ask Vienna if it was really okay for me to use it as it was intended, for a date with Jonathan. If I didn't, would it be weird? Would the donor wonder what happened? Would Jonathan wonder why his date hadn't contacted him? Would he be hurt or relieved? And would Jonathan wonder why I hadn't bid on him as I'd promised?

Sunday morning I decided to take my dress back to Dolce's rather than wait until Monday. I didn't want it hanging in my tiny apartment reminding me of last evening. I wanted to forget the whole scene.

Dolce hadn't said the dress was a loaner, but that's what I assumed. In any case, I had nowhere else to wear it and it was still in mint condition. Dolce would no doubt have it cleaned and sell it as a sample. So I folded it up with tissue paper around it and put it in a box. I dressed in my top-of-the-line jeans from France and layered a belted tunic over a long-sleeved sweater that made me feel warm and chic. Then I slid my feet into a pair of lightweight green Dakota slip-ons.

I hoped to see Dolce at the shop, since she lived upstairs, and maybe get the skinny on what happened after I left last night. If she wanted to confide in me, I'd be all ears, although our usual roles were reversed: she was the one with the social life, and I was the one who went home early, alone. I hoped the pilot was as good as he looked. She deserved some excitement in her life.

After I got rid of the dress and, hopefully, connected with her, I'd go to my health club and get a workout with the coach in the pool to prepare for my ocean swim. And then I'd come back and unpack all these cardboard boxes, and with a few odds and ends from Ikea, I'd turn this apartment into a charming small abode that would feel more like a home. I was full of righteous energy. I knew I had to act fast before I sank into a funk and started asking myself, What's the use?

I got on the bus with my Speedo classic double-cross-back suit tucked into a yellow Stella McCartney swim bag with a waterproof compartment for a cell phone or whatever, and the cardboard suit box containing the dress under my arm. I loved the dress, I really did, but what good did it do me if no one admired me in it except Dolce?

I stood in front of the old Victorian house Dolce had turned into a boutique and looked up at the top-floor window under the eaves, hoping to catch Dolce's eye, but I didn't see anything moving. Was it possible she hadn't come home last night? Maybe she'd reserved a room at the hotel so she wouldn't have to come home alone late.

I walked up the steps, set my bag and my box on the porch and rang the bell even though I had a key of my own. I didn't want to surprise her or catch her at an awkward moment. Maybe I should have called first. After waiting a few minutes, I finally got my key from the bottom of my big black leather bag. I put the key in the lock and leaned against the door. To my surprise, it swung open before I'd turned the key. I almost fell into the foyer.

"Dolce?" I called so as not to startle her into calling the security people. "It's me."

No sound. Nothing. Of course, she would be upstairs and not have heard me. Maybe I should just leave the dress and respect her privacy. I gathered up my stuff and took a few steps inside, closing the door behind me. The ridged rubber soles of my slip-ons made no sound as I walked in. That's when I saw her.

Vienna. She was lying facedown in the entry to the great

room. I knew it was her by the huge pink bow on the back of her dress.

"Vienna," I said, stopping abruptly just a few feet away. "What are you doing here? Are you okay?"

What a dumb thing to say. If she was okay, why was she lying there like that? She was not okay. I kneeled down next to her and realized she was not breathing. My heart started hammering. She must have fallen and hurt herself. Badly. I put my hands on her bare shoulders and turned her face to one side. She felt cold. There were ugly red marks on her neck. I stood up and screamed. My voice echoed against the walls, but no one came. No one heard me. My eyes filled with tears. I took my phone out of my bag and called 911. I told myself to stay calm. But it was hard when my hands were shaking and my heart was pounding. The dispatcher asked me a lot of questions. Like what was the nature of the emergency, my phone number, the address and so on. I finally finished and hung up.

I looked around. I wished I could do something for Vienna, but I was sure she was dead. And I probably shouldn't have touched her body at all. I wanted to leave, but the dispatcher had told me not to depart the scene. I wondered where Dolce was. I tried her cell phone, but she didn't answer.

So I picked up a bunch of hangers and hung them neatly on the clothes rack, knowing Dolce would want me to. She'd hate to have strangers see the boutique in such a mess. One hanger was twisted so badly I couldn't straighten it. After I hung my dress up, I finally went outside and sat on the front step, put my head between my knees and started shaking. It seemed like it took forever for someone to come.

They came in three or four cars, sirens screaming, and parked illegally in the no-parking zone in front of the shop. The men ran up the steps in their uniforms. San Francisco's finest.

"You're Rita Jewel?" the first stocky guy said after taking the steps two at a time.

I nodded. "I'm the one who called you. She's in there. Vienna."

He said, "Don't go anywhere," which wasn't necessary because when I tried to stand, my legs were trembling so violently I collapsed back down on the steps. I swiveled my body around to watch as they went through the front door and into the foyer. That's all I could see except for the camera flash going off. If you have to be photographed, it's good to be wearing a designer dress. I knew Vienna would be glad she was wearing it, especially if her photo appeared in the newspaper, which it probably would. After all, she was a socialite's daughter and her death was suspicious to say the least.

I finally got up and walked gingerly into the foyer.

"Hold it," a cop whose name tag said "Rowley" announced with his arm stretched out in front of me. "Stand back."

I craned my neck to look around him. "How is she?" I asked hopefully. Maybe I was wrong. Maybe she wasn't dead. She was just unconscious.

"Dead," he said. "Who are you?"

"Rita Jewel, I work here."

"On Sunday?"

"No, no, I just came to return a dress, and then I saw Vienna there on the floor, so I called you." I was breathing hard and hoping he wouldn't have any more questions. I wanted to get out of there. I turned to go.

"How'd you get in?" he asked.

"The door was unlocked, but I have a key. I work here," I repeated.

"Where you going?" he asked.

"Home."

"Nuh-uh," Rowley said. "Sit down. We've got some questions for you. First one, who is the deceased? Can you ID her?"

"Her name is Vienna Fairchild. She works here too."

"Okay. Wait outside." He shoved one of Dolce's folding chairs toward me, and I pushed it outside onto the small front porch and sat there, taking big gulps of fresh air. In the background I heard the cop talking to someone on his phone.

"Says she works here. Who? . . . Yeah, that's her. How did you know? Okay. Okay."

A few minutes later he came outside. "Don't go anywhere. The detective on the case wants to talk to you."

Uh-oh, by "detective" did he mean Jack? By "talk" did he mean on the phone? Maybe that was a good thing. Jack would say, "Rita is a smart girl. She can help us find out who did this. She's an amazing detective herself for an amateur. I want to talk to her." Of course he would say that.

I looked at the round-faced cop. Now what?

"Anyone else here?" he asked.

"My boss Dolce lives here." I looked up at the ceiling as if he'd be able to see through it to her apartment upstairs. "She has an office at the back of the shop. But I don't think she's there. She might be upstairs where she lives."

"I'll check it out. You come with me. Chief says not to let you out of my sight. You lead the way. Don't touch anything."

"But I already touched . . ." I'd touched everything—the

hanger, Vienna, her clothes. What did he mean by not to let me out of his sight? Why was that? Surely Jack didn't think . . . No, he couldn't. I walked through the shop, eyes straight ahead. I didn't want to see Vienna's body again, but I didn't need to worry, as it was now covered with a sheet. Rowley, the cop, came with me, and when we got to Dolce's office, I used my key to unlock the door. We went in. Since the whole world seemed to be upside down, I almost expected the place to be trashed. But everything in the office was just as we'd left it on Saturday. I sat down and used her Rolodex to find some numbers for him, like Vienna's next of kin.

"I should try calling my boss again," I said. "She'll want to know what's happened."

Instead, he took her number and called her. Like me, he got no answer, so he left a message that there'd been an accident in her shop and asked her to contact him as soon as possible. Then he gave his phone number and hung up.

"You say she lives upstairs?" he asked.

"Yes, but she's not there or she would have come down."

"Unless she didn't hear us," he said.

"You'd have to be deaf not to hear all this," I said. *Or dead*. I started to shake again.

Both Rowley and I jumped up at the same time. Was he thinking what I was thinking? That my boss had also been murdered? Anxiously I followed the lawman up the stairs to Dolce's apartment above the shop. Her door was locked, but the cop pulled an enormous key ring from his pocket and after a few tries, he unlocked the door. I didn't realize I was holding my breath until we'd made a tour of Dolce's place and found no evidence of foul play. In fact, it looked like no one lived there. That's how perfect it was, every cushion, every pillow, every towel in place.

Strangely, in the year I'd worked there, I'd never been upstairs before, so I took it all in and despite my ragged nerves, I couldn't help admiring her exquisite taste. No surprise there. We walked through the living room with its dramatic deep magenta walls and feminine floral print wing chairs on two sides of a faux fireplace.

For her bedroom Dolce had chosen a restful pale gray color for the walls—November Skies from Benjamin Moore if I wasn't mistaken. The bed was West Elm, which I recognized from their catalog, and the ultrasmooth linens that were guaranteed to soften with laundering and use were from Williams-Sonoma Home. I knew because they were just what I'd always wanted. Maybe if I didn't always blow my salary on clothes, I could upgrade my home furnishings. Back to the bed. It was covered with an Italian wool and cashmere blanket that begged to be touched. If I'd been alone, but I wasn't. It was clear no one had slept in it last night. That's what the cop said, and I had to agree.

"Know where your boss is?" he asked after we'd both peered into Dolce's walk-in closet where her entire wardrobe was organized by season and color. I don't know if he was impressed, but I was.

I tore my gaze from the lavishly patterned window shade in her bedroom and shook my head. "I haven't seen her since last night. We went to a charity auction thing at the Palace Hotel. I left early."

He asked me what time and where I'd gone afterward and how I got home. I didn't like the way he took notes. Who did he think I was, Vienna's killer? It was such a ridiculous idea I almost laughed out loud, but I was afraid I'd get hysterical and wouldn't be able to stop.

I was relieved when we moved on to the kitchen. Rowley

was wearing rubber gloves, and again he cautioned me not to touch anything. As if Dolce and her apartment had anything to do with Vienna. It couldn't be. It just couldn't.

Dolce's kitchen was the biggest surprise. I'd never heard her mention cooking for herself or for anyone else. She ate out or ordered in as often as I did, and yet she had a gourmet kitchen that had obviously been remodeled, since this house was built before the 1906 earthquake. It was small but ultramodern, with high-gloss off-white cabinets and stainless steel appliances, and just like the rest of the place, it looked untouched by human hands. Had Dolce cleaned up the place for some reason, or was it always like this? I reached up to open a cabinet, curious to see what kind of dinnerware she had, but the policeman reached out and smartly tapped my arm.

"I said, don't touch anything," he warned.

"But why? You don't imagine . . ."

"I don't get paid to imagine anything. I get paid to keep from contaminating the evidence."

"Evidence of what? Dolce had nothing to do with . . ." I stopped. We both knew that there was a dead girl downstairs—or maybe, hopefully, she'd been removed by now. And my boss was missing. And I'd found the body.

"And I get paid to bring the suspects down to the station," he continued. "Let's go."

Four

Bring the suspects down to the station? Did he mean me? I couldn't believe I was on my way to the police station with my swimming bag on my lap in the backseat of the police car. The last place I would have imagined myself when I woke up this morning. When we went downstairs, I saw that Vienna's body was gone, and so were most of the cops.

Dolce had not returned, and I was weak and strung out like I'd just run a marathon and come in last. Sweat was beading on my forehead and there were goose bumps on my arms. I wanted to go home, but for some reason I was being taken to the police station. Why me? I wasn't a suspect, so it must be because I happened to find the body. Of course it was. I was not going to just any police station; I was on my way to the main station where Jack Wall was now working.

"This is a big misunderstanding," I told Rowley from the backseat of his car.

"Yeah?" he said without turning to look at me.

"I'm actually a friend of Detective Wall. We've worked together on another case, which I'm guessing is the reason he wants to see me." I paused, waiting for him to confirm my idea. The cop said nothing. Probably part of their code of silence or something. "He does want to see me, right?"

He said something that sounded like "Yep" or "Huh." I tried to chill out by doing a relaxation exercise. First I sat back in the seat and kept my back straight. I put one hand on my stomach and the other on my chest, and breathed in through my nose and exhaled through my mouth—or did I have it backward? I'd once seen this on a cable TV program way before I'd ever dreamed I'd be involved in a murder investigation. *If* I was. I assumed I was, or why was I being taken to the station? If Jack Wall wanted to see me for any other purpose, he could call me.

I did my breathing exercises until we turned onto Van Ness. We took Van Ness all the way to Broadway, passing one of Vienna's father's dealerships, the showroom filled with expensive imports. Did he give Vienna one of them? If so, why didn't she drive it to work? More important, did he know about Vienna's death?

I leaned forward. "Uh, excuse me," I said to Rowley. "Have her parents been notified yet?" I replayed my conversation with Bobbi in my mind. What would she say when she heard her spendthrift stepdaughter was dead? What about her father, Lex, who, according to Dolce, supposedly doted on her? Or mother, Noreen? What a horrible job to inform the relatives of a victim. Was that Jack's job? Or was there a grief counselor who went to the houses in person like the military did?

He shrugged. "Guess so," he said. Obviously not his job to contact the family. What was his job? To walk me through Dolce's apartment and then escort me to the station? If I'd been at home, I would have continued with my exercises until I'd calmed down. It was hard to calm down in the backseat of a patrol car. At home I would have loosened my clothes, taken off my shoes and gotten comfortable to further improve my technique. But there's only so much you can do while on your way to see the detective you have a history with.

The best thing I could say about Central Station was that it was indeed centrally located. When we got inside the big, cold, featureless building, I had a few minutes to study the map of the district on the wall. It covered the financial area, Chinatown, North Beach, Fisherman's Wharf and three major hills, Nob, Telegraph and Russian Hill. The worst thing I could say about the place was that it had no character the way the neighborhood stations did, or at least the one Jack used to work at did. This one was all function. And the function was to intimidate and frighten suspects, I supposed, or even scare innocent citizens like myself into taking a vow of good behavior. As if I needed to. I felt guilty of something just standing there looking at the pictures of the officers who worked there.

The formal photo of Jack didn't do him justice. Maybe it was the uniform, which I'd never seen him in, and the hat that made him look so stern. Or maybe I'd just forgotten that he always looked stern no matter what he was wearing.

A moment later a policewoman came to get me to have my fingerprints taken. I pictured messy ink, but she said they had live-scan prints these days and I didn't need to worry. I wasn't worried about the ink, I was worried that my prints would be found all over Vienna's body. But maybe so would the murderer's. I could only hope they could sort them out.

After my session with the live-scan machine, Jack came out to get me. I was glad to see he was just as good-looking as ever, dressed as usual in top-of-the-line business casual. No uniform for him. In a pair of gray lightweight-wool flat-front trousers, a black cotton-blend sport coat over a dark striped shirt, he looked gorgeous and sophisticated but not really stern. Was this what he normally wore to work on a Sunday, or was he going somewhere afterward and if so, where?

"Good to see you," he said pleasantly as he shook my hand. "Appreciate your coming down." The last time I saw him, some months ago, he'd invited me to dinner as a kind of thank-you for helping him solve the murder of one of our customers. But there'd been no dinner, and I hadn't heard from him again. Until now. Should I remind him that he owed me? By the expression on his face, I decided, no, I shouldn't. Not now.

"Did I have a choice?" I asked.

"Not really."

He opened an office door bearing his name and waved his hand toward a chair. I sat down.

"Look, about my fingerprints. I know it's just a formality, I mean I could never kill anyone."

"I'm glad to hear it."

"But I have to tell you my prints will be all over everything. I found Vienna. I touched her. I picked up the hanger. Oh, my God, maybe the hanger is the murder weapon." I pressed my palm against my head.

"Don't worry about it now," he said.

"When should I worry about it?"

"I'll let you know."

I was sure of that. I took a deep breath and looked around the office. "Nice place you've got here," I said. "Big promotion?"

"More of a lateral move. I'm still a detective."

"Specializing in homicides?" I asked.

"I could ask you the same thing," he said.

I shook my head. He was referring to that other murder. The murder with which I really had had nothing to do other than that the victim was a customer and I was the prime suspect, which forced me to take an active role in solving the case. "Look, Jack," I said. "I had nothing to do with this and not much to do with the Jensen murder for that matter. Other than they both concerned persons connected to my place of work. I just happened to be in the wrong place at the wrong time."

"Such as in the shop on a Sunday morning. Do you want to tell me what you know about Vienna Fairchild?"

I knew it was pointless to ask "Do I have a choice?" again, so I didn't. Instead, I told him how I barely knew Vienna. But it turned out once he started questioning me, I knew quite a bit about her, including her so-called boyfriend, her father, her mother, her stepparents, her taste in clothes and where she was the last evening of her life.

"By the way," I said, "you and Vienna and I were all at the same function last night."

"That charity thing?" he asked. "Tell me about it."

"What can I tell you," I said, "that you don't know? You were there too. I saw you." I'd also seen the woman who bid on him, but if he didn't bring it up, neither would I.

"Don't worry about what I know or I don't know. I want to know what you know."

I blinked. I tried to follow, but my brain was getting tired by now. No big surprise after what I'd been through. I started telling him about Vienna's dress and her bidding at the auction and the last time I saw her in the ladies' room."

"I thought you saw her this morning at your shop," he said.

"Yes, but she was dead."

"How did you know?" he asked.

"I didn't until your officer told me. Although . . ."

"Yes?"

"She didn't seem to be breathing, and she had those marks on her neck." I shuddered. When I looked up, he was twisting a pen in his fingers and watching me closely. What had I said? Something incriminating?

"How would you describe your relationship with Ms. Fairchild?" he asked me as he leaned back in his chair.

"You mean when she was alive," I said, shifting from side to side. Why even try to get comfortable? That wasn't the goal. The goal was to get out of there. Jack's relaxed posture didn't fool me. He was trying to get me to speak without thinking, to say things I shouldn't if I wanted to walk out of here as a regular citizen and not a suspect.

"That's exactly what I mean," he said. "We'll get to the part about her death later."

I glanced at my watch. "Later? How much later? I have a swimming workout scheduled."

"On a Sunday?"

"Your office is open on Sunday, so is my health club. Some of us work during the week and we have Sundays off." Of course, Jack worked during the week and on Sundays too when he had a homicide on his hands.

"I'll try not to keep you much longer. Just a few more questions today."

Today? Were there going to be more tomorrow?

"I'll be honest," I said. "Even though I'm not under oath." Which I hoped he'd appreciate. "I was resentful of Vienna. She came to work for Dolce and took my place. She was a good saleswoman, and she worked on commission only. I got delegated to the stockroom, which I didn't like. So there you have a motive if you need one. I wanted my job back." I couldn't tell from Jack's stone face if he believed me—part of me was foolishly hoping he was so impressed with how forthcoming I'd been, he'd give me a pat on the back and send me on my way. But what the hell? He would find out sooner or later that Vienna had taken my place. Better he should hear it from me.

"Detective Wall," I said, trying to show respect and mindful that we were on his turf, "I think I've told you everything I know about Vienna."

"Have you?" he asked. "When was the last time you saw Ms. Fairchild?"

"You mean alive?"

"Yes, I mean alive."

"Last night in the ladies' room at the hotel. She gave me her winning bid."

"Really. Why was that?"

"Oh, oh, now I remember," I said as a lightbulb went off over my head. "She said she couldn't use it because her boyfriend would kill her." I couldn't believe I'd almost forgotten that. There, I'd solved the crime for him.

Jack raised his eyebrows. He was probably thinking the same thing: I can't believe you forgot to tell me that. Case closed.

"Do you know who this boyfriend is?" he asked.

"I asked her that. I said, 'Do you mean Geoffrey?' and she said 'Yeah, Geoffrey,' but you know, the way she said it, I'm not sure she meant it."

"What did she mean?"

"I don't know," I said, getting increasingly impatient. "That's the last time I saw her."

"Because you left the premises?"

"That's right," I said. "I went home in a taxi."

"By yourself?"

"Yes."

"What about your boss?"

"She was there when I left."

"How did she get along with Ms. Fairchild?"

"Famously. Dolce thought Vienna was terrific. Ask her."

"I intend to," Jack said. "Can you account for Dolce Loren's whereabouts for the rest of the evening?"

"No, I can't. I left early. She was still there."

"And then?"

"And then I went home." I couldn't believe he was grilling me like a suspect. I'd been straightforward with him, though I was beginning to wish I hadn't been. Why tell him how I felt about Vienna? He didn't need to know.

"Alone?" he asked.

"Yes," I said stiffly. "I went home and I stayed there until this morning about nine."

"Did you see anyone last night or this morning, a neighbor perhaps who could verify your presence?"

I did not like the way this was going. Not at all. "I didn't see anyone. Of course, you could ask the taxi driver, who would say he dropped me off at around ten last night." No response. "Do you have any idea what time Vienna was killed?" I asked.

"I'm asking the questions," he said.

"I understand that. I just wondered why Vienna would end up on the floor at Dolce's."

"That would be my question for you," he said.

"The answer is I have no idea," I said. "But I saw this program once where the killer took the body from somewhere to somewhere else to avoid suspicion or to plant suspicion on someone else. Maybe that's what happened. Someone wanted you to think that either Dolce or I killed Vienna. Or he was just bringing her back to the place where she worked for some reason." Jack didn't look impressed, but I continued anyway. "What I mean is, she could have been killed anywhere, like at the auction itself or in some back alley—although her dress looked perfect when I found her. Just the way it was when I saw it earlier that night. So I don't know," I admitted. "I assume you'll be questioning her family. Maybe they know. She was at the auction with them. At least I think she was with them."

"I appreciate the suggestion," he said, with just a tinge of sarcasm. Of course he would be questioning them. As well as Geoffrey. What did he think of my theory about moving the body? He didn't say.

"Geoffrey isn't her only boyfriend," I said. "I don't think so because she got picked up after work by different guys in different cars. A Porsche one day, a Lotus another day and an SUV."

"I don't suppose you got any license numbers?"

"No, why would I? I had no reason to spy on Vienna. That would be an invasion of her privacy and downright creepy."

"God forbid you should be creepy. Sorry I asked."

"Besides, how many Lotuses are there in town? You should be able to track this one down. And there's her room-mate, Danielle. She might know something." Like did she kill Vienna for not paying the rent.

"Thanks, Rita," he said as he entered something into his computer. Was it the persons or vehicles I'd suggested? Or had he entered some information about me? I'd have given anything to have a look at the screen in front of him.

"By the way," he said, "who was Ms. Fairchild's winning bid for? The one she gave you."

"Dr. Rhodes."

"Dr. Jonathan Rhodes at San Francisco General Hospi-tal," he said, glancing down at something on his desk. "Have you contacted him about it?"

"Not yet. Why, is there some reason I shouldn't?"

"Go ahead," he said. It was almost as if he was daring me. And what was I going to say to Jonathan? *I didn't bid on you because I couldn't afford it, but Vienna did and she gave me her ticket before she was murdered. How about that?*

He stood to indicate the interview was over.

"I just have one question," I said. "Are you sure it was murder?" Why did I ask? I wouldn't be here if she'd just died from a poisonous snakebite or a heart attack. I'd seen those marks on her neck. I knew.

"We're calling it a possible homicide while we wait for the coroner's report. From what you said about those marks on her neck—"

"Yes, but—"

"I appreciate your coming in, Rita," he said. "You're free to go."

I breathed a sigh of relief and stood up.

"Of course, we would appreciate it if you didn't leave town without notifying us."

I sat down again. "Is that usual?" I meant, was that usual for a nonsuspect.

"It's customary in a murder investigation."

"Then you must have the coroner's report and you know it was murder."

He didn't bother to confirm or deny it. All he said was, "You've been helpful, and we may need to call on you again for some details, names or addresses you may have left out or forgotten." He looked at a file folder on his desk. "Is your address and phone number the same?"

"Except I've moved to the third floor of the building," I said.

"Better view?" he asked. He'd been to my old place during the investigation of the other murder. But I had no idea where he lived, since he never followed through on that dinner invitation.

"Slightly," I said. "But a smaller place."

Before I left, he instructed Rowley to drive me to the health club as a way of making up for interrupting my Sunday. He also said the site of the incident—he didn't call it murder this time—had been cleared and was currently available. He handed me a card from a cleaning service that specialized in crime scenes and said we should call them. I said I'd give it to Dolce. I didn't tell him she was missing. He probably knew. I wanted to ask him if he needed any help solving this crime, but I knew better. I could just see the expression on his face of "Here we go again." I also realized it was not the time to remind him that he hadn't followed through on his dinner invitation, so I just said, "Good luck," and left.

I was too late for my water safety class, so I just snapped on my goggles, slipped into my Speedo and swam laps for a half hour. On a Sunday afternoon the pool wasn't very crowded. I was able to switch off my brain, and it was good for me to do something mindless after a day like this. Still, the vision of Vienna in her gown lying on the floor kept getting in the way of my zoning out.

I was full of ideas of who might have killed Vienna, but unfortunately no one had asked me. Surely the information I'd given Jack about what Vienna had said about Geoffrey, plus the possible other men in her life and her roommate as well as her fractured family life would give him some suspects other than me to work on, but as usual he hadn't shown his gratitude in a very demonstrative way.

I felt invigorated when I left the pool, and as soon as I turned on my cell phone, I saw I had a text message from Dolce to call her. At last she'd surfaced. I was so afraid of how she'd react to the news about Vienna, I went to a coffee shop, ordered an espresso and a blueberry scone, and found a quiet corner to call her after I'd fortified myself with the food and caffeine. Swimming always made me ravenous.

"Rita," she said. "I just got a call from the police. I don't believe it. Is it true? What happened?" She sounded hysterical.

"I don't know," I said. "I only know that I found Vienna this morning when I went to return my dress to the shop. She was lying on the floor in her dress with the pink bow. It was awful." Now it was my turn to fall apart. I started crying. It took me many minutes before I finally got hold of myself. All the while Dolce was trying to comfort me, but she was in no shape to be the comforter. What a pair we were.

"Where are you?" I asked when I caught my breath.

"I'm at home. I couldn't believe it when I saw that yellow crime scene tape across the entrance. There was an officer at the front door. I had to show my ID before they'd let me in."

"That's terrible," I said. "They told me they've finished with it now, thank God. And I have the name of the company you should call about the cleanup." I gave it to her, then I told her I'd tried to call her right after I found Vienna.

"I stayed at the hotel overnight," she said, "and had brunch this morning in the Garden Court."

"I'm glad you were able to enjoy it. I hear it's fabulous. Sushi, dim sum, crepes . . ." I was glad Dolce hadn't known about the murder or she'd never have been able to eat a bite of the delicious food in that beautiful room with the sun streaming in through the stained-glass windows.

I wanted to ask if she'd spent the night with the pilot and if so, had she had brunch with him too. But I held my tongue. She'd never pried into my personal life, and I certainly shouldn't pry into hers.

"The Palace Court was even more beautiful this morning than last night," she said wistfully. "I wish you could have been there."

"I wish I'd been there too instead of stumbling across Vienna's body in our great room."

"How awful for you."

"I'm the one who called the police."

"It must have been an accident," Dolce said.

"The police don't think so," I said. She'd find out sooner or later they were treating it like a homicide.

"They don't know everything. They don't know what a sweet girl she was. Nobody would have wanted her dead."

I couldn't say, "But somebody did." Why spoil Dolce's memory of her protégée ? I'd let Jack give her the bad news. He'd certainly want to talk to her.

In fact she hung up to take a call on her other line, a call I thought might be from Jack. He'd just want to ask her a few questions, like where she was last night and who had a motive to kill her assistant. Jack would see right away that Dolce had absolutely no reason to kill Vienna. Of all the people in Vienna's life, Dolce had to be number one on the list of nonsuspects. The question was, who was number one on the list of suspects? Me?

By the time Dolce called me back, I was at home on the edge of my seat. Literally. I grabbed the phone and sat back down on a wooden chair in the kitchen because my living room was full of boxes waiting to be unpacked.

"Oh, Rita," she said. "You were right. The police do think it was murder. They asked me all kinds of questions."

"Was it Detective Wall?"

"Yes, that's right. I can't believe he wanted to know where I was last night."

"That's easy," I assured her. "You were at the Bachelor Auction. And so was he. In fact loads of people saw you and talked to you. You're lucky because I—"

"No, I'm not lucky. I spent the night at the hotel and I wasn't alone."

I held my breath. Was Dolce going to tell me she'd spent the night with the dashing ex-pilot? That would be great news, great for Dolce's otherwise single existence and great in terms of having an alibi.

"That's good," I said.

"No, it's not. I spent the night with William."

"Did you tell Jack that?" I asked.

"Of course not. What would he think of me?"

I couldn't believe how old-fashioned Dolce was, thinking Jack would be shocked that a fifty-something-year-old woman would spend the night in a hotel with a man she wasn't married to.

"Besides," she continued, "then Detective Wall would call William and, I don't know, bring him in to verify my alibi. I can't have that."

"I'm sure he wouldn't mind if it's a matter of clearing your name in a murder investigation, would he?"

"I don't know and I'm not going to find out. I told the detective that I spent the night at the hotel alone."

"But, Dolce, you can't lie to the police."

"I just did," she said with a touch of defiance. Here was a Dolce I didn't know. "This is for your ears only, Rita: William is married."

"Oh," I said. Wouldn't you know it. Dolce finds an attractive man in her age bracket who she instantly hits it off with and he's married. "But his wife wasn't with him last night."

"I know. They're separated."

I breathed a sigh of relief. "Well, there you go."

"You don't understand. William is not just separated, he's in the midst of a nasty divorce, and he has to keep his reputation squeaky clean or risk losing everything. His retirement, his yacht and his condo."

"Yes, but, Dolce . . ." I didn't want to say "But you risk losing your freedom and your reputation," but I thought it.

"I can't talk about this anymore, Rita," she said. "I'm going to call the cleaning service, and then I'm going to bed. I'm exhausted."

I pictured Dolce curled up under her soft sheets and cashmere blanket, determined to stay there until morning. I knew she'd be at the door at nine tomorrow to welcome customers as if nothing had happened. She was the consummate saleswoman and would rise to the occasion no matter how she was hurting. The part I was worried about was her withholding information from the authorities.

I was full of nervous energy, tired from swimming and yet keyed up and eager to do something besides think about Vienna, Dolce or her new boyfriend. I wanted the time to fly, for it to be tomorrow already, when I'd be back where I belonged, in the front of the store selling clothes and accessories to San Francisco's most stylish and richest women. Was it wrong to be glad Vienna was gone? Probably, but I couldn't help it. She'd taken my place, both in Dolce's regard and in the store.

But did I want her dead? No. I'd just wanted her gone. I'd gotten my wish, but now Jack Wall had me on his suspect list. It remained to be seen if it was a good tradeoff. The best thing for me to do was to maintain my innocence and find the real murderer. Not that Jack wanted my help. He most certainly did not. He never had, even when I'd offered. Even when I'd found the murderer the last time I was involved and handed him over to Jack. If Jack was grateful, why hadn't he invited me over to dinner as he'd promised? Too busy? Too chagrined that I'd been the one who figured it out?

So Jack didn't want my help. Then I'd do what I could on my own without telling him or anyone. After hanging up with Dolce, I noticed the message machine on my home phone was flashing. When I pressed the button, I heard Dr. Jonathan's voice.

"Rita, what's going on?" he said. "You didn't bid on me. You said you would, but somebody else did. Whoever she is came up to me last night and said she was sorry she couldn't make it but she'd given her ticket to you. So do we have a date? Call me on my cell. I'm at the hospital treating seizures, chest pains, vomiting, overdoses, and one psychotic patient who just threatened to kill me. Just another beautiful Sunday morning at the hospital."

Five

I was glad to hear a friendly voice. Someone who didn't suspect me of murder. Someone who was healing the sick and
the crazy but didn't even know his supposed date for an evening at the Starlight Room had been murdered. I thought it
was better he should hear it from me than from the police.
Especially if he didn't have an alibi. Although Jack surely
wouldn't suspect an ER doctor who devoted himself to keeping people alive and who didn't even know Vienna, or would
he? I still wanted to know why she'd bid so much money on
him. Sure, he was a great-looking guy, but so were some of
the others.

I called Jonathan, but he didn't pick up. Maybe he was
taking out someone's appendix or else that crazy person had
possibly made good on his threat. So I left a message. Pushing the moving boxes aside, I made myself a cup of tea and
sat down at my authentic French bistro table with the

cast-iron base and aged white marble top. My dining room
table was folded up in the hall. Opened up, it would seat
eight, but I'd never had eight people to dinner. I'd never even
had one person to dinner, but one day I would.

Instead of an iPad, I took out an old-fashioned pen and
paper and drew a circle with Vienna's name in the middle.
Then I made a list of everyone I knew who was associated
with Vienna. Radiating from the circle I drew lines and put
a name on each line.

First there was her family. Her father, Lex, who would
have no reason to get rid of his darling daughter. I put a plus
sign next to his name. Her stepmother, Bobbi, who seemed,
judging by my one phone call with her, a bit resentful of
Vienna. I put a minus next to hers. Next came her mother,
Noreen, and her stepfather, Hugh, each name on a separate
prong. Then I wrote "Geoffrey" on a spike leading from
Vienna's circle, and three more spikes with blanks for the
names of other men she might be dating. At the very least,
I knew there were the guys who'd picked her up from work
at night, and I wrote the type of car each drove—van, sports
car and SUV. Then Danielle, her roommate, who definitely
deserved a minus based on my conversation with her. No
love lost there. But what good would killing Vienna do Danielle when she seemed to be most interested in the rent?
Maybe she had someone else who wanted to move in. Still,
it seemed like a weak motive for murder.

I finished by adding both Dolce's and my names to the
diagram, although I knew we hadn't done it. At least I knew
I hadn't, but I wanted to be an equal-opportunity fingerer
of suspects. I had to be if I wanted to be an unbiased aide
to the police whether they wanted my help or not.

I was about to give up and go to bed when Jonathan called me back.

"Rita, I just heard the news about that woman. Is it true?" he said.

"You mean Vienna being murdered? I'm afraid it is," I said. "I'm the one who found her this morning at the boutique."

"She was murdered while you were at work?"

"No, no, we're not open on Sunday. I went there to return my dress on my way to my health club and there she was. Lying on the floor in the same dress she was wearing last night with the p-p-pink . . . b-b—" My voice started to shake as the whole scene came back to haunt me. The sight of her body, her dress with the pink bow, the marks on her neck, the police, the accusations.

"But what was she doing there?" he asked.

I bit my lip and tried to stay calm, but my eyes filled with tears. I found a tissue and blew my nose. "I don't know. I keep asking myself that." I didn't tell him what I'd told Jack, that it was possible she'd been brought there from wherever she'd been killed. But if not, the question was still unanswered. What *was* she doing there? Why go to the shop in your fancy dress on a Sunday morning? Was she meeting someone? Possibly, but why hadn't she changed clothes? Because she hadn't gone home? But where had she gone? And with whom?

"So do we have a date?" he asked.

I blinked rapidly. I shouldn't have been surprised that Jonathan would take Vienna's death in stride and move on to the next event. It was part of his nature and why he was so good at his job. ER doctors probably had to be that way or they'd fall apart after one night on call. I liked that about him and resolved to be more like that myself.

"Sure," I said. I'd have to be certifiably crazy to turn down a date to the Starlight Room at one of the big hotels with one of the city's most eligible bachelors even though it was courtesy of a dead girl's generosity.

"What about next Saturday night? I'll trade off with one of my colleagues. He owes me and I need a night off."

"Sounds good," I said. "I've never been there. I hear it's very posh."

"Dinner and dancing. It beats a beef stick and stale coffee followed by a broken tibia, bronchitis and pneumonia. Save the date and I'll let you know more later."

So it's true what they say. It's an ill wind that blows nobody any good. An ill wind killed Vienna but brought two men back into my life. The only one still missing was Nick the gymnast, but he was laid up and out of the picture. Of course, it would be better if Detective Jack Wall didn't suspect me of murdering Vienna. On the bright side of the coin, it gave him a reason to seek me out. As for me, I wanted to help him solve the murder. Not just to save myself from a long messy trial, but also to see justice done. If my status as suspect number one threw us together again, so be it. I was confident he'd find the real guilty party sooner or later. With my help, of course.

I worked on my suspect list until I couldn't see straight. The problem wasn't that I didn't have enough suspects—I had too many. The problem was how to contact them and interrogate them without them realizing what I was doing. I also didn't want Jack to know what I was up to or he'd put a stop to it and tell me I was out of line.

I finally fell into bed. No top-of-the-line three-hundred-count all-Egyptian-cotton sheets for me, still I slept like a baby until my alarm went off. Sensing there would be a crowd at the shop, I dressed carefully.

First off, I went with bold bright lips and kept the rest of my makeup subtle. I didn't want to come off as totally retro. I did iron my hair, though, to give it a sleek, swingy, sexy but still low-key look. My work brings me in contact with women mostly, since we sell only women's clothes and accessories, but these days you never know who's going to turn up when there's been a murder on the premises. So why not try for sexy hair, I asked myself.

From my closet I pulled out a rather stark black cashmere dress that landed above the knee, paired it with black tights and wedge booties that I'd unpacked the first day I moved in, knowing there would be a day like this when I'd have to look my best. Then to contrast the low-key look, I tied a splashy red cotton necktie around my neck that exactly matched my lipstick. I wanted to say, "Look at me! I'm not guilty of anything but looking as good as I possibly can."

I knew I looked as good as I could, but my stomach was doing flip-flops. I also knew I should eat something like whole grains, fruits and vegetables, but I was in a hurry, and, frankly, nothing good for me sounded good. When I got off the bus near Dolce's, I stopped at a coffee shop for a soothing cup of chamomile tea to go. That ought to get me through the morning, depending . . .

I was relieved to find the front door devoid of any yellow crime scene tape and, once inside, to see the floor looked freshly scrubbed and waxed. So those crime scene cleaners had done a good job. I didn't realize I was holding my breath until I entered the great room, stepping gingerly over the place where I'd last seen Vienna's body.

"Good morning," a voice from the next room said.

I almost jumped out of my skin. It didn't sound like Dolce. In fact it was Detective Ramirez, who I knew used to be Jack Wall's assistant or whatever you call a detective that's beneath you in rank. She came walking toward me from the rear of the house, dressed, as usual, in an outfit all wrong for her figure. She was not in uniform, which might have covered her ample figure and given her some gravitas, which I assumed all officers of the law aimed for. Instead, she was wearing a pair of short shorts with tough boots and a striped surfer-inspired hoodie.

I knew it wasn't polite, but I simply stood there in the middle of the great room staring at this vision, a portly policewoman wearing a trendy outfit that accented her wide hips and stocky legs.

"Detective Ramirez," I said when I finally found my voice. "I hardly recognized you."

"Why not? Because I wear street clothes when I'm on duty and also when I'm not?" she said.

"That's right," I replied, not wishing to get into an argument over what she wore or didn't wear. "What brings you to the boutique so early this Monday morning?" And how did she get in?

As if I didn't know why she was here. She was surely at the boutique to grill both Dolce and me about the murder of our former salesgirl. But why her? Why now? And why didn't Jack tell me he was sending her?

"Your boss let me in," she said. "She said she'd be with me shortly."

"In the meantime, what can I do for you?" I asked pleasantly. I decided to assume she was there on personal business and treat her as if she were a regular customer. "A new bag? A pleated skirt? We just got some girly skirts in that look great with oversize sweaters in neutral colors." I don't believe in forcing styles on our customers. Instead I try my best to find them something they like whether I think it's appropriate for their body type or not. Which is why I thought, based on the detective's taste in clothing, that she'd go for one of our new skirts and sweaters. My job was to help everyone, whether wraith-like or chubby, find what they wanted and if they felt good about themselves, all the better for them.

"Not today," she said. "Actually this is my day off. As you see, I am dressed even more casually than usual. This is just an informal courtesy call. I've recently been reassigned to your neighborhood."

"Really?" I said, though I wanted to ask, "How recently? Just today?" Instead, I said, "So does your assignment have anything to do with the um . . . death of Vienna Fairchild over the weekend?"

"It could," she said. "I want you to know that even though I'm off duty, I'm available for consultation any time of night or day. Our goal at the SFPD is to cut down on violent crime in the area."

"I second that. Crime in the area is not good for business." I paused for a second. Enough pussy-footing around. "So do you have any suspects in the Fairchild murder? Any clues?" I asked. I didn't think she'd answer, but why not push the envelope? She'd never liked me, so why pretend otherwise?

She looked surprised at my audacity. What nerve I had asking direct questions. I decided if Jack had sent her here, I was going to let go of my inhibitions and ask her anything I felt like. Even if she wasn't on duty. Even if she refused to

answer. This was my chance to ask anything I wouldn't ask
Jack for fear of setting him off on a tangent. She could say
no and that would be that. I was used to being turned down.
I was also used to taking chances.

"That's for me to ask you, Ms. Jewel," she said. "In any
case, I'd be speaking off the record if I talked about clues,
since I'm not on duty today."

"Yes, yes, I understand," I said. I got the message or I
thought I did. But wait. If she wasn't working today, then
why was she here? To shop at an exclusive boutique on a
public servant's salary? "Call me Rita," I added. "All the
customers do."

"I'm not a customer . . . yet. And I can only be one on
my day off, Rita. So if I were here to question you—."

"Which you aren't," I said flatly, daring her to contradict
me. "If I can't show you anything in the shop or help you
then . . ." Then why in hell are you here? What *is* a courtesy
call anyway, I wondered.

"I do have a few questions," she said. "Nothing official,
just between the two of us."

Just the two of us? I didn't believe that for a minute.

"Are any of your customers friends of Ms. Fairchild's?

"I'm not sure," I said. "At Dolce's there's a fine line
between customers and friends. We like to think of our customers as our friends. And if this is in regard to the homicide, Detective Wall has already questioned me."

"I'm aware of that," she said. "But there are still more
questions."

"Of course," I said. "You have questions and I have questions. Naturally I'm always happy to help. I've never met
any of Vienna's friends, although I have actually seen one
of her male friends, a man named Geoffrey, and I've spoken

on the phone to some of her relatives as well as her room-mate, Danielle. Is that what you want to know?"

She was writing all this down on a pad of paper, not her Blackberry—so it wouldn't look official, I supposed. All the while pretending she wasn't there on business and yet she didn't even look at a single item on our shelves or racks.

When Dolce finally came downstairs, she invited Ramirez into her office and they closed the door. Dolce barely glanced at me. Just when I had a lot of questions to ask her. Question number one: Had she changed her mind about confessing to her whereabouts to save herself from being a suspect?

I went to the door and listened shamelessly. I had to know if Dolce was going to tell her what happened the night of the murder. Instead, I heard Dolce giving her fashion advice.

"Play up your curves with a high-waisted printed pant," Dolce was saying diplomatically.

"But won't print pants just make me look like an ele-phant?"

Dolce laughed softly. A laugh that said, "That's just ridic-ulous." She was so good at making others feel good about themselves. Not just good, she was a genius.

Now they were talking underwear. "You need five differ-ent bras," Dolce told Ramirez. "Smooth, strapless, sporty, a black T-back bra and a leisure bra that is comfy and soft."

A moment later Dolce came out of her office by herself, and I jumped out of the way. She was walking toward the great room, muttering to herself.

"Is everything okay?" I asked.

She nodded.

"Why is she here, really?" I whispered.

Dolce shrugged. "I don't know and I don't want to know.

I want to find her something to wear and send her on her way. Did she tell you it's her day off?" she said.

"Only a half dozen times," I said. "Maybe she says that so we'll relax, get comfortable and tell her what she wants to know."

"Which is?"

"Who killed Vienna."

Dolce shot me a look that said "No way." Then she opened a drawer in a highboy maplewood dresser and took out a striped sweater. "What do you think?" she asked.

"Horizontal stripes?" I said. "On Detective Ramirez?"

"Oh, all right," she said with a sigh. "But large women can't wear dark solids all day every day. And it's a change from her uniform."

"You're right," I said. "Go for it."

Dolce looked at her watch. "Open up, will you? I want everything to appear normal."

I looked at her. The new faux bob hairstyle complete with chic feathery bangs she'd achieved without professional help was perfect. She wore a little forest green velvet jacket with a pair of slim cocoa-color pants. But she had huge circles under her eyes that no makeup could cover. I felt so bad for her I wanted to give her a hug, but I sensed she wasn't in the mood. She just wanted to get through this day. So did I. So did everyone connected with Vienna, I'd bet.

Shortly after I opened the front door, the great room was full of customers. We're not usually so busy on a Monday morning, but this was no ordinary day. Everyone seemed to know about Vienna. San Francisco is a small town in some ways, even though we have a big-city symphony orchestra, world-class cuisine and unmatched breathtaking views from every hill. Gossip travels fast. And news of the murder had been covered on the local news programs.

"Where's Dolce?" Patti French asked the minute she stepped inside our hand-carved antique door.

"In her office. Can I help?"

"I can't believe it. I'm the one who sold you the tickets to the auction, aren't I? This is my fault. If I'd kept my tickets to myself, Vienna would be alive today."

"You mean—"

"It happened that night, didn't it? Right here, wasn't it?" She looked around eagerly, as if she might see signs of the murder, like blood, torn clothes or clumps of blond hair.

That was the question. Did it happen right here or not? "Patti," I said, "don't blame yourself. Vienna would have been at the auction anyway."

"I don't blame myself," she said. "I blame that madman who killed her."

I bit my tongue to keep from asking, "How do you know it was a man?"

Now a small crowd had gathered around Patti, whose voice was rising with every word. I knew everyone in the room except for one tall dark-haired young woman who was watching and listening like a TV reporter. I sincerely hoped she wasn't. A murder on the premises was the kind of publicity Dolce didn't need.

"Right here?" Monica Sayles asked breathlessly. "But what was she doing here after hours?"

I shrugged. Good question. How should I know what our newest employee was doing at the shop on a Sunday morning—or was it late Saturday night? Lured here by her attacker? An assignation with someone she knew? Or just a random break-in by a thief whom Vienna caught in the act? Or back to my theory that it didn't take place here at all and whoever brought her here wanted to blame Dolce or me.

I wondered if I'd ever be privileged to hear any inside information from anyone. Not if Jack Wall had anything to say about it. He wanted me out of his side of the investigation. Well, that wasn't going to happen. I'd be careful, I'd be discreet, but I wouldn't be left out.

I decided to move on to the small accessories alcove, still within hearing distance, but giving the impression that I wasn't eavesdropping.

I was just polishing an already perfectly polished silver pendant with turquoise beads when the dark-haired young woman I'd noticed earlier joined me.

"What can I do for you?" I asked. After all, this *was* a store and we *did* have things for sale. It was not just a gossip fest. It would be different if one of our customers actually knew anything, but so far, all I'd heard was questions. Why, when, how and where?

"I'm Athena Fairchild, Vienna's twin sister," she said.

I almost dropped the necklace, that's how startled I was. "Vienna had a twin sister?" I said, dumbfounded.

"Has," she corrected. "I'm still alive, though I must say I'm not feeling entirely confident about my chances after what happened to Vienna. This is a dangerous place." She gave a quick look over her shoulder as if expecting an assassin to burst in at any moment.

I stared at Vienna's twin. "But you don't look . . ."

"Like her? No, we're fraternal twins. We never looked alike. Never wanted to. Never dressed alike. Never acted alike. Never wanted anyone to know we were twins."

"How did you manage that?" I asked while gaping at her

outfit, a pair of very wide-legged jeans, definitely fuller flaired, not quite bell-bottomed, but seventies inspired for sure. With the jeans she wore a sporty jacket and a pair of Miu Miu wedge sandals. None of which Vienna would ever have worn. Too casual. Too sporty.

"Our parents got divorced when we were small. I went to live with my mother, and Vienna stayed with my father and his new wife."

"Bobbi," I murmured, remembering our conversation.

"Horrible woman," Athena said. "That's one thing my sister and I agreed on. We didn't have many happy family reunions."

"Otherwise you weren't close?" I asked. Athena certainly didn't seem grief stricken over her sister's death, but given their history, maybe it was understandable. And some people simply don't show emotion the way others do.

She shook her head. "I hadn't seen Vienna for years. I was sent to boarding school in the East, then college. My mother and Hugh would come to New York for the holidays. The only reason I'm here now is because of the auction the other night."

"You were there?" I asked.

"Mother insisted," she said. "She bought a whole table. She's very charitable that way. So is Hugh. So I flew in Saturday morning. But I left after the dinner. I hate those black-tie affairs. So boring. But what could I do? Mother knew Vienna would be there. How would it look if she didn't have her other daughter with her to balance what I call 'the Vienna effect.' I hear my sister bid up a storm on some hot MD."

"Mm-hmm," I said noncommittally. Now was not the time to mention that I not only knew the hot MD, but I also would be going out with him, thanks to her sister's winning bid.

"I was supposed to fly back to New York today, but my mother wants me here for the funeral. It's tomorrow, you know."

No, I didn't know. "I'm sure you're a big comfort to your mother," I said, because that's what you're supposed to say. To myself, I said, "Rita, you have to go. Everyone will be there, including the killer." That's how it happened at my last homicide. I went to a celebration-of-life gathering as well as the funeral for MarySue Jensen, one of our regular customers, and both events were eye-openers. It would be even better this time because now I knew what to look for: someone who cries too much, who falls apart, who is a little too sad and lets you know. It's a dead giveaway. If I was looking for a suspect who was overly distressed, it was not Athena. I wondered if she even cared that her sister was dead.

"My mother is freaked out," Athena said. "She's already had a call from a policeman who wants to interview her. Like she knows anything? Vienna didn't even tell her she was working here, just that she was coming to the auction. She sent me today to see if Vienna left anything behind, any clothes or jewelry? What happened to the dress and the necklace she was wearing to the auction, Mom wants to know. She doesn't want Bobbi to get her claws on anything, especially that necklace."

"I don't know where her clothes are," I said. "I'm the one who found your sister Sunday morning, and she was wearing the dress then—but not the necklace, come to think of it. You should speak to the police. Call the SFPD and ask for Detective Wall."

"I'll do that. The necklace belonged to our grandmother—it's a real heirloom piece, with an electric pink, pear-shaped tourmaline encircled in diamonds. Mom didn't know Vienna had it until that night and she wants it back."

Wants it back? I thought. How can she want it back if she never had it? "I saw it. It was gorgeous. I don't know why I didn't notice it was missing." Other than I was upset at finding a dead body. "Maybe your grandmother gave it to her," I suggested.

"I doubt it. Grammie is old and lives in a retirement home. She doesn't always know who's who or what's what. But she does know what's hers and what isn't. And that necklace is hers. She gets us mixed up even though we don't look anything alike. If Vienna asked to wear the necklace that night, Grammie might have loaned it to her. Vienna had a way of asking for things that you couldn't resist. I'll never forget her taking my favorite doll away from me when we were small and tearing her arm off before she was forced to give it back. Frankly, I'm not surprised she came to a violent end. What do they call it when you get what's coming to you?"

"Just deserts?" I suggested.

"That's it."

"You're not saying she deserved to die," I said, staring at her.

"No, of course not, just that I'm not totally surprised that she inspired someone to want to do away with her. Anyway, I want to know what happened to the necklace. Grammie once promised it to me. She doesn't remember, of course. But I do and Vienna did. Why else did she wear it the one night when I'm in town? You tell me."

What could I say? Because it matched her dress? There

was no love lost between Vienna and myself, but there was no point to adding to Athena's list of her sister's faults.

"I don't care about the dress, but I want the necklace," Athena said emphatically, tossing her long dark hair. Suddenly her eyes widened. "You don't think that's why she was murdered, for the necklace? It's valuable, but still, it wouldn't have the same sentimental meaning for anyone but family."

"I don't know why she was murdered," I said. "I'm not a detective." Though in all modesty I ought to be one after what I'd done to catch the killer of MarySue Jensen.

More to the point, Detective Wall didn't know about the necklace either. I couldn't believe I hadn't noticed it was missing when I found Vienna's body. That's how traumatized I was. Now I had something to tell Jack. Something important. "I remember seeing your sister and the necklace Saturday night just before she left the auction." I surely would have remembered if Vienna had been wearing the pink tourmaline when I found her. It was that stunning.

Athena was looking at me as if she suspected me not only of knocking off her sister but of taking the necklace too.

"It was beautiful, but not my style," I added hastily. "It was an antique and I'm the modern type."

She gave me a quick once-over, and I had the feeling she was not impressed with my modern style. It didn't matter. Her sporty style was not mine either. So there. You can't please everyone, can you?

At that moment Dolce came into the room. She was alone, so I assumed she'd finally shaken off the frumpy policewoman and maybe even sold her a few strategic pieces before she left. I had to introduce her to Athena, but I was afraid she'd go into shock.

"Dolce, this is Vienna's twin sister, Athena," I said gently.

Dolce's mouth fell open. Maybe I shouldn't have told her. She didn't need any more surprises. But her reaction shocked me. She threw her arms around Athena and hugged her as if she were Vienna reincarnated. "I'm so sorry about your sister," Dolce said, her voice trembling.

Athena appeared stunned as well. She held herself stiff and silent, as though unsure of how to respond.

"Athena is looking for Vienna's dress and jewelry, the things she was wearing Saturday night. I told her we had no idea where they were, but perhaps the police . . ."

Dolce released Athena and nodded, a tear trickling down one cheek. She may have been the person most affected by Vienna's demise. Using my theories, did that mean she was most likely the guilty party? No, a thousand times no.

"Athena says the funeral will be held tomorrow," I said.

"It's at Cypress Ridge Funeral Home in Colma at two in the afternoon, followed by a reception at my mother's house in Atherton. She's hosting that part; my father's in charge of the wake. He's completely broken up over it. So I have no idea what he has planned other than an open casket and an open bar. No speeches. So if you have something to say, save it for the reception."

Dolce nodded, and I hoped she'd have a chance to say how much she loved Vienna and what she'd meant to our business in the short time she'd worked there.

"Mother's going all out, and so is my father in his own macho male way. Nothing's too good for his little girl. Never has been. He's always spoiled her something terrible. When she tore the arm off my doll, he bought us each a new one. She didn't deserve it. She was livid when she heard for once he was being fair and he'd given me a car for graduation too."

"When was that?" I asked, peering out the window to see a late-model sports car in front of the shop.

"Just this weekend. I picked out an energy-efficient little roadster, but Vienna was dithering over whether to choose a Porsche or a BMW. That's my sister. Always trying to one-up me with her expensive taste. Me, I'm easy to please." She tossed her long loose hair over her shoulder again, and I thought she sounded just a little too smug about her taste and her superiority over her sister. Maybe being Vienna's sister required a lot of self-confidence. Even when you lived across the continent from her. I wondered what Dolce thought of her. I could hardly wait to call Jack Wall. Wouldn't he like to know Vienna had a twin sister with whom she was on the outs and who had actually been at the Bachelor Auction? But where was she when Vienna was killed? I was tempted to ask, but that was a question for a skilled professional, not me. For once, I held my tongue.

"Here's my phone number," Athena said, handing me a card. "Call me if you come across Vienna's dress or neck-lace. Mother's on a rampage, as you can imagine. See you tomorrow." With that, she turned and left.

There was a long silence in the shop while we both pon-dered this new arrival on the scene. What role would she play in the next act? A more important question came to mind. What was I going to wear to the funeral?

Six

I left Dolce to mix with the customers in the great room, and I took refuge in her office for a moment to call Detective Wall.

"I have some information for you regarding the Vienna Fairchild case," I said, unable to conceal my excitement.

"Go ahead," he said.

"Can we meet somewhere?"

"Is it that good?"

Now I was nervous. What if we met and I told him everything I knew and he just looked at me blankly, or even worse, he looked at his watch as if I was wasting his time.

"I think so, but if you're too busy . . ."

"I'll be at the coffee shop on the corner in fifteen minutes," he said brusquely.

I hung up, pulled out a pad of paper and made a list so I wouldn't babble on incoherently when I saw him. I started writing names and then remembered I didn't know the names of the other men in Vienna's life. Except for Geoffrey, whom Vienna had told us about. But who were the others? Had one of them killed her in a jealous rage? Or did Geoffrey? It made sense. If only I knew who the others were. Suddenly I remembered Geoffrey's last name. Hill. I did a quick search on Dolce's computer and found he was a graphic artist with a web site. There he was, "Geoffrey Hill, Designer of Web Sites, Logos and More." From the examples, I could tell he had a whimsical sense of humor. Had that appealed to Vienna? Or was that why she was dating someone else, several someones else. He was too off-beat.

From the photo on his site, I saw that Geoffrey was indeed the tall, lanky guy I'd seen outside the shop on his motorcycle. He was a creative genius according to the raves he'd posted from those he'd worked for. I called his number. I expected an answering machine, but he picked up on the second ring.

I told him who I was, then I asked if he'd heard about Vienna.

Would he burst into tears or what? He didn't.

"Yeah," he said. "The police were here already. I told them I didn't know anything. Except that girl was headed for trouble."

"What do you mean?" I asked.

"Come on," he said. "You knew her. You knew what she was up to. She was a user. She was using me to design a web site for her, just like she used me as a decoy in high school. First a Facebook page and then it never stopped. She was using your store too."

I couldn't let that go. "How do you mean? She worked here and she was a terrific saleswoman." I realized I was sounding like her defense attorney, but I didn't get the part about her being a user. She didn't use me or Dolce as far as I knew. We used her to sell clothes and accessories.

"And I'm not sure I did know her," I said. "Are you talking about other guys she might have been dating?" Maybe he was mad because Vienna had other boyfriends with better wheels than his. "I suppose you told the police everything."

"Everything they asked me."

"Did they ask you who the other guys were?" If only he'd say no and then tell me and I'd have an exclusive. I'd show Jack Wall I was one step ahead of him.

"You mean did I rat on Raold and Emery?" he said. "No. None of their business. They're not murderers. You ever meet them?"

"No, but I think I saw one of them or both of them pick her up. Does one drive a Lotus and the other an SUV?"

"How should I know? Do I hang with them, go riding around with them? No. I've got my own wheels," he said proudly. But I thought he did know what they drove. Guys always do, that's how they identify themselves.

"I know. I saw your motorcycle. Nice bike. So you don't think either one of them could help find Vienna's killer?"

"I told you I don't know." He sounded irritated. Where was that whimsical sense of humor? Maybe he was saving it for his paying customers. "From what she said, I first thought it was you who offed her. She told me you were stiffed when she took your place. I don't know anything about crime, but I know jealousy is one hell of a motive for murder."

"I did not kill Vienna," I said, incensed that yet another person suspected me of murder. "I wasn't happy about

Vienna working here, but I didn't kill her. Did you tell the police—I mean, did you tell them you suspected me?" I asked anxiously. That's all I needed was another person thinking I was guilty and blabbing about it.

"I might have said something," he said. "Can't remember. Since Vienna's murder, people have been calling me nonstop since the obit was in the paper. Friends, customers, whatever. I've got more business than I can handle." Then he hung up. I'd pushed him as far as I could and found out he'd probably told the police to check me out. At least I'd gotten something positive out of our conversation. Two names I'd been looking for. Raold and Emery. And it looked like Geoffrey had gotten something positive out of Vienna's death: his business had picked up. Already. Amazing what murder can do for a person's business. Kind of ghoulish, actually.

I couldn't believe it, but that's what I'd heard. I wondered how other many people were glad Vienna was gone. Besides me, of course.

My phone rang. It was Jonathan.

"We're all set for Saturday night," he said. "That still okay with you?"

"Of course. I'm excited. It's such a happening spot."

"That's what I hear. How are you?"

"I'm fine, but well, it's complicated. With the murder of Vienna, it leaves a hole in our sales force." I didn't tell him how happy I was to fill that hole. I didn't want to sound callous, as if Vienna's murder was either an opportunity or just an inconvenience. I didn't want to put a damper on our relationship by telling him I was a murder suspect.

"You must be really busy. You don't have to work overtime, do you?" he asked.

How like Jonathan to think of me and how I'd be affected.

"No, it's not like that. In fact, because she's not here any-more, I have my old job back doing what I love: selling clothes. The downside is that there's a murderer on the loose."

"Any idea of who it might be?"

"Not yet," I said, "but I'm working on it." There you have it, the contrast between Jonathan and Jack. Jack never wanted my input, whereas Jonathan thought I was worth listening to. It almost made me want to cancel my meeting with Jack. He didn't deserve my help.

"I have to run, Jonathan," I said. "See you Saturday."

"Pick you up at seven," he said.

I grabbed my Juicy Couture hobo handbag and headed for the door. Jack was waiting for me at the coffee shop, in civilian clothes as usual. Today it was a blue denim work shirt and a pair of five-pocket designer jeans. The truth was, he could wear anything anywhere and still look like he'd stepped out of *GQ*. He was sitting at a small table talking on his cell phone and texting at the same time. Like he couldn't waste a single minute of the day just having coffee with an informant. As if he was the only one with a time-consuming, important job. I knew he thought selling clothes and accessories was a trivial pursuit, but did he have to make it so obvious I was wasting his time? I had half a mind to turn around and leave.

"Coffee?" I asked, since he wasn't playing the role of host.

He put his iPhone and his Blackberry in his pocket and nodded. I went to the counter, bought two cups of coffee, laced them with cream and came back.

"Well?" he said. "What have you got?"

"It's the house blend," I said. "See if you can taste the subtle hints of bittersweet chocolate and the well-rounded toasted-nut finish."

"I mean what information have you got?" he asked, stirring his coffee with a stick.

Sometimes I wondered why I bothered with him. Why not just solve this murder myself and turn over the criminal along with the evidence to the police? Would I get any recognition even then? Not that I cared about being praised in public or in the newspaper; I just wanted to see justice served. I also wanted to tell him I knew about the new police program "Anti-Violence Skills for Ordinary Citizens" and that I wanted to be part of it. But first things first.

I pulled out my notes and stacked them on the table. "One," I said, "the funeral is tomorrow in Colma."

"Are you going?"

"Of course," I said.

"You can't pass up a good funeral, can you?" As if I didn't have more than one reason to go.

"I have to be there. She was my colleague, a fellow salesgirl. Besides I need to be on hand for Dolce. She'll be a wreck. She cared deeply about Vienna."

"More than she cared about you?"

"I know what you're thinking. I was jealous of Vienna. And sometimes I was. But it wasn't really like that."

"What was it like?" he asked, cocking his head to one side.

"We worked together. She was the new girl and had loads of potential."

"Is that it?" he said, setting his cup on the table.

I knew what he was thinking: I came all this way for you to tell me what I already knew.

I gritted my teeth. This wasn't going as well as I'd hoped. I wanted him to beg me for my insight or at least thank me. I should have known.

"Two, as for suspects, Vienna has a twin sister, Athena. I just spoke with her at the shop, and I can tell you there's no love lost there. Vienna tore the arm off Athena's doll."

"Recently?" he asked.

"No, when they were small. But you never forget those things. And Athena was at the auction Saturday with her mother and her mother's husband. But she left early."

"Did you see her?"

"No, I'm just telling you what she told me." I frowned. Maybe Jack knew more than I thought he did and was just trying to trip me up. Why was I surprised? He was a cop with a mission. He had ways and means I didn't even dream of and might not approve of. Plus he had a staff who got paid to follow his orders.

"Go on," he said. "You were going to give me some suspects."

I hesitated for a moment. I wanted badly to keep my information to myself, but wasn't there a law against withholding evidence? "What about those men in her life? There were others besides Geoffrey, which is why she couldn't go on the date she bid on. She gave me the impression that one of them would be angry about it. Maybe even violent. I have two names, but I'm not sure they're accurate."

"Where did you get them?" he asked, leaning forward, finally showing some signs of interest.

"From one of my sources," I said smugly. He couldn't force me to divulge who it was, I hoped. Because I still planned to grill Geoffrey more when I saw him, perhaps at the funeral. I'd forgotten to ask if he'd be there.

"The names are Raold and Emery. That's all I know. Except I do know what they drive." I gave him my list of the vehicles I'd seen picking her up. "As for motives," I said, "when I discovered her body, Vienna wasn't wearing her antique diamond and tourmaline necklace, and as you know, her neck looked like someone choked her."

"You think the necklace was worth killing for?"

"If you like jewelry."

He glanced at the hammered gold necklace I was wearing.

"Okay, I confess. I love jewelry. I also love bags and scarves, but I don't love them enough to murder anyone. For the record, I didn't murder Vienna for her necklace."

"I believe you," he said. "If you murdered her, I think you did it to get your job back," he said. "Your fingerprints are all over the murder weapon."

"Of course. I told you that. It's because I found her. I picked up the hanger. I was in shock. I wasn't thinking."

"How do you know the hanger was the weapon?" he asked.

"I don't know—I thought you just told me."

He shook his head.

"If it wasn't the hanger, what was it? It had to be."

"So your best guess is that the killer was either one of her boyfriends or a member of her family, do I have that right?"

"Well, yes. Murder is hardly ever a random act, right? More women are killed by husbands or lovers or family members than by total strangers. That's what I've always heard." If that's what I'd heard, he must have heard it too. He must have seen the statistics, and he knew I was right to focus on the men in her life. He just didn't want to give me credit. He never did.

He didn't agree or disagree. He just stood and said he had to go.

"I almost forgot. I read somewhere you're doing an anti-violence program for the community."

"Don't tell me, you want to join."

"I think I should. If it wasn't a man in her life who killed her, then there might be a serial killer out there targeting shopgirls and I could be next." I gave a shudder to empha-size my fear, but the truth was I just wanted an excuse to hang out with cops so I could work on this case undercover. I hoped that Jack didn't suspect my true motive, but he prob-ably did.

"Wednesday nights at the Central Station. Weapons training, ride-along program, victims' rights counseling. Is that really what you want to do on your Wednesday nights?"

I nodded vigorously. "It sounds fascinating. How do I sign up?"

"I'll put your name on the list. If you're serious about this."

"Of course I'm serious. Do I look serious?" I fixed my gaze on him and assumed a serious expression. His mouth twitched, and I thought he might be going to laugh, but he didn't. What would people think, Detective Wall has a sense of humor?

"The citizens' antiviolence program is more what I need at this point. It's already organized, and I think I could really benefit from it. Seeing as I work in a dangerous neighbor-hood."

"I hope you're not getting paranoid. You live in a big city.

You should take normal precautions. But not change your lifestyle."

How did he know what my lifestyle was? He'd been out of touch with me for months. "I appreciate your advice. I definitely want to set up a neighborhood watch program in my neighborhood too, in the future when the air clears. But not now." Why did I get the feeling he thought I was not only paranoid but also flakey, jumping from one thing to another, never completing any project. I'd show him. I'd learn to handle a weapon, I'd comfort the victims of violent crime, and I'd ride along on police calls. And more important, I'd solve the murder of Vienna Fairchild. With or without his help. I was pretty sure it would be without.

When I got back to the shop, Dolce seemed more like her usual cheerful self. The lines on her forehead had smoothed out, and she was smiling at one of our old-timers, who was completely unaware that there'd been a murder on the premises until a few minutes ago. I almost preferred my theory that the murder had taken place elsewhere and Vienna's body had been transported to Dolce's. If so, why? If so, who? If so, when?

I wondered if I'd ever be able to forget the sight of Vienna lying there, right where several women were now standing, holding up dresses, trying on shoes and gazing at themselves in one of the many full-length mirrors around the room as if it were just another day in Paradise.

I put my jacket and purse in Dolce's office and went back out to help customers find the right outfit for wherever they were going. The funeral tomorrow or a night on the town. I felt good knowing I myself needed something for both occasions, which meant a personal and professional challenge all wrapped up together. I loved seeing the place crowded with the usual shoppers, and some of them were actually buying instead of just standing around gossiping.

I spent a few minutes going through the racks looking for black dresses, although I was happy to tell anyone who asked that wearing all black to a funeral wasn't necessary.

"Black, navy, gray or any other dark colors are fine," I told everyone who asked me. "Even deep burgundy red or forest green."

"What about pants? Or do we have to wear skirts?" Buffy asked.

"Pants are fine," I said. "But no jeans. Not that anyone here would wear denim to a funeral. As for shoes, closed toes are not essential, but it might be best to cover up bright toenails." Although Vienna would have said the brighter, the better.

"What I hate to see," Pam Lockhart of the Lockhart Unfinished Furniture chain said, "is a black suit, black pumps and a string of pearls. How boring is that? I know Vienna wouldn't want us to look like penguins. She would want us to express ourselves the way she did."

I had a vision of everyone dressed in Vienna's out-there style. Slit skirts, metallics, oversize cardigans, leather pants and more. She'd been with us only a short time, but what a mark she'd made. What if everyone turned up looking like Vienna or wearing the clothes she'd sold them?

"Amen," said Barbie Washburn, one of our frequent customers. "You all can do what you want, but I'm paying homage to Vienna by wearing an outfit she picked out for me. It's not black, it's not burgundy and it's not conservative."

"Good for you," I said. What else could I say? "What is it?"

"I want to surprise you, Rita," she said. "What I want to know is, what is Vienna wearing?"

A sudden hush came over the room. I caught Dolce's eye, and she shook her head sadly. What was Vienna wearing? Who decided? It should be Dolce. Dolce adored Vienna, and she knew her taste. But Dolce wasn't family. We knew it would be an open casket.

"We don't know," I said with a glance at Dolce. "It's not up to us."

"We can't dress Vienna." A lovely woman named Sachi, who was new to the city, spoke up. "But we can honor her by dressing the way she did. The way she wanted us to."

I managed a weak smile. I should have been happy. It meant they'd all need new clothes for the funeral. No bringing out the black suit from the back of the closet, slipping into a pair of black pumps and throwing on a string of pearls. Vienna would have been horrified to see the mourners in ordinary mourning garb. I knew her well enough to know that much. But what would her family think? That it was disrespectful? I couldn't worry about everyone. I couldn't control what they thought or what they wore. I could only help those who wanted my help.

"Okay," I said to the group. I felt a surge of new energy. "Dolce and I are here to help you dress for Vienna's funeral. Whether you want to wear girly lace, knee-high boots, blazers, short skirts or long, leather and suede, or even a black dress. We've got it all."

There was a stampede toward the racks, hooks, drawers and stacks of clothes. It was like Christmas in a department store, which was an awful thought. How much nicer and customer friendly to do your shopping in a boutique like Dolce's where everyone knows your name and your taste in clothes and accessories.

I didn't know if it was because I'd been sequestered in

the back room, but I felt like a moth who'd just been turned into a butterfly, flitting from customer to customer. I was all about finding the right item and fitting it on the right person. Was it wrong to have such a good time getting ready for a funeral? I hoped not because I hadn't had so much fun since before Vienna joined us. As for the others who clearly loved having Vienna wait on them only last week, I think it must have been the joy of knowing they were still alive while someone else was not. If that was wrong, then we were all doomed.

"What about us?" was Dolce's question when we finally closed the doors at six o'clock, one hour past our normal closing time. "Do we go bold according to Vienna's taste or sober black with pearls as befitting our relationship with our colleague and friend?" Dolce asked.

I wanted to say she wasn't my colleague or my friend, but of course I didn't. I wouldn't burst Dolce's balloon for anything. It was the first time I'd seen her smile since yesterday. They call it retail therapy and they mean for the customer of course, but I can tell you retail selling is another kind of therapy and just as important.

"Maybe we can find something that says respect for her family and pays homage to the memory of Vienna at the same time," I said.

"Of course we can," Dolce agreed. "How about a mix of neutrals and brights?"

When I gave her a thumbs-up, she went to the rack of new arrivals and handed me a breezy girly dress in violet print to try on.

"It says spring to me," she explained. "And renewal. It's not black, but I don't think it's disrespectful."

When I came out of the dressing room, she was holding

a long, soft wooly shawl in lilac to wrap around my shoulders. I twirled around in front of the mirror, and she said it was perfect with a shoulder bag that hugged my body and a pair of velvet wedge sandals.

"That was easy," I said. "But I wonder, what would Vienna have thought?" I thought I knew. I thought she'd frown and then try to say something polite while inwardly she would be cringing at my lack of taste. But maybe I was wrong.

"She'd say it suits you," Dolce said reassuringly.

Probably because Vienna thought I was just as tasteless as my outfit. So what. Vienna was gone.

As for Dolce, she knew what she wanted. A magenta sheath with a beige blazer and a bag with a classic shape in a major color, combining neutrals and brights in one great outfit.

"What about your shoes?" I asked. "I know the rule is no painted toenails at a funeral, but this is not your usual funeral if I understand correctly."

"We'll see," Dolce said, suddenly somber. "Her family may not appreciate our flouting the rules this way. Still, I'd like to wear my new sandals with tights."

"You should. You absolutely should. That would look sensational and just what Vienna would want you to do."

"You think so?" Dolce asked. "Then I'll do it. It will be my tribute to her."

I so admired Dolce for her taste in clothes. At her age, not many women would take the chances she did. I only hoped I'd be on the cutting edge like she was when I was fifty-something.

"Do we need jewelry?" I asked, sitting on a leather footstool. I was exhausted. First dressing all those women and now us. I wanted to go home and watch something mindless on TV. Tomorrow was going to be one big day. It was my chance to look over Vienna's friends and family and figure out who killed her, all the while looking stylish and bereft.

"I'll just wear my diamond stud earrings," Dolce said. I could see she was tired too. The day had taken its toll on both of us. "But you go ahead and wear something sensational."

"I'll wear something with a long chain and a tassel or a pendant on the end, since that's what's in right now," I said. I didn't mention Vienna's beautiful tourmaline necklace. Why bring up a painful subject? It was gone. I'd like to know what had happened to it, and I wasn't the only one. I was sorry I'd ever mentioned the necklace to Jack. But he would have found out anyway. Maybe he was just waiting for me to say something first so he could pounce on me, which he did. I would love to be one up on Jack Wall, but it hardly ever happened.

I changed back into my clothes and left my outfit for tomorrow hanging in the dressing room. I said good night to Dolce and headed for home. From my seat on the bus I realized we were passing not far from my new favorite pizza place where the so-called vampire Meera worked. My mouth watered remembering how good the last one was, and I jumped up and got off at the next stop. What point was there going home hungry? I wouldn't be able to think or to sleep on an empty stomach, and I needed to be sharp and get my rest before tomorrow. I renewed my vow to get my new apartment into shape as well as to find a cooking school so I wouldn't have to eat out so often. But not now. Not when I was a suspect in a murder case. I had my work cut out for me.

Seven

I thought Azerbyjohnnie's would be the quintessential neighborhood hangout. But it was more upscale than I'd imagined. Before I went in, I read the menu in the window. Not only did they have some unusual designer pizzas from their wood-fired pizza oven, but they also offered hand-rolled pasta and house-cured meats. Then why did they hire an alleged vampire to man the phones and the reception desk? Even as a temp filling in for her friend, Meera seemed an unlikely fit for this kind of upscale ambience.

Maybe Meera gave it a touch of class or just a touch of weirdness, dressed as she was in her usual Victorian garb. In her long black dress with the round waistline, she actually looked a little like Queen Victoria, only not quite as stout as the dowager queen. Meera had a regal air about her, maybe because she thought of herself as an ageless vampire. Who was I to say she wasn't? Not to her face anyway. I'd read enough vampire books, even studied Romanian in college, and I knew better than to even hint that I had any doubts about her claims. The thing I wondered was, what did Victorian style or vampires or Romania have to do with Italian food? To her credit, Meera seemed right at home at the front desk of this Italian restaurant, and she seemed glad to see me but not surprised.

"I knew you'd come by," she said, tapping her forehead as if that's where she got her ability to know what the future brought. "How was the pizza I sent you?"

"Excellent," I said.

"Today you are here in person," she said. "Sit down and I will bring you the house special."

"No carp," I said firmly.

"Very well," she said with a sigh. "But you look like you need a glass of Grasa de Cotnari."

"I thought you'd have Italian wines here."

"We do, but this is my recommendation. When in Romania . . ."

I didn't say, "But we're not in Romania. We're in San Francisco at an Italian restaurant." I knew better than to argue with Meera.

Since it was early, there were plenty of free tables in the long narrow room with windows along one side. The few customers already there were dressed in business casual as if, like me, they were on their way home from work and didn't want to face an empty fridge.

Meera refused to let me see the menu, saying she knew what I would like. Maybe she was right. Aside from her carp recommendation, everything she suggested was delicious, starting with a shaved asparagus and arugula salad with a pancetta-caper vinaigrette, followed by an outstanding puttanesca pizza with Castelvetrano olive wedges. It was smudged with black from the gas-fired oven, crisp and tender at the same time.

"I love it," I told Meera when she came to my table to check on me.

She smiled knowingly and refilled my wineglass. I hated to think about how much this was going to cost me, but feeling so relaxed and mellow was worth the price after the day I'd had.

She slid into the booth opposite me. She glanced over her shoulder and said in a low voice, "I hear there was another murder. Someone in your shop."

"That's right," I said. Though there hadn't been a reporter on the premises that I knew about, it was impossible to deny it had happened. I wondered how she'd found out.

"I would be glad to help out in any way I can," she said eagerly, resting her elbows on the table. I recalled that she thought her special vampire powers gave her insight that mere mortals lacked. For her, death wasn't a problem, but she still appeared to love hearing about crimes, especially murder.

"I'm not the one to ask," I said firmly. That's all I needed was a vampire making inquiries on my behalf. Already some people thought I was a nutcase, too involved in the murder for my own good. Along with those who thought I was responsible for the murder.

"I will telephone to the police," she said. "I remember the last time we were dealing with the very dashing and handsome Detective Wall. He reminds me of someone I once knew."

When Meera talked about people she once knew, she sometimes mentioned figures out of the past, and I do mean the past, like the past century. It made one wonder if she really was a vampire—or maybe just a student of history.

"I am thinking that the detective might have some Romanian blood in him. He has a certain look," she said.

He did have a certain look. I wasn't sure it was because of Romanian blood in his veins. It was more of a tough-cop, smart-cop look.

"Do you have his phone number?" I asked.

Meera reached into the bodice of her dress, pulled out his card and waved it at me. I should have known she'd be prepared and that she'd remember Jack. Who could forget him? I could just hear her telling him that I'd recommended she contact him to help him solve his crimes. He wouldn't be happy about it, but at least he'd be civil, thank her for the offer and then tell her he had everything under control. But did he? Maybe he could use some help from someone who supposedly had powers outside the norm. Or maybe he'd tell me once again to stay out of his business. I was getting used to it.

"I have a way of communicating with the dead," Meera said. "That might be useful."

I knew she'd get around to reminding me sooner or later. "You mean you would ask Vienna who killed her?" That would sure save a lot of time and effort. If you believed Meera was really what she said she was, which I didn't, and neither would Jack.

"Nothing so direct," she said. "But I have ways of finding out."

What could I say? Go for it? She'd go for it no matter what I said, even if I told her not to. So I ate the last bite of pizza, drained my wineglass and settled the check, left a tip and said good bye. But before I left I asked her to give me a call if she had any word from "beyond." I could use all the help I could get unraveling this mystery. Even if it came from a delusional Romanian's contacts with the other world.

She said she would as if it were the kind of request she got every day. I was just glad she hadn't asked about the funeral. Meera was unstoppable about funerals. She loved the idea of the corpse turning into a vampire like herself. When I turned around for a last look at the restaurant, she was standing at the window, her face pressed against the glass, looking at me. For some reason the woman was making me nervous. Which I didn't need in my already unsettled condition. It wasn't her fault. It was just that I'd recently come face-to-face with Vienna's lifeless body and I couldn't get it out of my mind.

Eight

Around noon the next day Dolce and I closed the shop and got ready for the funeral. We debated whether to eat lunch first. I said I was sure there'd be a big spread at Vienna's mother's house after the funeral. After all, they were rich and could afford it. Besides, given what Athena had said, I was sure Noreen Fortner was eager to show how much she cared for Vienna by outdoing Vienna's father.

Dolce drove us to Colma in her latest rental car, a Hummer. After she was in an accident some months ago, she'd continued to rent one car after another. It gave her a chance to try out cars she'd never considered before.

She said the Hummer was the only thing left in the lot she hadn't driven except for some models she didn't want to be seen in. "It's not the H-1," she explained as we pulled out of her garage. "The H-2 is its little brother, but it still has the distinctive military style. They're extremely capable even when taken off-road. Even with me at the wheel."

"Dolce," I said, "you're not going off-roading, are you?"

"No, no," she said, then she admitted she'd been influenced by the car-rental man. "He told me it has a lot of muscle under the hood."

"I'm sure we'll be very safe also," I said, thinking of the vehicle's famed crashworthiness. At least until we got to the funeral home. Then all bets were off.

Cypress Ridge was one of many funeral homes located in the city of Colma, which boasts that it's home to around a thousand residents and over a million souls. It wasn't always that way. But in the 1920s the city of San Francisco ran out of room and sent thousands of the dearly departed to Colma to be reburied.

Once inside the Colma city limits, we saw several bumper stickers that proudly pronounced, "It's good to be alive in Colma."

"It's not a depressing city in spite of all the cemeteries," I said.

"No," Dolce said. "In fact, you could call the cemeteries in Colma a good place to study local history. Former mayor George Moscone is buried here."

"He's the one who was shot by a disgruntled San Francisco supervisor in the seventies," I murmured. Every year in November the city pauses to remember the mayor and Supervisor Harvey Milk, both of whom were murdered at City Hall.

"And Wyatt Earp is here too, buried together with his wife, Josephine. His original three-hundred-pound tombstone was stolen so many times they finally replaced it with a more modest slab of black granite. If we have time, we can take a look at it. I read that his funeral was attended by some of the Western movie heroes like Tom Mix. But his wife was so distraught she didn't go to the funeral. I don't think any of Vienna's family members will miss her funeral."

I slanted a glance in Dolce's direction, sorry to see tears well up in her eyes. I thought it would be good for her to talk about the past, but maybe not. I wondered how hard it was going to be for her to see Vienna's body lying in a casket.

I was glad Dolce was distracted enough to tell me stories of the famous people buried in Colma, but it was clear she couldn't forget why we were here. I was determined to try to keep her spirits up one way or another.

We drove into the cemetery, passing elaborate tombs and mausoleums. "Do you think the Fairchilds will build something like that for Vienna?" I asked.

"It seems like something out of the Victorian era," Dolce said. "Those were the days when you showed your love for the departed by building a huge monument to their memory. I don't think that's done so much anymore. But who am I to say what the Fairchilds will do?"

I agreed. I pictured a huge statue of Vienna sculpted in marble. She'd be wearing one of her crazier outfits. It would be different. It would be appropriate. But would it be possible for the two families to ever agree on how to honor her? I was anxious to see how the families would pull off this funeral. How would her father hold up when his favorite daughter was lying cold and dead in her coffin? Would her mother and father come together today for once? Or would her violent death just deepen the gulf between them?

As soon as we walked into the huge, high-ceilinged entry

to the funeral home, I expected to see a lot of cold marble.
Instead, there were earth tones on the walls and burgundy
and white carpets on the floors. My first impression was of
a sea of black suits. Were we right to go against custom and
dress for Vienna? I felt cold, disapproving glances come
my way.

"Look," Dolce said under her breath. "Have you ever
seen something like that before?" Just as Athena had promised, there was a bar, tucked into an alcove lined with dark
wood. Behind the bar was a waiter dressed in a tuxedo, serv-
ing drinks.

"Never," I said. But then how many funerals had I been
to? "Might as well join them," I said, taking her arm and
heading toward the bar. I thought it wasn't a bad idea at all.
I mean, who wouldn't want some alcohol to numb the pain
of losing a loved one? It might even bring the two warring
factions together. Instead of fighting over Vienna as they'd
done when she was alive, they could end up in each other's
arms, consoling each other.

I liked the idea of an open bar, but I warned myself to be
cautious, since I hadn't eaten any lunch and I feared the
effects of drinking on an empty stomach. The alcohol could
go right to my head. Of course, if others were in the same
boat, it could be a good thing to loosen a few inhibitions.
Someone might say something or do something to give him-
or herself away as the perpetrator of Vienna's murder.

That's where Detective Wall would come in handy. He'd
put two and two together, maybe even hear a tearful confession, then jump in and make an arrest, and voilà, he could
wrap up the case without a lot of footwork. Was that why
he was attending this funeral? I had to confess that was my
motive. Even if I didn't get to witness a confession, I'd at

least get a feeling for the players in this drama. I would be disappointed if there wasn't some sort of drama, considering the situation.

As soon as I had in hand an Alexander expertly made with crème de cacao and Dolce was sipping something called an Acapulco made with tequila, we stood on the sidelines watching the crowd. So far I didn't recognize anyone, but that was because we didn't know any of Vienna's friends or relatives except for her twin, Athena. We'd seen her mother and father along with their significant others at the benefit.

"Saturday night at the auction, we never actually met any of Vienna's family, did we?" I asked Dolce.

She said no, but we already knew her stepmother, Bobbi, who was one of our customers. We were soon joined by our favorite oldster, Miranda McClone. She was holding a glass filled with a frothy substance she said was a banana daiquiri, while her husband had ordered a scotch and water. "Such a novel idea, serving drinks at a funeral," she said, giving both Dolce and me a once-over. "You girls look just fabulous," she said. "I should never have worn black. It ages a person at least five years." Since five more years would put Miranda close to ninety, I was glad to be able to assure her that it wasn't true in her case—and I meant it.

"With that hat, you look absolutely marvelous," Dolce told her. She was right; the wide-brimmed hat with the tassel, feather and beads was the perfect accompaniment to a plain black suit. The only drawback was that she hadn't bought the hat at Dolce's. She couldn't have because Dolce hadn't had much of a hat selection this season. A fact Dolce must have been acutely aware of as she gazed raptly at Miranda's choice of headwear.

"The hat certainly spices up your outfit," I added.

Miranda smiled and kissed me on the cheek. She smelled of Ralph Lauren's latest scent, Romance. One of the reasons I loved working at Dolce's was for the contacts I made there. The customers were so much more than customers. I was telling the truth when I said they were also friends. Miranda was one of my favorites. She never gossiped, never had a bad word to say about anyone.

I was thinking that maybe we too should have worn hats. Just seeing this spunky eighty-something all turned out made me feel like I'd neglected to get completely dressed. Almost as bad as forgetting to wear shoes.

"Have you viewed the, um, body yet?" Miranda asked us. "Or do you prefer to remember her as she was? I know some people do. I'm a good friend of her grandmother, Jane Marlow, on her father's side, and I know Jane is most upset about this whole thing. The police telling the family they're being investigated. I ask you, what is the world coming to?"

Neither Dolce nor I had an answer to that. Did this mean Jack was zeroing in on some particular member of the family? I was afraid to ask.

"Look, there's Lex standing at the door," Miranda said. "He was so fond of little Vienna. He gave her everything she ever wanted. Do you know Bobbi? Yes, of course you do. That's her in red. I know it's an unusual choice, but she's quite original, which is why I admire her so much. Doesn't follow the crowd. She explained to me that this is not a time to weep, it's a celebration of life. This is Lex's way to honor his daughter. The party after the funeral will be held at her mother's house in Atherton. It's an awkward situation, but I believe they're handling it well, don't you?" she asked us.

"Oh, definitely," I said. "Bobbi's dress is outstanding," I said. Actually I thought it was bizarre for Bobbi to be wearing bright red to this funeral. Especially knowing how she felt about her stepdaughter.

Dolce took a sip of her drink. "I believe red is traditional among the Ashanti tribes in Africa. Maybe Bobbi has some connection."

Dolce also knew how Vienna felt about her stepmother, and she wasn't about to compliment her in any way. No matter what she said, I could tell by the look on her face she thought the red dress was completely inappropriate. Of course, we weren't following tradition by not dressing in black, but we weren't trying to stand out either. We'd leave standing out to the customers we'd helped find outfits for, namely Sachi, Pam, Monica and Barbie, who were now mixing and mingling in the crowd.

I just couldn't wait any longer to view Vienna in her casket. I left Dolce chatting with Miranda and I slipped into the huge high-ceilinged viewing room with sunshine coming through the skylights. There was soft music playing, and the people in the room were speaking in hushed voices.

Instead of rushing up to view Vienna in her coffin, I held back, afraid of seeing her, afraid of bringing back the shock when I'd found her body. I'd have to look at her. Otherwise I'd regret it, but I wasn't ready yet. Maybe after another drink. I procrastinated by saying hello to her sister. Athena was greeting people while she stood next to the guest book. Her hair was long, layered and more voluminous than I remembered. She was wearing a black taffeta scoop-necked dress with a chiffon-trimmed grosgrain sash and black stiletto heels.

"You look great," I said. "Love your dress."

"Thanks," Athena said. "I wish you'd tell my stepmother that. Bobbi just told me I wasn't a bridesmaid and this wasn't a cocktail party. Even at my sister's funeral she had to say something snarky."

"She's probably terribly upset and she's not herself," I said. Though I wasn't sure why I was defending her. I scarcely knew the woman, and what I knew of her I didn't particularly like.

"Oh, she's herself all right," Athena said. "And if she's upset, it's because Vienna is the center of attention and not her." She looked around the room. "So, who are all these people?" she asked. "Like the guy who just came in wearing a kilt. What's up with that?"

I turned around to see a guy wearing a red and black tartan plaid kilt with a white shirt and black jacket. On his muscular legs he wore white kneesocks. I wouldn't have been surprised to see him haul out a bagpipe and play a dirge for Vienna.

"You don't know him?" I asked.

She shook her head. "But I'd like to. That's why I'm in charge of the guest book, so I can find out who's who. Watch me go."

With that, she strode across the room, the guest book under her arm, and sashayed up to the kilted guy. I knew it wasn't Geoffrey, but could this be either Emery or Raold? Or someone I didn't even have on my list of suspects? Neither of those names sounded Scottish, but you never knew. If only I had a guest book. What excuse did I have to go up to strangers and ask who they were and how they felt about Vienna? None.

I could hardly say I was investigating her murder. They'd say, "Oh, are you with the police?" Or, "Are you with the family?" All I could say was, "I found the body. I'm the chief suspect. I have to find someone else besides myself who had a motive and the opportunity to kill Vienna." Unfortunately I had both according to Detective Wall. I searched the room for someone who looked suspicious. Someone who either looked too sad or too happy to see Vienna in her coffin. But most people were standing around talking, completely oblivious to the body in the middle of the room. Almost as if they were at a cocktail party. I didn't see the mourner in chief, Vienna's father. Maybe he was too overcome with grief to face her body. Or maybe he was still playing host by the bar.

I should just grit my teeth and look at her. I might have a flash of insight. Maybe she'd send me a message from wherever she'd gone. It could be, "Look for a man in a kilt." Or it might be, "Don't overlook the obvious." Or what about, *"Cherchez la femme"*?

I inched up to the coffin. When I got there, I closed my eyes for a long moment, hoping for a moment of clarity, or at least a pathway into the spirit of Vienna. But I got nothing. Vienna had never communicated much with me when she was alive, so why did I expect her to get in touch now that she was dead?

"I can help you," I wanted to tell her. "I can catch your killer, just send me a sign."

"Are you okay?"

My eyes flew open. It was Detective Wall standing next to me at the coffin, his expression somewhere between concerned and puzzled. He'd managed to look conservative but drop-dead male-model stunning at the same time.

"I'm fine," I said, embarrassed to be caught unawares, my eyes closed like a sleepwalker. "You look like you just stepped out of *Vogue Hommes International*."

"Just trying to fit in," he said. "Wouldn't want anyone to think I was here looking for a murderer."

"But you are."

"It's my job."

Whether he wanted to or not, Jack always stood out no matter where he was or what he was wearing. Today it was a single-breasted, two-button dark blazer with a stylish white pocket square, a pair of narrow flat-front slacks, a buttoned vest and a pair of Steve Madden dress shoes.

"I thought maybe you were asleep," he said. "I was afraid to wake you."

"I was trying to communicate with Vienna."

"Tell her you were sorry?"

I stared at him. I was still avoiding looking into the coffin. "For what? That she took my job? That she broke Dolce's heart? That she had to die on Sunday morning, leaving me to discover her body . . ."

"Never mind," he said, obviously tired of hearing me rant. "How do you like her dress?"

I finally forced myself to look at her. I gasped. "It doesn't matter what I think of it, it's what Vienna would have thought that counts."

"What's that?" he asked.

"I . . . I don't know. She loved to shock people, so maybe this dress is exactly what she would have wanted. The glittery stretch fabric is fun, flirty and it hugs her curves. It's just . . . It's just that it's more appropriate for a party than a funeral." And it wasn't anything like anything she'd ever worn that I knew about. A long-sleeved dress with shoulder pads? A touch of forties glamour to my way of thinking. I wondered what Dolce would think. Where was she?

"So who dressed her?" Jack asked. "Someone who loved her or someone who hated her?"

I shook my head. "I don't know. I think she looks fine. It

was a bold choice. Maybe not something she would have chosen, but still gutsy. That's her stepmother, Bobbi, over there. Why don't you ask her who did it?"

"I hate to interrupt any private grieving," he said.

Was he serious? Jack was ruthless when it came to investigating a murder. And now he was afraid of hurting someone's feelings?

"Don't worry, Bobbi isn't grieving. Just the opposite is my guess. If you're looking for suspects, she should be on your list. She was at the auction, and she's jealous of Vienna's hold over her father, Lex."

"You're up on your motives, I see."

"Motives and opportunity, isn't that what it's all about? Just FYI, there are some men here to check out."

"Emery and Raold? They have alibis."

"Very convenient. What about Geoffrey? I think she'd dumped him for someone else. Not sure who." Not sure but I was going to find out.

"I have Geoffrey's statement."

"And the man in the kilt," I said.

"A cousin who flew in from Scotland," Jack said. "He was on the other side of the world when Vienna was killed."

"So who didn't have an alibi?" I said. "Besides me?"

"You don't really think I'd give you a list, do you?"

"No, but I'll give you a list of possibilities and you just shake your head or nod." I didn't wait for him to shake his head or roll his eyes, I just started naming names.

"What about her stepsister, her stepmother, her ex-boyfriend or, I don't know, her roommate, who I'm guessing is the woman over there wearing a sporty watch with a bunch of sparkly bracelets and a matching ring I could swear were Vienna's. She's the one talking to the cousin in the kilt. Have you checked all those alibis, because I think I could give you their motives without half trying."

Jack just looked at me as if I'd gone completely insane.

"Anyway, you admit there is a list. I'm *not* the only one. How about this?" I asked. "I come down to the station and take a lie detector test."

"Do you know how many convicted spies have passed a polygraph test?" he asked.

"So now I'm a spy as well as a murderer. I can't believe we're having this conversation." Didn't Jack know that someone like myself who was guilty would never volunteer to take the test. Or else he or she was innocent, as I was, and would pass with flying colors.

"I can't believe we're having this conversation at a funeral home in the presence of the deceased," he said with a glance around the room. I didn't blame him for averting his gaze from the coffin. No matter how good she looked, it was downright eerie staring at a dead woman you once knew.

"You started it," I said under my breath. I would not be blamed for disrespecting the dead. "I'm just defending myself. For your information, speaking as an Aquarius, Saturn has been in my house this past week, so I've been trying to broaden my mind. I know you don't want my help, and you won't let me take a polygraph test, so I'm backing off." Of course this was a lie, and I don't think he believed me.

"Rita," he said, glaring at me.

I don't know what else he was going to say, probably another warning not to meddle. What else was new? Tired of trying to clear myself, I turned away from the coffin and went to join some of Dolce's customers dressed just as they said they would, in true Vienna-homage outfits. It made me relax and smile as we exchanged hellos. They said they'd gotten some strange looks, but they didn't care. They were here to honor Vienna.

A few minutes later I saw Athena standing with her mother, Noreen. Her eyes were red and swollen. I wanted to introduce myself and offer my condolences, but they were in the midst of a conversation.

"I blame your father for this," Noreen was saying to Athena between sniffles. "He always gave her everything she wanted. Why else did she choose to live with him instead of me? Because he gave her everything she ever wanted, that's why. You see what happened? No wonder she crossed someone who did her in. She thought she was entitled. See where that got her."

I stood listening shamelessly while they talked. It was all useful information. Maybe even crucial. Some nuggets I already knew, like the fact that Vienna thought she was God's gift to retail and to the men in her life. The two women scarcely noticed me.

"Mother, Daddy is the only one here who even gave a damn about Vienna. Yes, he spoiled her, but at least he cared about her. You'll have to find someone else to blame for her murder."

At that point the two of them looked at me. They knew I'd been eavesdropping. I flushed guiltily, but I stayed right where I was.

Nine

I wanted to say, "Don't look at me," or else I wanted to run out of the room, but of course that would have made me look guilty. So I smiled weakly and said I was sorry for their loss.

Athena and her mother stared blankly at me for a second, then went on talking as if I wasn't there.

"You have to speak to Daddy," Athena told her mother. "Now of all times. He looks awful."

"I can't face his wife, that bitch. She always calls me Norma, like she can't remember my name is Noreen."

"You don't have to face her. Look, he's over there with one of his car salesmen. At least you could thank him for hosting this thing, whatever it is."

"It's a cocktail party, not a funeral," Noreen said with a frown. "Totally inappropriate. Just like your father. He has no idea what's proper under the circumstances."

"Well, that will just make your reception at the house look that much better."

"At least Lex will see I know what a wake is and how well I've done without him," Vienna's mother said. "All right, here I go."

I watched as she sucked in her breath, smoothed her hair and started across the floor toward her ex-husband. I would have loved to hear their conversation, but I'd have to imagine what went on by their gestures. As it happened, they hugged and cried. That much I could see. What I wanted to hear was who they suspected of killing their daughter.

All I needed to do was walk casually across the room, and I heard Lex Fairchild telling Vienna's mother, "I swear, Noreen, I'll kill him if I find him."

There was only one person he could possibly mean by that: the murderer. How was Lex going to find him? I wished I knew. I wanted to ask him if he had any clues, but I was afraid to face him. I really hoped I could find the murderer first and turn him over to Jack before Lex killed him.

I didn't have the opportunity to hear any more because just then Lex's wife in her shameless red dress came out of nowhere, grabbed his arm and told him it was time to leave.

I swear I saw sparks fly between her and Noreen. If Lex hadn't been there, there might have been a real catfight.

I could only hope I'd have more chances to hear more at the reception or wake or whatever you call it. I caught up with Dolce a few minutes later, after Vienna's parents had had their brief emotional meeting.

"Looks like the place is clearing out," Dolce said, her eyelids fluttering. "I hope you can drive to Atherton because I'm feeling a little woozy."

I gave her a quick scrutinizing look and was glad I'd had

only one drink. How many had she had? I couldn't blame
her for wanting to anesthetize herself from the pain of losing Vienna, the daughter she never had. I used to think I
was that daughter, but even though Dolce only knew Vienna
briefly, she'd really loved her. Despite the fact that Vienna already had two mothers, she had Dolce too. Maybe Vienna
needed all that extra attention. But in the end it didn't help
her stay alive. I admit that Dolce's fickle affection hurt me,
but then, I was still alive and Vienna wasn't.

"Did you hear anything interesting?" I asked Dolce after
the burial as we drove south on the freeway toward the
exclusive suburb of Atherton.

"No, but guess what? Vienna's mother asked me to speak
at the wake at her house," she said. "That's what she called
it, 'the wake.'"

"Really? That's nice of her. She must realize how much
you meant to Vienna. You gave her a job. You were her
friend. What will you say?" I was a little worried. Dolce
had reclined the front bucket seat and was leaning back with
her eyes closed and her shoes off. I was afraid she'd fall
asleep or into a stupor and I wouldn't be able to pry her out
so she could give her speech.

"I don't know," Dolce said, opening her eyes to peer at
me. "I have to write it down or I'll say the wrong thing. You
have to help me."

"Of course I will," I said. "You should say something
about what she loved to do at the shop and how she was so
good at it. And what you remember about her, what you'll
never forget. It's important to be personal, don't you think?"

I was glad nobody had asked me to speak. If I had to say
what I'd remember, I'd say how proud she was of her sales
ability and her taste in clothes compared to mine and how

generous she was to give me her benefit ticket. But was that generous, or was it just a way of getting out of a date she didn't want?

If it were me who'd been asked to speak, I'd go against the tide and take the opportunity to ask if anyone knew what had happened to her necklace. There's a question I wanted answered. I was sure Jack did too, but he wouldn't admit it. I couldn't help but believe that the necklace had something to do with her murder. And wasn't that the best way to honor the deceased, by trying to find and punish her killer? But no one had asked me, and it didn't look like they were going to.

When we got to the address on the card they gave us at the funeral home, we pulled into a circular driveway filled with limos and other expensive cars. And a motorcycle. I assumed it must be Geoffrey's. I looked forward to a chance to talk to him. Dolce and I sat in the car for a few minutes staring in awe at the property with the towering redwoods forming a backdrop behind it. The house was two stories, a historical Tudor estate on several manicured acres of lawn. A place Vienna might have chosen for her wedding, if she'd had one. If she didn't get married at her father's house, which I assumed was equally beautiful.

"I can't go in there," Dolce said.

"Why not? Of course you can. You're going to give a speech, which we're going to write right now." I was getting worried, but I couldn't let it show. I pulled a small pad of paper out of my purse and began to write.

"First an introduction," I suggested. "How you met. What you noticed about Vienna. Why you hired her. How she stood out."

Dolce nodded, but she didn't say anything. I wrote a few

notes about Vienna's unique style, her ability to sell snow to Eskimos or whatever the equivalent was in the fashion world. "What else?" I asked Dolce.

This time she didn't open her eyes. She just sat there without moving. My anxiety level was rising. "Dolce, they're counting on you. These are family and friends of Vienna. They're not there to judge you. They're there to hear your memories of her. Special memories. They might not even know Vienna had a job and that she was so good at it. Tell what a great saleswoman she was. You can do that, can't you?"

"I don't know, Rita," Dolce said in a small, sad voice. "Can't you do it?"

I froze. Imagine me telling Vienna's family and friends what a wonderful person she was. I could just hear the crowd saying, "Who's she?" I was nobody. Not to Vienna.

"They asked you. They want you. You knew Vienna in a way that no one else did. You gave her her first job. A job she was great at. Wasn't she?" I asked, knowing full well what Dolce thought.

She nodded. "The best," she said.

I tried not to let the words hurt me. "You're supposed to say how the deceased made the world a better place," I said. "You can do that. Everyone knows that fashion is a way of brightening people's lives and helping them feel good about themselves. Vienna had a special talent for bringing out the best looks in the customers, right?" I jotted that down without waiting for Dolce to comment. If I waited for her to agree, we'd never get through with this eulogy.

I looked up to see more cars approaching, parking, and mourners getting out and going in through the wide front doors.

"You'll feel better when you get something to eat," I said as I got out, then walked around the car to open the door for Dolce. This was purely selfish. My stomach was growling and my head was pounding. I just hoped Dolce wouldn't have anything else to drink. One more drink and she'd be unable to even remember her own name much less read the words I'd written on the scratch pad.

I was not disappointed by the buffet Vienna's mother had prepared. Just the opposite. I was blown away by the spread and hungrier than ever. Actually Noreen must have ordered it, judging by the presence of the caterer's truck parked behind the kitchen. As I made my way around the long table in the dining room, I filled two plates with tiny appetizers like salmon wasabi bites, spinach and ricotta tarts, grilled lamb skewers with a spicy chutney, and a few individual-size baby back ribs. Just for starters. There was another table with more selections and an entire room dedicated to desserts. I'd have to come back later.

I moved to the patio then where I saw Dolce talking to Patti, who'd sold the auction tickets, and her friend Caroline, also one of our customers. I was dismayed to see Dolce was holding a drink. Of course, it might be something nonalcoholic, but I doubted it. I greeted Patti and handed Dolce a plate.

"Here you are," I said. "You must be hungry. Let's sit down." I took Dolce's arm and we walked on a brick path toward a second, covered patio next to a sparkling pool. Caroline and Patti came with us, and we all sat down at a glass-topped table.

"I was just telling Dolce I feel responsible for selling her those tickets," Patti said, shaking her head sadly. "If I hadn't . . ."

"Vienna would have gone to the auction anyway," I said. "Her whole family was there. It's not your fault."

"I'm glad you feel that way," she said. "Her mother was very upset with me."

"She'll get over it," I assured her, taking a bite of lamb from the skewer.

"But Vienna won't," she said.

I had to agree. "But whoever murdered Vienna, did he or she have anything to do with the auction? I wonder if it was all about something totally different, an old score to settle, an old dispute." I looked up, gazing hopefully from Caroline to Dolce to Patti, hoping they'd agree with me because that's what I wanted to believe. But none of them was any help at all. They just shook their heads. I should have known. These were the subjects I should be discussing with Jack, if only he'd let me. If only he'd ask for my help. If only we could brainstorm. Good luck with that. It wasn't going to happen. I'd just have to figure it out by myself.

I was glad to see Dolce was eating. That should help her settle her nerves and be prepared to give her remarks. When we'd eaten everything I'd brought, I offered to go get some coffee and dessert for all of us. The more, the better—and a chance to look over the crowd.

The desserts were displayed in the library on a large table. There were about a dozen kinds of cookies, from macaroons to Mexican wedding cookies to classic chocolate chip to shortbread, oatmeal current, and lemon bars. Then there were several kinds of brownies, and numerous cakes, all labeled in case there was any doubt. Opera, lemon meringue, German chocolate and so many more. I couldn't decide between fresh-fruit Bavarian with fresh raspberries

piled high above the many layers or a simple devil's food
with a rich, thick frosting.

I was standing there, mesmerized by the vast selection
of mouthwatering desserts and plates of hand-dipped chocolate candies, when a young man walked in. He didn't look
like Geoffrey—at least, he didn't resemble the photo I'd
seen on Geoffrey's web site—but in a dark suit and tie,
maybe it was him. Or was it Emery or Raold? Whoever it
was, however he was connected to Vienna, I had to see what
I could learn from him.

"Quite a library, isn't it?" I said, waving my hand toward
the shelves of books that lined the walls. I was impressed
by the way the fiction was arranged alphabetically by the
authors' names and the nonfiction by subject matter. I wondered if they employed a professional librarian or had set it
up and managed it themselves. Maybe Noreen's husband
Hugh was the intellectual. I hadn't met him yet.

"I wouldn't know," he said. "Not much of a reader myself.
Besides, they usually don't let me in here."

Sorry I'd chosen the wrong subject for an opening, I tried
something else.

"Quite a selection of desserts, isn't it?" I asked brightly.
Who could deny that?

He nodded, then he took a cookie and stood there
thoughtfully eating it.

"Are you a friend of Vienna's?" I asked. I couldn't go
wrong with that unless he just said, "No, I'm the caterer,"
or told me he was the DJ in charge of playing suitable music.

"Was," he said. "She's dead."

"I know," I said.

"You?" he asked.

"I used to work with her at a boutique. We . . . I'm in sales."

"You're the one who sold her that dress she was wearing today?" he asked, brushing the cookie crumbs off his hands.

"No, I can't take the credit or the blame for the dress. I don't know where it came from. What did you think of it?"

"She looked good," he said. "Better than when she was alive. Maybe because she didn't choose it herself. I don't know who did."

"She had a sense of style, and she wasn't afraid to take chances," I said. It was something I wouldn't mind someone saying about me at my funeral.

"Took too many chances," he said.

"How do you mean?" I asked, hoping no one else would find the desserts and interrupt what could be an important conversation. I stood still as stone, silently pleading for him to say something revealing, though he was hardly the chatty type. Was he going to tell me she was selling drugs? Running a prostitute ring? Robbing banks after hours? Stealing money and a necklace from her grandmother?

"Playing fast and loose," he said.

"With who? With what?" I asked.

From another room someone was ringing a bell. He jumped as if he'd been burned.

"What's that?" he asked, his eyes wide with fear.

"It must be time for the program," I said. "I don't think we've met. I'm Rita Jewel."

"I know. I heard about you. I saw you at the shop, but no one knew I was there. I'm Paul."

"Paul?" I said startled. Yet another man in her life.

"You've heard of me? What did they say, I'm her crazy uncle?"

"No. Are you?"

He laughed harshly. "That's what Vienna called me. It's her fault I got sent away. We had an argument."

"Recently?" I asked, startled. Was he going to confess that's why he killed her?

"I came today to set things straight with the family. They should know the truth about Vienna."

"Isn't it kind of an awkward time to do that?" I asked as the bell rang again.

"I have to leave town soon, so it's my only chance. They don't even want me here." With that, he set his plate down and started toward the door. I followed him. I didn't want to miss the program and the accolades, but I didn't want to lose this guy either.

Just then Noreen came down the hall. She put her hands on Paul's shoulders and said, "Where have you been? I told you you could only stay for a few minutes. You're not supposed to run off. They're looking for you."

I strained my ears. So they were connected after all. But how? They walked back down the hall toward the huge living room where chairs had been set up with a podium in front of the fireplace. I was surprised to see Noreen escort Paul out the front door where two burly men were standing, apparently waiting for them. I stepped outside to watch from the front steps.

Paul threw his arms in the air, and the men closed in on him, linking his arms with theirs. Then all three headed toward a long black car in the driveway. Just before Paul got in, he turned toward me. I looked around, hoping he'd fixated on someone else. No, it was me, and only me. Noreen was gone.

"You," he shouted, twisting his body, trying to get away

from his handlers. "Rita Jewel. You're the one who killed her. She told me you hated her."

"No," I burst out, even though I knew I shouldn't say a word. He was out of his mind. He didn't know what he was saying. And yet I couldn't help defending myself. "It wasn't me," I shouted.

I watched while the two men hustled Paul into the back-seat of the car. They got in the front and took off with a roar of the engine. In a moment the car had disappeared down the long driveway. Was I the only one who had seen this scene, whatever it was? Or was Noreen watching from the window to be sure he'd left? Had my voice carried all the way to the mourners who were assembled inside? From somewhere the classical music that had been only back-ground became louder. I could only hope the music had drowned out my parting words with Paul. I was left to won-der, who was Paul and where had he gone?

Despite my anxiety about Paul and his baseless accusa-tion, I had to be sure Dolce was in place with her speech. When I quietly crept back inside, I half expected everyone to turn and stare at me. They would have horrified expres-sions on their faces. Maybe even a few wagging fingers. But I was relieved to see they seemed oblivious to the crazy man's wild statements. No one looked at me, and Dolce was in the front row seated between two of our customers, Mon-ica and Patti. I was torn between making sure she was okay and taking a seat at the rear of the room and fading into anonymity.

Out of the corner of my eye I saw Athena walk down the hall. Still feeling unsettled by my exchange with Paul, I fol-lowed her into a charming garden room filled with wicker

furniture and a fountain splashing water into a small pool.
"Athena? Sorry to bother you."

Startled by my arrival, she dropped a folder she was holding, which I assumed contained the speech she was giving
today. She turned and looked at me.

"I just met a man I'm a little worried about," I said.

"Was it Paul?"

I nodded.

"Don't worry," she said. "He's harmless. It's all taken
care of. He's gone now. He wasn't supposed to be here, but
he talked them into letting him out for the funeral. He was
very fond of Vienna, didn't want her to get hurt."

"He said he had an argument with her."

She sighed. "Who didn't? Anyway, he says a lot of things
that may or may not be true."

"Who is he?" I asked.

"Uncle Paul, my mother's half brother. He's not quite
right in the head. He's been in an institution for years. I hope
it didn't upset you."

"Was he out the night of the Bachelor Auction?" I asked.
If he was, and he was crazy, wouldn't the police like to know
about it? And wouldn't the family try to conceal it to protect him? Where was Detective Wall when I needed him? I
thought he was supposed to be here.

Athena coughed nervously. But she didn't answer my
question. Instead, she said, "We'd better go in. It's time for
the program. I think it will be quite moving. As long as no
one tells the truth," she muttered.

I took a chair in the back of the room, while Athena stood
with her back against the wall. I couldn't help being nervous. There was no way I could find my way to the front to
sit next to Dolce. She was on her own. I only hoped she had

the notes in her hand. She wasn't the only one who wanted to say something about Vienna. Many people stood, went to the podium and spoke into the microphone. As it turned out, there was no program, it was just an open mike. I guessed that was the way the family wanted it. Even Bobbi, who was now wearing a Kay Unger stretch satin sheath dress, got up to say how much she missed her stepdaughter. Had someone told her to change out of her red outfit?

I buried my face in my hands. It was so difficult to listen to Bobbi and know she was lying. Or was she? Had she changed, or was her bark really worse than her bite? Did all stepmothers resent the attention their husbands paid to their first family? I glanced to my right and was surprised to see that Detective Wall was standing to the side of the room, no doubt taking in every detail, every expression, every word that was said.

When had he arrived, and what exactly was he looking for? Probably the same thing I was: a hint as to who was responsible for Vienna's death. I was sure it was there, hidden behind someone's sad mask of mourning. Someone who pretended to be crushed by Vienna's death but who was in fact responsible. If only I was smart enough to figure it out. I'd clear my own name and get some respect for solving the mystery at the same time. I told myself that the murderer was most likely here in this room and I'd better pay attention.

But my mind wandered. The speeches were all so maudlin, so teary and so rambling. For once I wished someone would tell the truth. Vienna had her good points, but she had some flaws too. I guess it was too much to ask that a dead person be criticized at her own funeral. I shuddered to think what they'd say about me.

Rita was selfish and self-centered. She couldn't cook to save her life, but she was a wonderful salesman. Clothes were her passion, and she was devoted to her job. Until it was taken away from her. Though accused of a heinous crime, two in fact, Rita wouldn't hurt a fly. She was kind and generous to a fault. Rita had many friends, among them her well-dressed customers, three good-looking men and a self-proclaimed vampire.

My mind skipped around when I knew I should be paying attention. This was my big chance to catch someone out and out lying or saying something that was just a little off. I sat up straight when Dolce got up. She was holding the notes I'd written for her. I held my breath and willed her to get through it without falling apart.

To my relief, she did a fine job, saying that Vienna was eager, ambitious, helpful and hardworking. Then she deviated from the notes. I so hoped she wouldn't go off topic to talk about the clothes she sold many of women here in this room.

"Vienna was our super saleswoman at Dolce's, my boutique," she began. I winced. I thought *I* was her super saleswoman. Never mind. This was not my funeral. And it was good PR for her to mention the shop. In case any woman here didn't know about us, they would now.

"One of our customers once asked Vienna why it was that women had to wear uncomfortable clothes like tight skinny jeans, clingy shirts and five-inch high heels that made them trip over themselves while guys got to dress in loose, baggy clothing and shoes as comfortable as slippers. It just didn't seem fair."

Dolce paused, and everyone including myself waited for

the answer. I held my breath. Was Dolce making this up, or had it really happened?

"I'll never forget what she said," Dolce said. " 'Beautiful clothes don't have to be uncomfortable. You just have to find the right brand and the right size of jeans, pants, sweaters and shirts and dresses. That's my job,' she said. 'To help you find what you're looking for so you can look and feel your best.' "

Dolce looked around. I caught her eye and smiled encouragingly while I thought, when had Vienna said that and why hadn't I heard about it? Dolce smiled back. "That was Vienna," Dolce continued. "Always thinking of others. Always helpful and kind. We'll miss you, Vienna." She left the podium, her eyes filled with unshed tears, and sat down. I was so proud of her. I couldn't wait to tell her what a great job she'd done. But I had to wait for yet more endless, tacky, sentimental memorials that I was sure Vienna would have ridiculed. I must remember to make out a will and leave instructions for my funeral. No open mike. No sappy testimonials to how wonderful I was. Just lots of good food and humorous, self-deprecating remarks about me.

When the last person had finally spoken, Noreen stood and thanked everyone for coming. Many left, but some headed back to the tables for more food and drink. In the foyer with its polished mahogany floor, bold striped wallpaper on one wall, and a spectacular lady's slipper orchid with dark purple flowers dramatically placed in front of a huge oval mirror, I grabbed the opportunity to speak to the well-dressed detective.

"What did you think of Dolce's remarks?" I asked Jack, knowing any question about who he thought the murderer was would go unanswered—not just unanswered, but ignored and greeted with a frown and another warning.

"She has a point," he said.

I looked him over. "But you don't fit the pattern. No loose baggy clothing for you or shoes like slippers. You don't dress like a typical cop."

"How many typical cops do you know?"

"Professionally—too many. Socially, not enough." I stared at him, willing him to remember the dinner he'd promised me. When he didn't say anything, I swallowed my disappointment and continued. I was not here to socialize or to eat, I was here to learn something about Vienna's murder.

"How did you like the program?" I asked. "Learn anything?"

"Maybe," he said. "Did you?"

"I thought you didn't want my input."

"I don't want you to go off investigating. But if you hear anything or see anything suspicious, then of course I'm all ears."

"In other words, this is a one-way street. I tell you what I know and you tell me nothing. Except that I'm your number one suspect. Or am I?" I asked. Of course he wouldn't answer, but I had to keep trying. What did I have to lose?

Instead of answering, he asked, "Who was the guy who left before the program?"

I should have said I didn't know. Jack didn't deserve my help, but I blurted out everything like a gushing fountain. I couldn't help it.

"His name is Paul; he's a relative and a little bit crazy. In fact, he's gone back to his institution. He said some interesting things."

Jack wouldn't give me the satisfaction of saying, "Oh, what were they?" He just stood there as silent as the orchid on the table, waiting for me to talk. If only I had the chutzpah to walk away or to wait him out, but I didn't.

"Well, he said that Vienna played fast and loose." I stopped. Jack said nothing. Gave nothing away by his expression. Something he was taught at the police academy, I supposed. "He said she took too many chances and that he'd had an argument with her. And he'd come to tell the family the truth about Vienna."

"That's it?"

"What more do you want?" I asked.

He didn't answer.

Was there any point in telling Jack that Paul had accused me of murdering Vienna? Why should I contribute to my own problem? I shouldn't. No one is required to incriminate themselves, are they? But again I seemed to have no control over my mouth.

"Then he said he thought I was the one who'd killed her, that Vienna told him I hated her. I didn't hate her, and Vienna wouldn't have cared if I did. She was that confident. You see how ridiculous his accusation is. The man is crazy. He didn't know what he was saying."

"Then why did you listen to him?" Jack asked.

"I was merely being polite. Maybe you don't think I'm capable of it, but I do try. I didn't know he was crazy at the time. I just thought he was another guest, a relative, which he was. What do you think I should have done? I'm getting used to being accused of murder by madmen." I didn't say Jack was a madman, but if he came to that conclusion, I couldn't stop him.

That's when his mouth twitched again, a sign he was

getting ready to leave or that he thought what I'd said was almost too ridiculous. Imagine, suggesting that a San Francisco police detective was crazy. It boggles the mind.

I didn't know about Jack, but I'd learned very little today.

A waiter came by with a tray of champagne. I snagged a glass and so did Jack. I took that as a sign neither one of us was ready to leave. Not until we'd made some kind of progress.

"What if Paul escaped from his institution, had an argument with Vienna, perhaps at the Bachelor Auction, then followed her to the boutique where he strangled her and took her necklace?" I suggested.

Jack took a sip of his champagne and raised an eyebrow.

"Why did she go to the boutique?" he asked.

"I'm not sure," I confessed. "Maybe she wanted to change clothes without going all the way home. Leave her dress on a hanger and slip into something couture but still casual. Perfectly acceptable and totally okay with Dolce. I've been known to do it myself. As I did Sunday morning when I found her body. Dolce always said the shop was not only her home but ours too. The clothes were there for her customers of course, but for us too. After they're worn by one of us, Dolce has them dry-cleaned and puts them on her bargain rack."

"If I were Vienna, I would have changed into a pair of loose tweed trousers and a long cashmere sweater in a diamond pattern," I continued. "And a pair of ballet flats from the new Maria Sharapova collection we just got in. Perfect for more casual after-the-formal activities. And what a relief to change out of her dress, which was beautiful but had to be constricting."

"Was anything missing from the shop?" he asked. "The

clothes or the shoes you mentioned. You'd know, wouldn't you?"

"I didn't notice," I said. But of course I would have or Dolce would have and we hadn't. I wasn't discouraged. We'd been too distraught on Monday—and too busy helping the would-be funeral goers choose outfits—to take inventory. "Let's just say it's possible it happened that way. Vienna went to the boutique; Paul, who was angry about something, followed her; and before she could change clothes, he killed her. He's crazy. He couldn't help it. It makes sense to me. In which case, you can follow up, arrest him and if he's found guilty by reason of insanity, your work is done. He's already under wraps, under lock and key except for family funerals, I'm guessing, where he accosts an innocent guest and accuses her of murder. It's embarrassing for the family, but that's all." I really liked this scenario. It was all so neat and clean. Sometimes I amazed myself.

As I basked in the glow of self-congratulation, I had to step aside to allow guests to walk through on their way out the front door. It was time to leave. I'd done everything I could. Watched Dolce give a touching speech, showed that I was a bona fide mourner and finally solved the murder. Maybe Jack wasn't totally convinced, because I made it look too easy, but he'd come around when he ran out of suspects and time. He had to.

"Good to see you again, Detective," I said on my way to find Dolce and pay our respects to our hosts. "If there's anything else I can do for you, let me know."

I could just hear him saying, "Anything *else*?" in an incredulous tone, as if I hadn't done a thing for him. But I had. And I'd continue to try to help him or at least shake up his current theories, whatever they were. What else could he do to me but haul me down to the station again for more questioning? His case against me was weak. At least that's what I hoped.

So I went back into the living room and made my way through what was left of the crowd. Dolce and I said good-bye to Noreen and went out to the car. On the way we passed the motorcycle parked in the driveway, which reminded me of Geoffrey. Why hadn't I seen him today? Or had I but didn't recognize him because he'd blended in in a dark suit and tie? I told Dolce to get in the car, since she looked like she was about to collapse, and I circled the parking lot on foot hoping Geoffrey would turn up. He did.

Ten

Just as Geoffrey was putting his helmet on, I hurried over to say hello. "I'm Rita Jewel from Dolce's," I said. "We spoke on the phone."

He frowned. "How'd you know it was me?"

"I saw you one day when you picked up Vienna from the shop. And I saw your picture on your web site."

"Oh."

"How did you like the wake?" I asked, hoping he'd say something I could wrap my mind around. Even though I'd just solved the murder myself, I didn't want to leave any stone unturned, so to speak.

"Only one I've ever been to. Kind of weird. So that guy you were talking to in there, he's the cop, right?"

"Yes, he is. Isn't he the one who interviewed you?"

"No, it was a woman. She came to my studio. Asked some

questions, then she left. Wanted to know where I was Saturday night."

"I didn't see you at the auction," I said.

He snorted. "I don't do that charity crap."

I wanted to say, "What do you do?" but I didn't. I knew what he did for a living, but I didn't know where he was that night. He didn't tell me.

"They find the killer yet?" he asked, a little too casually I thought.

"Not that I know of. I mean, Detective Wall wouldn't tell me if he had. I'm just an ordinary citizen. If and when he solves this case, I'll probably read about it in the paper." It was probably true. The idea made me furious. After all I'd done for the police. And yet no one appreciated me. "Those other guys you mentioned, Raold and Emery, were they here today by any chance?" I didn't want to pass up an opportunity to meet all the men in Vienna's life, just in case my case fell apart.

"Yeah, they were. I don't know why. Maybe to get some free food. They didn't know her that well."

Didn't know her that well? Then why had they picked her up after work? Or didn't they? "I suppose they left already then?" I craned my neck to look back at the house. How had I overlooked two twenty-something guys who I wanted badly to meet? I hated to leave without checking out everyone I could.

He shrugged, straddled his motorcycle and turned the key in the ignition. I got the message. He'd had enough of me.

"Okay," I shouted over the roar of the motor. I realized I wasn't getting much out of this interview and I'd been dismissed. "Good to meet you. If you have any other ideas about who killed Vienna . . ."

"Besides you?" he said, his eyes narrowed. He didn't really think . . . Yes, maybe he did.

"Since I didn't do it, I'd like to know who did."

"Got it," he said. But the look he gave me wasn't reassuring. I had the distinct feeling he still thought I was guilty. Join the club. Had he told Ramirez that? Because I was sure she was the woman cop he'd mentioned. I watched while he tore out of the circular driveway. Then I went back to the car intending to tell Dolce I needed to run into the house for something I'd forgotten. But she told me she was feeling unwell and wanted to leave. I'd think of another way to meet these guys. Dolce and I drove back to the city.

I awoke Wednesday morning feeling like I'd hit a brick wall in the investigation of Vienna's murder. Frustrated, I decided that I wouldn't participate in the antiviolence program at the Central Police Station where I'd probably see Detective Wall and he'd once again make light of my brilliant observations. Not only that, but he'd make me feel like he was waiting for me to give up and confess I'd murdered Vienna. So instead, I'd go for a less-strenuous activity like a cooking class at Tante Marie's Cooking School and try to forget all about Vienna. Her funeral was over; it was time to get on with the living.

Easy for me to say, harder to act on. Just walking up the steps to the front door of the shop made my heart pound and my legs shake. What if the door was unlocked just as it had been that fateful Sunday that now seemed like eons ago? What if I opened the door to find another body lying there? It could happen. If word had somehow gotten out this was the place to dump bodies. What would the cops do then? Would Jack Wall blame me? Probably.

But this time I'd at least know what to do. Better yet,

what not to do. I would not touch anything. Nothing. I would immediately call the police. I wouldn't even turn the body over to see who it was or if she was dead. It didn't matter. I had to think of myself first for a change. I had to protect myself from baseless accusations.

Today the door was locked. Of course it was. I used my key to unlock it and walked in. There was no one lying on the floor. I straightened my shoulders and proceeded into the great room. The morning sun bathed the merchandise in golden beams of light. The clothes were back where they belonged. With Dolce's permission, I'd moved the bright citrus colors favored by Vienna to a small alcove. She didn't want to be reminded of Vienna any more than I did, for different reasons.

We got through the day somehow. When I told Dolce about my cooking class, she thought it was a great idea. "Every woman, whether she has a career or not, should know how to cook. I wish I'd learned," she said as I stood in her office at five o'clock. "Maybe if I had, things would be different."

I hated to see her so down in the dumps. So it was true: her spotless kitchen was not used for cooking.

"It's not too late," I said. "Take the class with me."

"I can't. I'm wiped out. Have a good time," she said. She looked pale and tired. It had been a slow day. Just what we expected after the blockbuster day when we sold all those funeral outfits. Good day for Dolce, since she didn't have to go into full sales mode, but bad for me. I was bored and antsy. Glad I had plans for the evening that involved self-improvement and food.

Dolce seemed ready to fall apart. I could understand that. Her favorite girl had been murdered right here on these premises, unless she wasn't. In any case, Dolce might be feeling guilty. If Vienna hadn't come to work here, would she be alive today? Was it something about her work here that had led to her demise? Or was the reason she'd been found lying on the floor here just because it was a convenient spot for some vagrant to attack her? I wished I knew.

I told myself there was nothing more I could do. It was time to stop obsessing over Vienna, was time for some "me" time instead of Vienna time. The woman had taken over my life since the day she first appeared in our shop. And she continued to cast a long shadow over me even after she was dead.

What had I ever done to deserve this? I'd given up my lunch hour so she and Dolce could go out together. I'd meekly retreated to the back room so she could be the bright new salesgirl racking up sales and making friends with women I used to think were *my* customers. Did I complain? Did I beg Dolce to let me back into the showrooms? Did I ever utter a harsh word to or about Vienna? No, no and no.

I took the number twenty-two Fillmore bus to Eighteenth Street, the heart of Potrero Hill where Tante Marie had her cooking school. Good choice, I thought as I walked up a steep hill toward the school, catching a glimpse of the Bay in the distance. *Potrero* is Spanish for "pasture," the hill so named because it was given as a land grant to Don Francisco de Haro in 1835 to graze cattle in the *potrero nuevo*— the new pasture. That's what it said on a historical marker on the corner.

Potrero Hill, once used for farming and shipping, was now a sunny neighborhood even when the rest of the city was socked in with fog. I passed cafés and restaurants, shops and narrow frame houses that lined the streets. Each house, no matter how small and modest, boasted a garden of sorts or at least a flower box or a tree in front of it.

Tante Marie had chosen a storefront for her cooking school, showing a frugal and a practical nature. Inside the front door was a desk where I registered and paid a fee for the class, and in the back was a huge kitchen and several rows of chairs.

I'm not sure if there really was a Tante Marie; if there was, I didn't meet her. Instead, I learned our teacher for tonight was Guido Torcelli, who looked like the quintessential Italian chef unless you think all Italian chefs are rotund. Guido was tall and lean with flowing gray hair and a thick accent. I was disappointed to hear this was a demonstration class, not hands-on. I really needed to get some experience. After all, I could watch cooking classes on television any time, but what I was paying for was to have a professional like Guido watch me and tell me what I was doing wrong. I guessed I hadn't read the fine print, although, to tell the truth, I was so eager to start my new life filled with cooking and exercise, I'd just impulsively rushed right into this class tonight. I know that's my problem. I'm impulsive and I don't always do my homework, but who wants to think everything over before acting? If I did that, I'd never get anything done.

I was reassured when Guido said we'd all participate in the class in some fashion or another. He didn't say we'd do the actual cooking, but anything was better than nothing, which was what I'd be doing if I was home tonight.

He said that after the demonstration we'd sit around the table, eat the food and drink the wine and discuss how it all went together. Everyone would have a complete folder of all the recipes he'd made tonight. Since I was tired after my immersion in Vienna's funeral yesterday, I really didn't mind sitting there watching Guido. He'd been a TV chef, a cook-book author and a cooking teacher for years. Seeing him up close and personal was worth the price of the class.

I took a seat in the front row, with a good view of Guido, his assistant Marco and his rack of tools and equipment. First Guido told us about his weeklong cooking classes at his fifteenth-century farmhouse in the Chianti Classico wine and olive oil country just outside Florence. I positively sal-ivated even though we hadn't seen a bite of food yet, but I imagined myself in the farmhouse rolling out fresh pasta, deep-frying zucchini flowers and simmering rich sauces on top of the vintage farmhouse stove. I had to go. Maybe I could combine the cooking classes with some shopping for Dolce.

Tonight's menu was prosciutto, pear and pecorino salad; halibut baked in a bag with clams, mussels, fennel and anchovies; and Sicilian-scented cracked wheat. I was on the edge of my seat. It all sounded so delicious. When Guido asked for a volunteer to chop the pears and grate the pecorino cheese, I jumped up and went behind the table before he could call on anyone else. I thought he was going to hug me he was so glad to see such enthusiasm. And of course he was Italian and very demonstrative. A minute ago I'd been glad to sit and watch; now I was up in front with the masters.

I found I had a lot to learn about chopping. How to hold the knife, how to keep from slicing my fingers off. All important stuff. Then there was the cheese, where I was only in danger of grating the skin off my fingers. I mixed up a dressing of balsamic vinegar and olive oil according to the recipe and poured it over the pears and the delicious, sliced-wafer-thin proscuitto.

And on to the fish course. I wanted to continue to help, but Guido asked for another volunteer. Was it because I had made a tiny mistake like sloshing too much vinegar in the vinaigrette so that Guido's assistant Marco had to work with it, adding more oil then more vinegar and a dollop of mustard until he got it right? Maybe it wasn't my mistake. Maybe it was the recipe that wasn't correct.

Guido reminded us to always taste, taste, taste. I should have done that, but I didn't trust my own taste buds yet. Guido said that would come with time and experience. When a new volunteer came up to take my place and work with the master, I reluctantly sat down and watched.

Guido explained how to be flexible when at the market. If your recipe calls for halibut but the halibut at the fish store doesn't look so good, what to do? The Italian cook knows that halibut is a flat fish. I scribbled "halibut—flat fish" on my notepad. Because not being an Italian cook, I hadn't known that.

Guido continued. "The Italian chef knows that flounder, turbot and sole are also flat fishes, and the sole is on sale. You're in luck! And just because your recipe calls for spaghetti it doesn't mean you can't use linguini."

I wrote it all down. What an amazing eye-opener it was. Substituting one kind of fish or one kind of pasta for another. Something I never would have dared before I came to this class.

"As for the cheese, you might be out of pecorino, but you've got Parmesan, which will work just fine," he said.

Of course I didn't have pecorino or Parmesan or any kind of cheese or pasta, but that was okay. I'd head for the store and stock up. Right after I bought some new pots and pans and cleaned up my new kitchen. I was filled with resolve and enthusiasm.

While the fish was baking in its bag, Guido made the Sicilian-scented cracked wheat. It was supposed to be so good for you that I couldn't believe it would taste as good as he said it would.

When everything was ready, we all took our seats around a long farmhouse table set with rustic hand-painted plates and wineglasses. I was glad to find a spot near the head of the table where Guido had taken his place. His assistant Marco came around to heap our plates with the salad, the baked fish and the cracked wheat.

I was in heaven. Between bites I told Guido I loved to eat but I had no idea how to cook anything before I came there tonight.

"And now you will have a little dinner for your friends and show off, yes?"

I nodded. That was exactly what I'd do. I had the menu. I had the recipes, and I had the plan to inaugurate my new apartment with a small dinner party.

When Marco served small cups of espresso coffee, I decided I'd buy an espresso machine. But what to serve for dessert? I asked Guido and he suggested gelato. Perhaps he sensed that trying to make something Italian like cannoli or tiramisu would push me over the edge on my first Italian meal. Although today there was no mention of dessert.

"There are many gelato brands available here in your country," he assured me. "Of course not the same as in Italy, but . . ." He shrugged and poured himself some more wine. "Don't forget to look over our line of cookware. I couldn't do without it and neither should you."

That did it. When dinner was over, I headed for the adjacent shop where the clerk was kind enough to help me choose all the pots and pans I'd need to duplicate the dinner we'd just had. I could hardly wait to do it myself.

But once out on the street loaded down with boxes and bags, I felt my enthusiasm fade. I was back in the real world where I was planning to give a dinner when I didn't really know how to cook.

Not only that, I also didn't know where the next crime I'd be blamed for would be committed. I set my bags down and checked my phone messages. I was surprised to find that Nick the gymnast had called. When I found a taxi, I sat in the back and listened to the message he'd left.

"Hello, Rita," he said. "My aunt has told me about your appearance at the pizza restaurant. So you have heard about my accident? Why haven't you come to see me? I am calling you to suggest to you a meeting outside in the good weather because my doctor recommends exercise and not staying inside resting so much, although I do not go to the gym to work just now. Tomorrow I propose to bring a typical picnic lunch of Romanian specialties of course. Can you meet me at the Palace of Fine Arts at the Marina Green near my house at twelve o'clock noon? Please tell me that you can and that we are still friends. It is a favorite place for picnic, reminding me of Romania sometimes."

I normally didn't take more than a half hour for lunch because Dolce needed me, but I thought I deserved a treat after all I'd been through. So I called Nick back and told him I'd meet him there. I didn't ask what happened to his

Romanian guest/girlfriend. I just hoped she wouldn't come along on the picnic. Not that I was worried about competition. I was afraid of being left out of a conversation in Romanian. I did remember a few important phrases from my language studies, like *Doresti sa dansezi cu mine?* It means "Would you like to dance with me?" Very useful in certain situations. But when two Romanians get together, I've noticed they tend to speak fast and slur their words, making it likely that nonnative speakers such as myself will be left on the sidelines trying to make sense of the conversation, but afraid to chime in.

To show off a little, I said, *"Multa sanatate,"* before I hung up, which I believe means "Get well soon," and Nick chuckled appreciatively, unless perhaps I hadn't pronounced it correctly and it meant something entirely different.

A Romanian picnic on the green in the sun was just what I needed. Especially when my companion knew nothing about the murder of Vienna. The subject of crime or my now-deceased coworker would not come up unless I brought it up, which I wouldn't. Whereas at work, Vienna's murder hung over the shop like a dark cloud. Never far from our thoughts or our conversation. Even if Dolce or I kept quiet, a customer was sure to ask about Vienna, her family or her funeral.

Maybe I was the only one who felt it, but I couldn't help looking at every customer and wondering if she was capable of murder in general and if she'd killed Vienna in particular. Isn't everyone capable of killing someone if they have a strong motive like revenge or lust or jealousy or hate or blackmail or greed? That was a question I would like to ask Jack if I wasn't afraid he'd jump to the wrong conclusion—that I excused myself from killing Vienna because I had a good strong motive. I didn't. I had no motive at all except for wanting my job back. And jealousy over Dolce's fondness for Vienna. I sighed. No wonder I was suspect numero uno.

Nick didn't know Vienna; he didn't know Dolce or any policemen. His world was all about gymnastics, exercise, Romanian immigrants and Romanian food and Romanian visitors from abroad. I could only hope he hadn't read about Vienna's murder in the newspaper. I hadn't. Surely one of our customers would let us know if there was anything. I did wonder how her murder had been kept out of the papers, seeing as she was from such a prominent family. Maybe that's how it worked: prominent families used their influence to keep ugly incidents out of the print media. Although they hadn't been able to keep the news from the TV crew.

The next day I dressed casually in a pair of Joe's Jeans, which everyone knows are very flattering, making your legs look longer and lifting your butt. I paired them with a print T-shirt and a jean jacket tied around my waist—though I made sure the jacket only partly covered my lifted butt. I knotted a print Hermes silk scarf around my neck and propped my sunglasses on my head. On my feet I wore soft suede spring open-toe shoe booties with dark socks.

Dolce said she loved my outfit, and she was delighted I had a lunch date. I knew she would be. She's just like that. Always wants the best for everyone. I wanted to ask if she'd heard from William Hemlock. Instead, I told her about my cooking class and said I was going to invite her to dinner. Then on a whim, I added, "I'd like to invite your new friend William too. How would that be?"

"Fine," she said, but I couldn't tell if she meant it. Whatever she said, I was determined to pull it off. I'd invite some others too, like Nick, since he'd invited me to lunch. We wouldn't talk about Vienna's murder. We wouldn't talk shop at all, not at my first real dinner party.

As for Dolce's lunch, she said she'd order something from the sandwich shop and have it delivered and I was to take a long break and have a great time with the Romanian gymnast.

It was a gorgeous day, and I'd never been to the Palace of Fine Arts before. I'd seen it from a distance but never stopped to admire the reconstructed historic old building, which was built on fill from the 1906 earthquake. When San Francisco got the nod to host the World's Fair in 1915, they held the Panama Pacific Exposition on this unstable land near the Bay. The only building left today was the Palace of Fine Arts, or rather, this rebuilt copy of it, which is where I found Nick, sitting on a bench, a large basket at his side. Eyes closed, he was wearing straight-cut jeans, a scarf casually knotted around his shirt, which was half unbuttoned, and a male purse or messenger bag hanging over his shoulder. His face was tilted toward the sun, his long legs were stretched out in front of him, oblivious to the joggers, skaters and dogs on leashes who paraded by.

"Nick," I said.

His eyes flew open. He got up and kissed me on both cheeks, Romanian style.

"How is your tendon doing?" I asked with a glance at his leg.

"Much better, thanks, although I cannot use the high bar for a while yet. I am glad to see you again."

"Me too. Thanks for inviting me," I said with an eye on his picnic basket. I'd skipped breakfast today except for the coffee and a bagel that one of the customers had brought me.

So far every Romanian dish I'd ever had had been delicious—but I still wasn't brave enough to try the pizza with carp Aunt Meera had suggested. I could only hope there wasn't one of those in his basket.

I didn't have to worry. After we found a spot on the grass next to the small lagoon under the Roman-style columns of the Palace, Nick spread out a cloth and opened his basket. A quick glance told me there was no pizza of any kind inside.

"You have not been to my country, no? If you had, you would know that on Sunday we always go to the country for a picnic."

"What a wonderful custom. Americans like to picnic too. Even during the week. It must feel strange to you," I said, accepting a small crusty meat pie Nick called *strudel cu carne* from an earthenware container he'd packed in his basket, "to see so many people enjoying the weather any day of the week." Even I was amazed to see all these people out playing on a weekday. Did they have jobs? Didn't they have to work?

"Strange but very nice. I am still surprised at all these American people who can picnic today like you and me without work," he said with a glance at the passersby who ate, talked, walked or bicycled past us. "Very good country," he added. "In Romania we mostly live in big apartment buildings, so even more necessary to go out on weekend for picnic. So once in the outside Romanians don't sometimes know how to behave. They turn up music on small radios so loud we cannot hear ourselves speak. Then they must cut down branches for making a small fire to grill small boxes of *mici*. After that they return to their car and drive back to the city, leaving behind a mess."

"But that's terrible," I said. "Who cleans it up?"

"No one. So that is the waste that pollutes our beautiful forest and stream." He reached into his basket and handed me a small dish of Romanian potato salad with onions and olives, and a fork.

"But wait," Nick said, "this is not end of story. There is good news. We too have green revolution and new rules. Now people must take away trash for themselves. It is a very good idea, I think."

After learning about the Romanian picnic culture, I was able to inform Nick about the history of the Palace of Fine Arts, which I'd researched that morning in Dolce's office on her computer. I pulled some notes from my pocket and began my lecture.

"The Palace of Fine Arts was built in 1915. But years later it began to crumble away, since it was only built for the World's Fair. So in the sixties they rebuilt it following the same pattern."

"So new," Nick said.

"Yes, compared to Romania where you have castles that are from the Middle Ages, right?"

"Yes, but this looks old."

"It's supposed to. The original architect, Bernard Maybeck, got his ideas from Greek and Roman architecture. The people who rebuilt it wanted to keep it looking old."

"Like the columns and the dome," Nick said as he opened a small cheese he called *cascaval* and cut me a slice. I tore off a piece of bread and ate it with the plum brandy he poured for me. "Romanian picnic tradition," he explained as he lifted his paper cup. "To your health."

"What a nice tradition," I said. Nick went to find the men's room inside the Palace, and I lay down and rested my head on my jean jacket. I'd just closed my eyes for a moment when I heard someone say, "Rita. Rita Jewel?"

I sat up and saw a man in shorts and a helmet on a bike who'd stopped on the path and was looking at me. I didn't think I knew him.

"Emery Grant. Heard you're looking for me."

I blinked rapidly. Yes, I was looking for him, but not now. Not today. Not here. First, how had he recognized me? Second, did he know I'd be here? And finally, I knew why I wanted to see him, but why did he want to see me? I would have thought he'd try to avoid me as did everyone connected with Vienna these days.

"What do you want?" he said, dragging his bike across the grass.

I was so startled I almost forgot what I wanted to ask him. But when he stood looming above me, I had to defuse the situation. Following Romanian tradition, I offered him a drink of *tunica*, which he accepted. Once he saw the ornate bottle it came in, he couldn't refuse. He sat on the picnic cloth next to me.

I hated to bring up the subject of Vienna's murder today when I was taking a well-deserved break from the tension. I especially didn't want to muddy the atmosphere between Nick and me. I didn't want him to know anything about it. It was so good to spend an hour with someone who was in a different world than the one of funerals, police interrogations and family feuds that I was in every day, where everyone suspected everyone else. Since Nick was conveniently gone for the moment, I decided to make the best of the situation.

"I . . . how did you know me? How did you know where to find me?" I asked.

"I saw you when I went to pick up Vienna," he explained. "You worked in the shop with her."

"Yes, I know," I said, slightly annoyed to be caught at a disadvantage. He knew who I was. If he was guilty of killing Vienna, why stop and say hello? Why not keep his distance and out of sight?

"I went to the store to see you today, and your boss told me you'd be here. I just want to get one thing straight. I didn't kill her. Why would I?"

"Why come all this way to tell me?" I asked. "Why don't you tell the police you're innocent?"

"Because they didn't accuse me, you did."

"You did know Vienna," I said.

"Yeah, of course. We went to San Francisco Prep together. When she came back to town, she looked me up."

"You came to pick her up from the store, didn't you, in your . . . Lotus?"

He shook his head. "Do I look like a drive a Lotus?"

Out of the corner of my eye, I saw Nick ambling toward us across the grass. He would be so confused, and I didn't want to go into the whole long story. Not now. Not ever really.

I didn't answer his question about his looking like he drove a Lotus. I wasn't very knowledgeable about cars. I decided to cut to the chase.

"If you didn't kill Vienna, who did?" I asked breathlessly as Nick drew closer.

"Hah. That's what everyone wants to know. Could be any number of people. Sure it wasn't you?" he asked.

I shook my head vehemently.

"She wasn't exactly the most popular girl at our school. For one thing, she cheated on tests and she cheated on her boyfriends, but somehow she never got caught. There were people out to get her. To pay her back."

This was news to me. Would it be news to Jack? "So did you tell this to the police?" I asked.

Before he answered, Nick joined us. "Hello," Nick said with a curious glance at the newcomer.

"Nick, this is Emery, a friend of a friend. Just stopped by to say hello."

Nick, who was instilled with the Romanian spirit of hospitality and generosity, shook his hand and refilled Emery's cup.

"So, uh, would you be willing to share your information with others?" I asked, meaning the police.

"No way," he said. "That would be inconvenient. No names. I've got to live in this town. If someone I know did anything wrong and he knows I ratted him out, I could be next. So don't go telling them I know anything."

Was he kidding? Was he really afraid he'd be killed like Vienna was? On a sunny day having a picnic and drinking Romanian wine, it didn't seem possible.

He glanced at Nick. "Who's he?"

"Sorry, I should have introduced you. Meet Nick Petrescu. He's a Romanian gymnast. He speaks very good English."

"Okay," Emery said with a brief nod to Nick as he

nimbly got to his feet. He turned to me. "You got my message, I got yours. This is it."

"Wait," I said. "Give me your number. In case I need to talk to you."

As I reached in my bag for a pen, he called out some numbers, which I quickly jotted down on a scrap of paper Nick handed me. The more I saw Nick, the better I liked him. He didn't accuse me of anything. Didn't ask me to do anything. He provided me with food, and he even treated this guy politely, a guy whom he didn't even know.

When Nick brought out a thermos of hot coffee and a bag of *cornulete*, crisp Romanian cookies rolled in cinnamon and sugar, I was so content I'd almost forgotten my worries. As long as no one else came riding by on a bicycle to tell me he did not kill Vienna, I would call it a perfect day.

Maybe it was because I so badly needed a break from work and from everyone who was connected to the shop. Or maybe it was just because Nick was a kind and caring friend. Here he was suffering from a torn tendon and yet he'd been able to put together this wonderful lunch and had even suggested this historic spot, though he was far from being a native. It made me want to visit Romania with someone like him for a guide.

I wondered what my detective friend would think if I told him I was leaving for Romania. Would he put out a warrant for my arrest? Put me under shop or house arrest? Take my passport, which I didn't have, to prevent me from leaving the country? Since I didn't have enough money for a plane ticket to Bucharest, I decided to hold off and just pretend I was there. Sitting on the grass gazing at the Corinthian columns of the Palace mirrored in the lagoon, it was almost like being in Europe, I thought, though I wasn't sure, since

I'd never been there. Why else would Nick have chosen this spot for our picnic? Surely because he felt at home here. I was feeling so much at home myself I hated to get on the bus and go back to work. I finished my coffee, looked at my watch and told Nick I had to leave.

"Thank you so much for the picnic lunch. It was delicious. Now it's my turn to invite you."

He smiled widely. Probably thinking: It's about time Rita repaid me for all I've done for her. And me with my torn tendon.

"I'm going to have a dinner party," I said. "Uh, next Sunday night." Thinking fast, I knew I was busy Saturday night, but I planned to have all day Sunday to prepare the salad and the fish in the bag. "I hope you can come. I've taken a cooking class, and I want to show off what I've learned."

"How nice that will be," he exclaimed. "You are living in the same place?"

Nick had visited me when I hurt my ankle and even then he'd supplied food for me.

"Same address, but I've moved upstairs to a smaller apartment." It was so much smaller I was wondering how to fit everyone in because I intended to invite everyone I owed. Never mind. I'd worry about that later.

Nick walked me to the bus stop. He was limping, but he assured me he'd improved a lot since his accident on the high bar.

"I hope you had a friend or someone to help you out besides your aunt Meera."

He didn't say anything for a moment, and I wondered if he was going to mention the Romanian woman I'd overheard speaking to him while I was standing outside his apartment.

"Yes, other people have been kind to take care of me,"

he said at last. But no names were mentioned. It was none of my business really.

I thanked him again and waved good-bye from the bus stop.

While on the bus I called Jonathan and left a message inviting him to my dinner. I'd be seeing him on Saturday night, but I wanted to give him enough notice so he could find a substitute if he was on the ER schedule for Sunday.

Eleven

When I got back to Dolce's, I hurried inside, worried I'd taken advantage of my boss's good nature by dragging out this lunch date. The place was crowded with customers, which made me feel guilty I hadn't been here to help. Dolce looked overwhelmed as she handed a slip dress to a slim twenty-something I'd never seen before and a preppy shirt to someone else at the same time.

I immediately went into my sales mode, helping our customers two and three at a time, finding pieces to mix and match. A silk shirt here, some funky shoes there, a girly skirt and a tuxedo jacket to pull it all together.

I felt like I had a new lease on life. So that's all I'd needed—a break from the everyday stress of being a murder suspect. I'd even forgotten about Emery, glad he hadn't ruined my picnic with Nick. How tactful of Nick not to ask me any questions about him, like who he was or what he was talking about.

Smiling at the thought, I finished helping Sharon, one of our good customers, find the right leather handbag to go with her new off-white pants outfit. When she gasped at the prices, I reminded her, "A leather bag is an investment that you will keep forever." But I did give her a choice between one in faux leather and a real leather satchel. Naturally she chose the satchel.

Out of the corner of my eye I saw a young woman come in the front door, the same woman I'd seen at the funeral home wearing sparkly bracelets that had belonged to Vienna.

"Can I help you?" I said, rushing to the foyer where she stood looking a little lost.

"I'm Danielle, Vienna's roommate," she said.

What was she doing here? She couldn't be shopping, could she, because she sure didn't fit in with the typical Dolce clientele: rich, married women who wore real jewelry and belonged to the social set. Even in the designer clothes she wore, which I recognized as Vienna's. Did Dolce know who she was? I hoped she wouldn't come in and make a scene. I remembered she had a temper.

"I'm here to pick up Vienna's stuff," she said.

"What stuff?" I asked.

"You know. Whatever she left here."

"Did her parents send you?"

"Nobody sent me. Look," she said, fixing me with a steely stare, "Vienna skipped out without paying the rent. She owes me."

"I hardly think being murdered qualifies as skipping out," I said tersely.

"How do you know she was murdered?" she asked,

placing her hands on her hips. "What, was there a bullet hole in her head? Maybe she had a heart attack."

A heart attack? I only wished it was that simple. I shuddered at the thought of the image I'd seen that morning. Just days ago. No wonder I couldn't get it out of my mind. Seeing Vienna's prostrate form on the floor with those marks around her neck had been bad enough; now I was being asked to verify her murder, by her rude roommate no less? It was more than I could take. Why had I even bothered to talk to this woman?

"I'm only going by what the police told me," I said stiffly. "I'm sure they'd be glad to explain it to you. Let me give you the card from the detective on the case. You can call him."

"Detective Wall?" she said. "I already saw him. And I told him what I thought."

"Does he know you're wearing Vienna's clothes?" I asked, deliberately eyeing her coat and shoes.

She flushed. So I was right.

"He didn't ask me if I was wearing her clothes. What difference does it make if I wear them or some homeless person wears them, which is what her parents would do with them, donate them to a shelter. So if she left anything here, like the above-the-knee suede boots she bought or her designer sunglasses, give them to me. I'll appreciate them than anyone else. And like I said, Vienna didn't pay the rent up front, so she owes me. Either I take her clothes or I get some money."

"Maybe if you tell her father . . ." I suggested.

"I thought about it, but I don't want to bother him right now. Instead, I'll just take whatever I can get here. So what about your boss? Vienna said she'd given her a bunch of stuff. Where is it?"

Dolce had given Vienna a bunch of stuff? Like what, I wondered. And where was it?

"How should I know?" I asked. "How do you know Vienna anyway? Did you go to San Francisco Prep with her?"

"Yes, but I wasn't in her crowd. She was a preppie. Always looked like she should be on the cover of a Ralph Lauren magazine. Then she went away to school and she changed her style." She paused and looked around the store. "Perfect place for her to work, if you can call waiting on rich spoiled women work."

"What do *you* do?" I asked.

"I work at home," she said.

I hadn't asked her where she worked, I'd asked her what she did. I tried again. "How convenient," I said. "What kind of work is it?"

"I'm a writer."

"I love to read," I said. "Maybe I've read some of your books." Which wasn't likely unless she wrote paranormal romances where mortals fall in love with vampires. Because that was my reading material of choice. Nothing too heavy or challenging.

"I don't write books," she said. "I write the fortunes for fortune cookies."

"I always wondered who wrote them. In fact, I got one once I didn't understand. Maybe you wrote it." It was so complicated I couldn't remember it. "Something about not stepping in the same stream twice."

"That wasn't mine. Mine are easy to understand. Like, 'A golden egg of opportunity falls into your lap this month.'"

I just stared at her. What a great job, I thought. How hard

could it be to come up with that kind of thing? "I thought you had to be Chinese to write those."

"Some people are. I'm not. Being a professional writer is a great job. You get to work at home. You can wear a pair of sweats all day. But it doesn't pay that well. And there's no job security. One day they say your fortunes aren't any good anymore. They're tired or boring or repetitious, or they hire someone who's cheaper. I have good taste. I love champagne, but I can only afford beer. I admit I was jealous of Vienna's clothes and her rich parents. What did she do to deserve what she got?"

"You're not the only one who felt that way," I said. "Someone else resented her. Someone killed her."

"Well, it wasn't me," she said.

I didn't know whether to believe her or not. It seemed like too many people were eager to declare their innocence. But I knew how she felt. I was one of those people.

"If you wear sweatpants all day, why do you want Vienna's clothes? They're on the cutting edge. You can't even wear them to the Safeway or you'd be stared at."

"I'll worry about where to wear them when I get them," Danielle said in her snippy way. Then she walked past me into the great room. Fortunately both Dolce and her customers were busy looking at some new jewelry we'd recently gotten in. Danielle looked around from the racks of formal dresses to the shelves stacked with scarves.

"No wonder Vienna wanted to work here. All this great stuff. I didn't think she needed the money because she could just ask Daddy."

"I thought everyone at Prep was rich," I said. I could hear the jealousy in Danielle's voice. However she denied killing her roommate, she would have to admit jealousy was a common motive for murder.

"Most everyone was rich," she said. "But some of us were on scholarship. Some of us were jocks, some were nerds, some were geeks."

I noted she didn't say which group she belonged to. From looking at her, I couldn't tell. All I knew for sure was that she was trying to get something for nothing.

"Listen," I said when I saw Dolce giving Danielle a curious look, no doubt wondering who the hell Rita was talking to for so long when she should be helping other customers. "I'll ask my boss if Vienna left anything behind and I'll call you."

Danielle seemed torn between going or staying. Finally she said she'd call Dolce later. She'd just opened the door when I thought of something. I rushed over and asked quietly, "Did you see the necklace Vienna was wearing the night of the big benefit, the night she was murdered?"

"Was it made of diamonds and a huge pink stone?" she asked.

"Yes," I said.

"Nope," she said. "Never saw it." Then she turned and left. I just stood there staring at the door she'd just walked out of. What else could I do, rush out after her and demand an explanation?

"Who was that woman in the trench coat?" Dolce asked me later when she'd closed up.

"Vienna's roommate, Danielle. Did you recognize the coat?"

Dolce turned pale. "Oh, no, that was Vienna's coat. What did she want?"

"You won't believe this, but she wanted any clothes that

Vienna left here. I didn't say anything because I thought you wouldn't want to deal with her at this point. Especially since she wanted something from you. She thinks she deserves the clothes because Vienna was behind in the rent. In fact, I gather Vienna didn't pay any rent, so Danielle thinks she's been stiffed."

"So she wants a dead girl's clothes," Dolce said with a shiver. "Don't you think that's kind of macabre?"

I nodded. "I told her I'd ask you, just to get rid of her. I hope none of the customers heard what she was saying. They would have been disgusted with good reason."

"Vienna did leave some clothes here. She picked out a few outfits, and she was going to collect them later." Dolce blinked rapidly. I couldn't stand it if she cried again. I hesitated about continuing the conversation, though I wanted to ask if Vienna had actually paid for the clothes. Or did Dolce give them to her? Or none of the above.

"I was wondering," I said, propping one hand on the ornate door frame between the showroom and the alcove, "if that's why Vienna came back here that night. To change clothes. Just to get out of her beautiful dress and into something more comfortable, more casual. Maybe a short flouncy skirt with a wool blend cardigan and a pair of Sorel boots. Knowing Vienna, she might add a sleek beret and a cozy scarf that can feel so good at night in the city. Does that make sense?"

"But why not go home to change?" Dolce asked. "Where she'd have even more clothes to choose from?"

"Home being her apartment, the one she shared with Danielle? Maybe she didn't feel at home there, and after speaking with Danielle just now, I can understand why she might not. You knew Vienna better than I did. Any idea how she felt about her roommate or why she came here that night?"

I probably should have asked Dolce sooner, but it was kind of forbidden, the subject of Vienna's murder. Dolce really cared about Vienna and maybe even felt partly responsible for it, since it happened here.

"All I know is that Vienna and her roommate were not close. I don't even know if Vienna ever spent any time at that apartment," Dolce said. "Still, I wouldn't mind giving her Vienna's clothes. There's a leather jacket, so soft and thin it's almost like a shirt, and a pair of faux suede booties that look Victorian, and a pair of polished knit sweatpants. I certainly don't want them, and they should be worn by someone. They're classy and expensive."

Just like Vienna. Dolce didn't say it, but I knew that's what she thought. I wanted to know if Vienna had paid for the clothes, but I didn't want to seem nosy. After all, that was between Vienna and Dolce. If Dolce wanted to give them away to someone else, paid or unpaid for, she should. I noticed Dolce hadn't answered my question about why Vienna would have come here after the auction. Was she avoiding my question, or wasn't it worth answering?

"What about you?" Dolce asked.

"Me, wear Vienna's clothes?" I asked. "I couldn't." Even if she'd never worn them, it was too weird. Besides, we didn't even remotely have the same taste.

"You're right. Of course you couldn't wear her things. You and Vienna were totally different. She had such an out-there fashion sense. Being older, you're much more conservative."

I didn't know if I liked that description. It made me feel old and tired and out of touch. Was it possible I'd slipped into middle age without knowing it? Had it taken the arrival of a fresh new face to point out to everyone that I was a has-been?

"I like to think I'm just as trendy as the next person," I said, trying not to sound defensive. Although if the next person was Vienna, I obviously was not.

"Of course you are," Dolce said soothingly. "I'll give the clothes to her roommate. Her parents won't want them. It would just make them miss her more."

I didn't think her stepmother would miss her at all, but I didn't care if Bobbi got anything out of Vienna's death. And her mother had enough clothes already, and the money to buy whatever she wanted. What would Vienna want? Hard to say. She hadn't spoken favorably about anyone. Not friends, not her sister or her mother. Her father was another matter. I had a feeling he was her favorite parent. And why not? He gave her everything she wanted. Or so I'd heard.

"What about her sister? Maybe we should ask her if she wants Vienna's clothes."

"I don't think so," Dolce said, then she pressed her thumbs against her temples. "Again, from what I saw, she has totally different taste. Now I'm going to take two aspirin and go to bed."

"Good night," I said, heading toward the door. "Oh, and that little dinner party I mentioned earlier today? It's on Sunday night, and please, invite William as well."

"Rita, that sounds lovely," Dolce said. "I didn't know you could cook."

"I took that cooking class," I said. Then I felt silly. How could I hope to give a dinner party after one cooking class? My resolve was slipping away. But now that I'd asked both Jonathan and Nick as well as Dolce and her pilot friend, I couldn't back down.

"Good for you," Dolce said. "I wish I'd done that. It's too late for me, but not for you. Of course I'll come."

Dolce seemed more enthusiastic than the last time we'd discussed the diner party. "What about William?" I wanted to ask, but I didn't. I was almost afraid to invite him after what he'd said about how he cooked his steak Diane, but as my aunt Alyce always says, "In for a penny, in for a pound." Which I believe meant that once I'd extended the invitation, I had to go ahead and make the best of it.

I went through the motions at work on Friday, but my real energy was focused on my date for Saturday night. I was glad I had Saturday off, though I knew it would be hard on Dolce to handle the customers by herself. I needed a day off. I'd had it up to here with Vienna's murder. I was stuck having too many suspects and sick of being suspected myself. I wondered when I'd hear from Jack Wall again. Of course I didn't want to answer any more questions about Vienna unless I could ask questions in return. And that wasn't going to happen. Not in this lifetime. It was always interesting to joust with my favorite detective, but not so interesting to try to turn his attention to other topics when he refused to respect my opinions—or humor me, at the very least.

As usual, Dolce threw herself into the project of what I should wear to the Starlight Room with Jonathan. "I'm glad you didn't have to pay for this date," she said as she hung three of four dresses on a rack for me to try on. "Because I don't know if it's exactly your scene."

"Really? Whose scene is it?" I asked.

"Let's just say you're a little young for it."

"Good," I said, "I want to feel young and fun for a change. There are times when I feel old and conservative."

I didn't mention that that was because of Vienna's and Dolce's earlier remarks. I didn't ever plan to say anything negative about Vienna in front of Dolce.

"Then let's see what says young and fun," Dolce said, looking at the dresses she'd pulled out. One was a gypsy dress with a long flowing skirt. She suggested wearing it with leather lace-up wedge boots, which would have been fine on someone else. On me it looked sloppy. Next she showed me a white faux-fur jacket, black leggings and a pair of killer heels. The whole outfit was dramatic, but I could hardly walk in those heels and the fur coat made me feel claustrophobic. Dolce was unstoppable. Her next choice was an ultrashort party dress in silver lamé with an A-line shape. Worn with Hue black tights studded with sheer dots it was dramatic and young and fearless.

"The A-line shape makes your legs look longer and slimmer and lets you eat and drink whatever you want," Dolce pointed out enthusiastically.

I didn't like to think that my legs were normally short and fat and that I usually couldn't eat and drink what I wanted. But of course Dolce was only trying to be helpful. She added a wide bracelet and a pair of festive sparkly peep-toe shoes to my outfit.

"I think I like it," I said, standing in front of the mirror. It made a statement. It said, "I'm out of my element and that's not a bad thing. I'm out on the town. I'm dressed for fun."

It wasn't anything I'd wear anywhere else. I hoped I wouldn't have to pay for this dress, which I'd probably only wear one night, because just a glance at the price tag left me breathless.

"It's perfect for the Starlight Room," she said. "You'll see."

I wondered what else I'd see. Would everyone else be in the conservative outfits I'd heard they wore there? Would any of our customers be there? What would Vienna have worn if she'd gone with Jonathan? Maybe the diaphanous black dress I imagined wearing to the Venice Film Festival, which I was sure Vienna had been to or, if not, was planning on going.

"And with it," Dolce said, "you must wear this faux-fur black jacket from the Armani Exchange and carry a clutch bag that says 'Party on.'" She smiled at me, and I didn't have the heart to spoil her fun by telling her I was having second thoughts. Was this really what people wore to the famous nightclub on the twenty-first floor of the hotel to drink and dance and ogle the other customers? I was going to find out.

At least Jonathan said all the right things about my outfit when he picked me up on Saturday night. At first he stopped and stared, looking a little shocked, but in a good way. I did look different from my everyday working-girl self. After all, isn't that the point? If you're going clubbing on a Saturday night, you should look different.

"You look . . . different," he said after he'd walked up the three flights of stairs to my new apartment. I'd spent an hour shoving all my moving boxes into my tiny bedroom so that the place looked almost spacious, with nothing much in it except for my expandable dining room table and a stack of folding chairs I intended to use tomorrow for my dinner.

Then he added, "Sensational, I mean."

I told him he looked fabulous and I meant it. He was as handsome as ever. This time in a retro vintage suit. Some men might look silly or pretentious dressed in a seventies-style narrow, double-breasted dark suit with a fitted striped shirt and tie. But not Jonathan. His sun-bleached hair gave him a beach-boy casual look that I, a transplanted midwestern girl, found irresistible. Who would guess he was an ER doctor, dedicated to saving lives every day and night except for tonight.

"I like your new place," he said.

"It's small, but I love the neighborhood," I said. "My very first dinner party at my new place is tomorrow night. I'm taking Saturday off to get ready. Sorry for such short notice, but I hope you can make it."

"Of course I can. I'll trade shifts with someone else if I have to, but I'll be here. What can I bring?"

"Nothing. I have everything under control." That was a lie. I had nothing under control, but I had all day tomorrow to do it. Plus I knew what it should look like and taste like, and I knew how to do the chopping. I was so touched he'd make such an effort to show up.

I breathed a sigh of relief. My party was shaping up. Besides Dolce, Nick and Jonathan, maybe Dolce's new boyfriend would come. It seemed a little lopsided. I had to think of someone else. Tomorrow I'd call around and fill in the guest list. If the weather was nice, we could have drinks on my deck so the guests could appreciate the view of the Bay reflecting the last rays of sun.

Jonathan drove downtown and parked in a garage near the hotel. It was exciting just to be out on the town, walking among the well-dressed and the underdressed and the tourists wandering around Union Square.

"You know why it's called Union Square, don't you?" Jonathan asked as we hurried across Powell Street to avoid the cable car that headed up toward Nob Hill. "During the Civil War the supporters of the Union used to gather here to rally round the North."

"I didn't know that," I said. How much I appreciated being with someone so knowledgeable and so modest at the same time. "You're not a native. How do you know so much?"

"Maybe it's because I'm not a native. I love this city, don't you?" he asked, taking my arm as we entered the hotel.

"Oh, yes," I said, but I loved it a lot more before I got involved in two separate murders, both because I worked at Dolce's. I'd started thinking of it as a homicide capital, which wasn't fair, but there you are.

"You know what people told me before I accepted the job at San Francisco General?" he asked. "That I should bring a tent because I couldn't afford the exorbitant rent here. And bring a lot of sweaters and jackets because of the fog. And sell my car. Buy a bicycle and a Muni pass."

I laughed lightly. I was sure glad Jonathan hadn't sold his Porsche or we'd have had to come here on the bus or his bicycle. Being ecofriendly myself, I didn't mind using alternative transportation but not in my silver lamé dress.

"There's so much to see and do here," he said. "Have you been up the Filbert Steps to Coit Tower, walked across the Golden Gate Bridge or watched the sunset from Ocean Beach?"

"No, I haven't. But I have been to the Palace of Fine Arts."

"That's on my list," he said. "As soon as I get off this night schedule, I'm definitely going to see it. So you recommend it?"

"Definitely. It reminds me of Italy. Not that I've been to Italy, but if I had, it would remind me because of the Roman columns and the views and the swans in the lagoon."

In the elevator to the twenty-first floor of the hotel, Jonathan asked the question I hoped he never would.

"So who is this woman, Vienna, who bid all that money and then gave the ticket to you?"

The wood-paneled elevator stopped, and we stepped out onto a red carpet. I had a momentary reprieve while I thought of what to say.

Twelve

"The woman you mention was Vienna Fairchild," I said. "She died unexpectedly Saturday night."

As usual Jonathan, being an ER doctor, was not shocked hearing of an untimely death.

"Not at my hospital, I hope," he said.

"No, it happened at our shop. Or at least I think it did. I'm the one who found her on the floor in her dress with the pink bow."

"What was the cause of death?" he asked as we stood at the entrance of the nightclub waiting to be seated. "She appeared to be in good shape when she told me she couldn't use her winning bid."

"I, uh, don't really know. You're right. When she gave me the ticket, she looked fine. The police are investigating her death," I added reluctantly. I felt Jonathan had the right to know. If he didn't know already.

"The police? Why is that?"

"They think she was murdered," I said. I really didn't want to talk about Vienna, her life or her death, but it seemed she followed me everywhere. First she took my job, then she almost took Jonathan. I guessed I should be grateful that she gave me this evening with him.

"I didn't see anything about it in the papers," he said.

"I didn't either. Her parents are very big city boosters, so I wonder if they used their influence to keep it quiet. She was lying on the floor of the boutique when I came in last Sunday morning. I called the police, and things haven't been the same since."

It was a relief to get it off my chest, to confess that Vienna's murder had disrupted my life and not feel selfish and self-centered admitting it. Even if I weren't on the suspect list, there was no getting around it. Her death affected my job, my boss and the atmosphere at my work.

"That must have been a shock."

"It was. I'm still having nightmares."

"About finding her body?" he asked.

"About being suspected of killing her," I admitted.

"That's ridiculous," he said. "It's obvious you couldn't kill anyone."

"I appreciate your confidence in me," I said. If only everyone I knew felt that way. "I wish it was that simple. But my fingerprints were all over the place according to the police." I couldn't believe how easy it was to talk to Jonathan. I could tell him things I hadn't been able to talk about to anyone. Being a doctor, he'd probably had a class in listening attentively to patients, the better to understand their health problems. Or maybe he was just naturally a good listener.

"That's awkward for you," he said sympathetically.

The mâitre d' motioned us to follow him. We were greeted by a blast of fifties music and a huge bouquet of fresh flowers that almost obscured the rich red velvet upholstery and the chandeliers dripping with crystal. I was immediately transported to another San Francisco than the one I knew.

Jonathan ordered the Starlight's signature drink, a cinnamon-rimmed brandy concoction called a Cable Car, for each of us from the bar. When they seated us at a linen-covered cocktail table at the window, I took the opportunity to look around, not only at the spectacular view of the city spread out below us but also at the other patrons. At first glance it seemed that we were the youngest people in the place. There were middle-aged men, one in a shirt unbuttoned to show off his gold chains, and women in dresses that made mine look like a high school prom dress, and not in a good way. In general I would rather be underdressed than the opposite.

When the waiter came, we ordered a Green Goddess salad for me and a Caesar salad for Jonathan. After consulting the waiter, we decided to share a plate of petite lamb burgers and a selection of mezes—hummus, pita bread, olives and feta cheese.

"There's a woman at the next table who keeps looking at you," Jonathan said.

I turned. It wouldn't have surprised me to see a Dolce's customer at this popular nightspot, and there she was: Leigh James and a man that might or might not be her husband. At first, I didn't recognize Leigh, but I definitely recognized the dress. It was the black Dior couture dress with the sheer sleeves that Vienna had sold her.

I remember overhearing Vienna tell her, "You look absolutely smashing in that dress. It makes you look ten pounds lighter and twenty years younger."

"Really?" Leigh had said, obviously loving the flattery.

"You know that same diaphanous Dior dress was seen at the Venice Film Festival last year. I can't remember who wore it, but it's beautiful and a steal. You can wear it everywhere. A dress like that never goes out of style. You'll wear it over and over. It's worth every penny when you think of it that way."

Well, that was all it took for Vienna to wrap up the sale and the dress. I wondered at the time if Vienna had actually been at the festival or had just seen the dress in a picture from the event. Or maybe neither—maybe she'd made it up? No, that wasn't possible. Whatever I thought of Vienna, I had no reason to suspect her of lying about the clothes she sold.

I thought at the time that I should learn something from Vienna, like salesmanship, but given her sudden death, I really hadn't had enough time to learn a thing. And maybe I never would have, given my jealousy of her position in the store. I liked to think I was good at sales, but compared to Vienna? She'd sold more in the short time she was with us than I had in any month I'd worked there. It hurt me to admit it, but I had to, at least to myself.

Leigh waved to us, and a moment later she got up and came to our table. I said hello and introduced her to Jonathan. I didn't say he was a doctor. He once told me that he's constantly being asked for advice even from utter strangers when they find out what he does for a living. I didn't want to hear Leigh ask him what to do about her heart palpitations or bunions, corns or warts. I couldn't inflict any additional advice-seeking stranger on him, not on his night off. And I vowed never to ask him anything about my health unless he asked, which he often did.

"Rita, it's so good to see you again," Leigh said to me. I can't believe Vienna is gone, can you? I keep expecting her to show up in a bright Christian Lacroix dress with some eligible young bachelor to dance the night away. Then I remind myself she's dead. She was so young, so vibrant, so alive. How could she be dead?" she asked, shaking her head sadly.

What could I say? I just murmured something about how shocking it was and how much I missed her.

"Wasn't the wake at her mother's house just beautiful?" she asked. "Dolce did a wonderful job. I was so proud of her. I don't know how she got up there and spoke the way she did. I was so nervous and overcome with emotion, I couldn't have said a word if they'd asked me. But I'm wearing this dress tonight in Vienna's memory," she said, smoothing the sleeves. "I'll always think of her when I wear it. That's why I came over to say hello. I knew you'd appreciate it."

"The dress looks fabulous on you," I said. I wondered how often she would wear it. Maybe Dolce's customers went out on the town every weekend, which was why we sold a fair number of these dresses. I told myself that nobody who'd ever bought anything from Vienna would want to kill her. Instead, they wanted to thank her for making them look better than ever. That was her gift. So who didn't like her besides half of her high school class, especially the jealous girls? Who didn't like her besides one of the guys she'd been dating who hadn't made the cut? I should get a copy of her yearbook and just go through the names. I'd bet anything Jack hadn't thought of that.

"Isn't this place just too glamorous?" she asked us. "I love it. Have you seen Harry Denton?"

"No," I said. I didn't want to admit that I didn't even know there was a real living, breathing Harry Denton, as in Harry Denton's Starlight Room. I'd thought he was one of those gone-but-not-forgotten San Fran celebs, like Lillie Hitchcock Coit—the firefighter and eccentric character whose bequest to the city resulted in Coit Tower, which stands atop Telegraph Hill—or Domingo Ghirardelli, who made his signature chocolate at a factory located in what is now called Ghirardelli Square. But Leigh said the owner and host of this famous nightclub was often on the premises himself.

"There he is over there." Leigh pointed to a jovial bald man with glasses who was greeting customers at the bar. "When you're in the mood for a nightclub, this is the only place to go. I mean it. Have you seen the powder room? Don't miss it. It's right out of the thirties. Just gorgeous."

When Leigh went back to her table, Jonathan and I got up to dance. Passing other tables, I noticed more than a few older men with much younger women. What was going on here? I was glad that Jonathan still had a full head of hair and a great beach-boy tan, thanks to his graveyard shift at the hospital giving him days free to surf in Santa Cruz. I didn't think anyone would mistake him for my sugar daddy.

Jonathan was a great dancer; whether the music was forties swing or modern hip-hop and pop, he led and I followed. Was there anything wrong with this guy? I couldn't think of it.

When we went back to our table, the waiter brought our food and we chowed down, hungry after all that exercise on the dance floor. I ordered a Napa Crush made with white wine, a liqueur and a white peach puree. It was delicious.

Jonathan had a coffee. We danced some more, then a portly older man came up to tell Jonathan how much he appreciated his care when he'd been treated for a heart attack at the hospital a few months ago. They started talking about his current condition and whether it was okay to resume playing tennis. That's the thing about Jonathan: he is sincerely interested in every one of his patients.

I took the opportunity to pay a visit to the powder room, which was every bit as sensational as Leigh had described. Looking in the mirror, I could almost imagine I was as glamorous as a movie star from the thirties. Then I sat on a red velvet–cushioned love seat, took my cell phone out of my clutch and called Dolce to get Vienna's father's phone number while I had a chance. I told Dolce I had a couple of questions to ask him, and she didn't press me for more information.

I promptly dialed Lex Fairchild's number. When Bobbi answered, I asked if I could borrow Vienna's high school yearbooks.

"Why?" she asked.

"I just want to see what kind of school it was."

"I can tell you what kind of school it was. It was expensive. Cost more than most colleges. And it's snobby. You've got to be rich to go there. Here's the kicker: it's not the tuition; it's what you have to have to keep up with whoever. So Vienna had to have a little sports car, which isn't good enough now. Oh, no, she has to have something faster and more expensive. And the clothes and the school trips. Hawaii in the spring. Mexico at semester break. But does Lex say anything? No, he just hands over the money."

"Well, could I speak to Mr. Fairchild then?" I asked.

"He's not here," she said a little too quickly.

I didn't believe her, but what could I say except, "Could you have him call me?" I didn't wait for her answer; I just gave her my number, hung up and went back to join Jonathan at our table.

I supposed I could have told Bobbi the truth, that I was looking for a clue in those books that would help us identify her stepdaughter's killer. So much for my taking the night off from thinking about murder. Jonathan and I left a little later, after he gave the waiter his winning bid certificate and left a hefty tip.

We drove home through the city. I felt more like I belonged here than I ever had. Jonathan said he'd had a great time, and I did too. Neither one of us mentioned Vienna, but we both knew we had her to thank for this evening. Before he left, Jonathan said he'd see me the next night. He was sure he could find someone to fill in for him at the hospital and he wouldn't miss my first dinner party for anything.

"I'm a little nervous. I've never baked a fish in a bag before."

"What kind of fish?" he asked.

"It's supposed to be halibut with clams and prosciutto, but . . ."

Under the streetlamp Jonathan looked a little pale.

"What's wrong?" I said as if I were the doctor and he, the patient.

"I'm allergic to shellfish," he said. "Not that it matters. I can eat whatever else you're having."

"I'm glad I found out now," I said. But was I? Now what was I going to do? "I haven't bought anything yet. We'll have something else." As if I had a whole book full of recipes. I'd go online and find something.

"Please," Jonathan said, "don't worry about me. Make whatever you planned. I'll be fine."

I smiled and nodded, but inside I was in turmoil. I had no idea what to do. This was all Chef Guido's fault for teaching me how to make only one thing. And now I couldn't do it.

The next day I hit the supermarket early. To say I was nervous was putting it mildly. I had never had a dinner party before, not even a dinner party with one guest. Tonight I had too many male guests but not enough women. I wracked my brain to come up with someone else, but I had enough on my mind with the lack of a menu.

Hoping the shelves full of fresh produce and the meat department with its slabs of pork, beef and chicken would inspire me, I strolled the aisle of the Marina Safeway pushing a cart and looking, looking, looking for inspiration. That particular Safeway is a known hook-up spot for young singles like myself, but today I didn't even glance at the single male shoppers. I had more important things demanding my attention. I told myself it was no big deal if the store didn't have exactly what I needed. If I knew what I needed. As our chef said, it was all about improvising.

I was standing at the meat counter when Lex Fairchild called me back. I was surprised that Bobbi had actually told him I'd called. He was very brusque. For all I knew he blamed me for Vienna's murder. He said he'd drop the yearbooks off at Dolce's that morning. I told him we were closed but he could leave them at the front door. He agreed, but he didn't see what good it would do.

"Vienna was very popular at Prep. She was Spring Fling princess and the vice president of her class. Everyone liked her," he said.

"I'm not surprised," I said, trying to be mindful of his loss. "She was popular at work too. She had a real eye for fashion and helping customers look their best. I only wish I could be as good as she was," I said. And that was partly true. If I could be half the saleswoman she was, I'd be happy.

That seemed to mollify him. At least he must have realized I was on his side. "Let me know if there's anything else you need," he said gruffly.

I thanked him and went back to staring at the vast selection of meat. Too vast. How could I choose? Fortunately a kind butcher in a white apron asked if he could help me. I practically leaped over the counter to give him a grateful hug.

"I'm having a dinner party tonight," I said. "And I don't know what to have. I was going to do a fish dish with halibut and clams, but one of the guests just told me he's allergic to shellfish."

"How about a pork roast?" he asked. "On sale today. Nobody's allergic to pork that I know of." He held up the roast so I could see it. "A lot cheaper than your halibut and shellfish too."

"But what do I do with it?"

"Put it in your Crock-Pot with some wine and onions, sugar, vinegar, soy sauce, ketchup and a few other things."

"A few other things? What other things?" So far he'd named everything I didn't have.

"Here's a recipe," he said, taking a three-by-five card from a stack on the counter and handing it to me. "It's easy. It's foolproof."

I studied the recipe. It did sound easy. Brown the pork roast in a pan, then put it in the slow cooker with the other stuff and cook it all day.

"Okay, I'll do it," I said, feeling the weight of responsibility fall from my shoulders until I realized there was a catch. "Only I don't have a slow cooker." Why hadn't I bought one at the cooking school? Was it because a professional chef would scoff at a lowly Crock-Pot?

"Doesn't matter," he said. "Just cook it on top of the stove or in the oven for a few hours in a big heavy pot."

I breathed a sigh of relief. Thank heavens I'd bought one of those. But what did "a few" mean, three or four?

"What should I have with it?" I asked, hoping I wasn't pushing my luck. I looked around. I was his only customer. He didn't seem to mind helping me. Maybe I wasn't the only clueless single woman he'd ever seen about to give her first dinner party. "Something simple."

"Hmm." He leaned over the counter, his forehead furrowed. "How about some seasoned rice or buttered noodles and a green vegetable? And you can't go wrong with a loaf of crusty bread. Just put it in the oven for ten minutes before you serve it."

I just hoped I could remember everything he'd said. I wanted to ask him which green vegetable, but even I was embarrassed to utter such a simple question. And maybe there'd be someone in the produce department who could help me.

I put the roast he'd wrapped up for me into my cart, then I went up and down the aisles, filling the cart with the ingredients printed on the pork roast recipe card, like onions and vinegar, things that the experienced cook would already have in her pantry.

I moved on with determination and speed. The bread was easy, the noodles obvious. But the selection of green vegetables was enormous. I finally decided all on my own to buy some broccoli. I liked the look of it, and I'd heard it was good for you. I'd figure out how to cook it later.

"Oh, miss."

I turned around. The butcher was waving to me. "Applesauce," he said. "Don't forget some applesauce with your pork. That's what you need. And about those noodles."

I stopped and waited, holding my breath.

"Even easier, you could put some small potatoes around the roast, during the last half hour. Save you a lot of trouble."

I thanked him profusely, waved to him and followed his suggestion by buying a jar of organic applesauce and a bag of small red potatoes. I hoped that was what he meant.

I was sure I'd forgotten something. On the bus ride home with my bags of groceries, I thought—wine. And I thought—dessert. And I thought—another woman guest. I said to myself, "Forget it. That's it. I can't cope with another single thing."

When I got home, I followed the pork roast recipe by browning the meat in a large pot and adding the rest of the ingredients, and then I put the whole thing into the oven. Exhausted, I lay down on my bed. If I'd had a couch in the living room, I would have lain on it, but I'd had to leave my sofa behind when I moved upstairs because it wouldn't fit. It was old anyway. I'd inherited it from a friend who was leaving town.

I drifted off and slept until my phone rang. It was Nick.

"Rita, how is your dinner coming?" he asked.

"Just fine," I said sniffing the air. The roast smelled divine, tangy and homey. I couldn't believe it. It was like a miracle. And I'd done it myself. "How are you?"

"Very well," he said. "I have a question. My aunt would like to come along. It's all right, yes?"

I sighed. Maybe it was a Romanian custom to extend hospitality to whoever wanted to join the party. What could I say after Nick had just entertained me with a picnic lunch? "Of course," I said. "I would be happy to see her. I only hope the food will be up to her standards." By that I meant it wouldn't be the Romanian food or pizza with carp that she seemed to favor.

"Never mind about that. She would like to see how you live and so forth," he said. "And of course she will bring some wine from our country, which is the custom."

I wasn't sure how I felt about that, knowing the reputation of Romanian wine, but it would be a conversation piece anyway. And got me off the hook as well.

"That's very nice of her. I'll see you both at six."

I jumped up and peeked at the pot in the oven. The sauce looked rich and savory. I was a genius. I turned the oven down to low and hopped on the bus to go get the yearbooks from Dolce's.

Fortunately the bus came on time and fortunately the yearbooks were stacked on the front porch of the boutique, so I didn't even have to get out my key or bother Dolce, though I did want to know if her friend William would be coming to my dinner or not. It didn't matter. I'd be ready at six. I was anxious to go through the yearbooks, but I promised myself a day and a night off from thinking about Vienna. Besides, I still had work to do. Clean the apartment, wash the windows and set the table.

If I'd been murdered, I doubted Vienna would have spared more than five minutes to think about my death, let alone try to solve the murder. She'd probably just expand her empire to the entire boutique. She and Dolce would go to New York for Fall Fashion Week to see the runway shows

as I'd always wanted to do. They'd study the new trends.
They'd stay at the Waldorf Astoria and eat at Sardi's or
Keens Steakhouse. But I was alive and I could still do all
those things. Just as soon as I figured out who killed Vienna,
I had a feeling my karma would change. I'd be rewarded,
preferably in this life, for catching her murderer.

As the hours passed, I grew more and more nervous. I'd
put the table with folding chairs in the living room and set
places for six, which was tight. But the fact that the walls
were bare and there wasn't much furniture made the partial
view of the bridge from the clean windows more prominent
and more beautiful.

I was so busy polishing the wineglasses, filling a pitcher
with ice water and inserting the potatoes around the roast,
I didn't have time to worry about Meera startling everyone
by claiming to be a vampire or about putting the two men
in my life together under one roof. I refused to consider
whether someone would ask about Vienna, which would
cause an awkward silence or Dolce to burst into tears.

At five I decided to change my hair from straight to vol-
umes of waves by washing and blow-drying it, spraying it
and then curling it with a curling iron. More spray and I then
I got dressed in a pair of baggy trousers with a ruffle at the
waist that gave the pants, though tailored, a feminine flair.
With them I wore a fitted black tee. I wanted a completely
different look than the one I had at Dolce's. I wanted to send
a message that even though I was a savvy businesswoman,
I knew how to relax at home and have fun.

At six I was ready, but I was still startled when the front
doorbell rang. There was no going back now. My stomach
churned with anxiety. I glanced at myself in the hall mirror.
I leaned over, shook my head of wavy hair so it didn't look

like I was trying too hard. Then I checked out my apartment once more, trying to see it with fresh eyes as they would. Would they feel sorry I had to live in such a tiny space? Or would they envy my view and the location in trendy Telegraph Hill, walking distance to Coit Tower and the picturesque Fillmore Steps? Would they like the roast in the oven, or would they just say something polite, then stop for takeout on the way home? Would there be too many awkward silences, or would everyone talk at once?

I pushed the buzzer and called, "Come in," not knowing which guest it was. It didn't matter.

Of course Meera would be the first to arrive along with Nick. She was wearing a princess-style Victorian outfit. Her long dress was made of gray silk with a modest white collar, a full skirt and banana-shaped sleeves. If you asked me, I'd say she resembled a governess out of *Jane Eyre*. I didn't say that, because she was a guest and I was sure she didn't think of herself as the governess type, but rather as the lady of the house. She carried a large plate covered with a towel, and Nick had two bottles of Romanian wine under his arm.

"I hope you like this red Feteasca Neagra, and a white wine from my country, Tamaioasa Romaneasca. Both very high quality," he explained as he set them on the kitchen counter.

Since I wasn't up on my Romanian wines, I was glad to know he'd brought the best. I thanked him and handed him a corkscrew.

"What a fine home you have here," Meera said. She set her plate down on the table and looked around. "Small but right for you. I bring some *mamaliga* balls," she said, lifting the cloth off her dish to reveal a dozen crusty yellow balls of something that smelled wonderful. I was beginning to relax a little. Here was the wine and the appetizers that were missing. "I hope you like them."

"They look delicious," I said.

"Do you know *mamaliga*?" she asked. "They are made of cornmeal porridge. I cook it until thick, then make a ball with the hands and stuff with smoked sausage and then fry them."

"What a lot of work," I murmured, impressed that she would go to all that trouble to bring me this Romanian dish.

"It was taught to me by the cook of our last queen. They are very popular."

"The *mamaliga* or the royal family?" I asked.

"Both very popular," she said. "Although we do not have kings and queens on the throne anymore, we still eat *mamaliga*."

The doorbell rang again, stopping a possible story about the Romanian royal family and her connection to it. It was Dolce and William. I was ecstatic to see them together, and Dolce looked flushed and happy. But maybe that was due to the long flight of stairs up to my apartment. William looked even better than I remembered, with his salt-and-pepper hair and wearing a casual sweater and slacks. He too had brought some wine, which he opened. And Dolce, bless her heart, had stopped by my favorite bakery and brought a banana cream tart.

"I didn't know if you'd have time to bake anything," she said with a wink. She knew perfectly well I couldn't bake anything if my life depended on it.

I wanted to ask about William, and how she'd invited him or had he called her first, but I didn't get a chance. I just thanked her profusely and put the tart in the fridge. When Jonathan arrived casually dressed in designer jeans, a rugby shirt, a cashmere sweater knotted around his neck and retro suede sneakers, I introduced him to everyone. Nick gave him a long look. I didn't say he was my doctor, but maybe Nick guessed. Maybe he remembered that I'd been treated by him after a fall from a ladder. Nick had been wary. He wanted me to see a specialist, but one look at Jonathan and I knew he was the doctor for me. I thought, ER doctors have to know how to treat everything, especially a concussion and a sprained ankle. And I was right. My head had healed, and my ankle was as good as new.

We all went out on my deck to watch boats on the Bay and drink wine. Meera passed the *mamaliga*, and everyone exclaimed at how good they were. If they wondered who Meera was, they didn't ask. I saw a few curious looks in her direction, but in San Francisco every day is Halloween, where it's okay to dress up and pretend to be someone or somewhere else.

I looked around at my eclectic group of friends enjoying the view and the wine. It was just the way I'd imagined my life in San Francisco would be. Dinner parties chez moi, good company, well-dressed men and women, laughter, good conversation. What more could I want from life? It would be nice if murderers didn't keep killing those I knew, but mostly life was good. I loved my job, especially since Vienna was gone, and there were two men in my life.

Meera talked a lot as usual. But I didn't mind as long as she was amusing and entertaining. She told how she'd learned to make *mamaliga* in her country, but she refrained from saying she'd been on earth for more than one hundred years and planned on staying around indefinitely. So possibly everyone just thought she was eccentric and liked to role-play, which was most likely true.

I almost forgot to cook the broccoli, but I threw it into a pot at the last minute and took it out when it was very crisp. I tossed it with a little butter and chopped almonds, a combination I'd read about somewhere. Dolce helped me transfer it to a large bowl. Then I put the roast in the middle of the table surrounded with potatoes and onions and the rich gravy that magically appeared when I took it out of the oven. So the butcher was right. The meat was so tender it fell apart as I cut it.

We all sat around my small table, everyone helping themselves to the meat, the vegetable and the applesauce, bumping elbows, spooning sauce on their meat and potatoes and spearing stalks of broccoli, while William and Nick kept everyone's wineglass full.

I was giddy with success, which is always an omen that something is about to go wrong. I should have known. But I didn't. When I heard the doorbell ring, I was again startled. I looked around the table. Everyone I'd invited was there. Keep talking, I silently ordered my guests. And they did. As if they were old friends.

I got up, went to the door and called, "Who's there?"

"Detective Wall," he said from the bottom of the long stairway. "Sorry to bother you."

What was he doing here, and how did he get in through the front door? "This is not a good time," I said with a glance over my shoulder. My guests were still talking and laughing and enjoying themselves. I hated to think of what a damper the presence of an agent of the law would put on my dinner party. I assumed this was not a social call. I assumed he had more questions for me. But why here? Why now?

"I won't take up any of your time. I just need something you have."

Hmm. What could that be? "I don't have anything," I said.

"I think you do. I'm coming up."

"I'm having a dinner party."

"I won't disturb you."

"You already have."

"Rita, don't make me get a search warrant."

"I wouldn't dream of it," I said as I closed the door to my place with a loud slam. I could just picture him sighing, frowning at my lack of cooperation, racing up the three flights and lifting his fist to pound on the door. Or firing a few shots in the air as a warning. I wouldn't put it past him.

I gave up, grabbed the doorknob and pulled the door open.

Thirteen

···

As usual Jack wasn't wearing a uniform. Instead, he was dressed in his customary San Francisco casual. Today it was khakis. If I had any doubts about khakis making a comeback, I could now throw them out the third-story window. Jack Wall would never wear anything that wasn't totally in style. In the past, like last week, khakis were not serious enough for business wear but not cool enough for after hours, and if today wasn't after hours, then I didn't know what was. I read that most men have on average eight pairs of jeans. But khakis? How much would you bet the average well-dressed San Francisco man had zero to none.

It's a fact that men prefer jeans to casual slacks and with good reason. Stylish, well-fitting jeans are an essential part of a man's wardrobe. As long as they're not too short or too long. Pants should cover the ankles and tops of the shoes. A glance at Jack's feet told me his pants, while not denim, fit the requirements. Khakis have a way to go, but if Jack Wall was wearing them, it shouldn't take that long for them to rank higher than they had. The beauty of khakis is that they go with everything, especially with the dark tan Dunlop shirt Jack was wearing.

While I stared at him, he was staring at me as if he expected me to invite him in. What, in the middle of my first dinner party?

"Look," I said.

"I'm looking for some yearbooks. I understand you have them."

What could I say? He knew I had the books. Someone had told him, probably Lex. But did he have a court order or would he really get a search warrant, or did he just rely on his authority and his ability to intimidate to make me hand them over? At least that's what they'd use on TV crime dramas—court orders or intimidation.

"Why do you want them?" I said. I didn't want to admit I had them, although he probably knew that.

"Why do *you* want them?" he countered.

"If I tell you, you'll tell me to mind my own business."

"Possibly," he said. "Let's cut to the chase and give me the books."

"How did you know I had them?"

"You're a smart girl. How do you think I knew?"

"Lex told you. You know he's not the only one who had copies. Everyone in the class had them. Why didn't you ask the school . . . Prep?"

"They're closed today."

"So you're desperate."

"I'm working."

"And I'm having a party."

"I'm sorry to intrude. Just hand over the books and I'll go." He held out his hand. That's how confident he was. But I'm stubborn.

"Get your own books," I said.

He shook his head as if he'd never heard anything so audacious as my refusal to hand them over. I'm not entirely sure we wouldn't have come to blows over it if Meera hadn't interrupted.

"Officer Wall," she said, suddenly sneaking up behind me. "I said, who is that arriving so late? Nice to see you once more. Not too late to try one of my Romanian corn-meal dumplings. Have you ever had *mamaliga*?"

I never expected Meera to go into hostess mode. That was my role. But then nothing she did should ever surprise me.

Jack just stood there looking from me to Meera until she couldn't stand the uncertainty anymore. Brushing me aside, she took him firmly by the arm and escorted him into the living room. I wished I'd had the nerve to do that. Only I would have escorted him down the stairs and out the front door. Sure enough, someone had pulled up an extra chair and set another plate on the table, no doubt assuming as Meera did that he was a guest arriving late.

"Everyone," Meera said, "meet our friend from the police, Detective Jack Wall, a little late, but never mind."

Now everyone thought he was someone I'd invited but somehow had forgotten to set a place for. I guessed that was better than knowing the truth: that their hostess was a mur-der suspect and the officer who suspected her was here to put the squeeze on her and not in a good way.

Fascinated, I watched while Meera put a generous serv-ing of pork roast, potatoes, applesauce and broccoli on his plate as well as a crusty *mamaliga*. I suddenly remembered

I'd forgotten about the bread. But with *mamaliga* on the menu, who needed bread?

Dolce filled Jack's wineglass and gave me a knowing look. I smiled at her as if I were delighted with the way things were going. Maybe she too thought I'd invited him. If she was worried, she didn't let on. I hoped that no one knew the truth. That no one suspected his real purpose in ringing my doorbell on a Sunday evening. As if I'd invite three men to dinner at the same time. Unless I owed them. I owed Jonathan, and Nick too, of course. So I gave up and just pretended this was how I'd planned it.

Dolce looked better than I'd seen her since Vienna died. She was smiling frequently, talking often and even eating a second helping of pork. But then she was sitting next to her friend William, who was giving her admiring looks between bites. If that wouldn't cheer a person up, I don't know what would. And if nothing else came of this evening, this dinner was worth having if it brought them together. Of course, maybe they were together anyway, but if so, why hadn't Dolce said anything? Why hadn't I heard her mention his name? Or taken a phone message from him?

After I cleared the table, I thought Jack would leave. Not without the yearbooks of course, but I expected him to make another attempt or pull out a search warrant and demand them. Instead, he let Dolce serve him and everyone else a piece of the scrumptious pie she'd brought while I poured coffee. He even leaned back in his chair and laughed at something William said. Jack Wall laughing? He caught my eye, and I shook my head signifying that I was shocked and stunned by his erratic behavior. From stern lawman to genial guest. Was he just softening me up so he could walk out with the yearbooks? He'd do it no matter how I acted. I wondered what would happen next. An earthquake? Another knock on the door?

Even though Meera loved the spotlight, telling stories of life in Romania and of historical figures she claimed to have known, she had to give way to others who wanted to talk. I couldn't believe it. It gave me courage to think I'd done something right. I'd invited interesting people. I'd served interesting food, and it had all come together despite the party-crashing detective, who, much to my surprise, stayed until everyone else had left.

"Wonderful party," Dolce said as she and William stood at the door. "Don't hurry in tomorrow. You have a lot of dishes to do." Then she peered over my shoulder to see that Jack was standing behind me.

"Good night, Detective," she called merrily. "How nice to see you again."

As they all trooped down the stairs, I turned around to face him. He was holding the yearbooks in his hand. My mouth fell open in surprise. I don't know why. It was typical police procedure. Don't ask, just take what you want.

"I didn't want to trouble you any further," he said by way of explanation.

"How thoughtful," I said. What else could I say? The man never quit. First he stays for dinner when he wasn't invited except by Meera. Then he goes into my room and takes the yearbooks. "I don't suppose I can have a look at those before you go."

"No time for that," he said. "But as you said, they're available other places from other people. You won't have any trouble finding some books to look at." He went to the door. "Thanks for the dinner."

"You're welcome. What next?"

"What about the antiviolence program I signed you up for. You were a no-show."

"I know. I'm sorry. I should have called. Things have been a little hectic." .

"You mean without Vienna."

"Yes, I mean no. It's not that. It's . . . everything. I'm training for an open-water swim." It wasn't exactly true. I was thinking about training for an open-water swim. And it sounded good. Better than saying I was at a dead end thinking about Vienna and her friends and family and hadn't had the energy to join the police for a ride-along or weapons training no matter how much I could use the practice in defending myself. I wanted Jack to think I had a life other than the shop. Maybe tonight he'd seen that.

"Where are you training?" he asked.

"At my health club, and the swim is from the Marina to Alcatraz."

"Then I gather you're not afraid of sharks."

"Sharks?" No one had said anything about sharks. I acted nonchalant, as if sharks were the least of my problems. Actually they were. "I'm more afraid of the police arresting the wrong person."

He gave me a half smile. "Relax. It's not going to happen as long as everyone tells the truth."

"I assume you are referring to the Vienna Fairchild case?" I said. "Is there anything else I should be concerned with?"

"You should be concerned with the fact that you lack an alibi for the night of the murder."

"Surely I'm not the only one," I said.

"No, you're not."

Was he referring to Dolce? She said she wouldn't involve

her new boyfriend in her alibi, but what if it came down to proving she wasn't at the scene of the crime, which she couldn't do without him. Then what?

"The only person you should worry about is yourself. You have enough on your plate with your job and your social life. Leave the rest to me."

"How can I do that when you suspect me of murder?"

"Try."

I sighed loudly. He said good night, then turned and took the stairs two at a time down to the street. Why shouldn't he rush off? He'd gotten what he came for and more. He'd gotten a free dinner. And he'd had a look at my friends. Maybe he'd been analyzing them, wondering if one of them, probably Dolce since she was under his microscope and had no ready alibi for Saturday night, was the most likely suspect.

Now he would go home or back to work and pore over the faces in the yearbook just as I'd planned to do tonight, trying to decide who among Vienna's high school friends and foes had had a motive and the opportunity to kill her. I liked to think I knew more than he did about the people in Vienna's inner circle. He very likely didn't agree. Maybe he thought I was full of myself. Little Ms. Amateur Detective who was coasting on her last case, which she'd solved purely by chance.

His lack of confidence in me just made me more determined to get to the bottom of the murder before he did. Maybe Vienna's murder had nothing to do with what happened in high school. Maybe by taking the yearbooks, he was off on a tangent to nowhere. He'd spared me from the needless task of looking through them. I would go in a different direction. But where? Which one?

....

By the next morning I'd changed my mind. I had to get those yearbooks. If Jack hadn't wanted them enough to come to my house, crash my party and take them, I wouldn't have been so sure they held the answer. But now I was. I decided to pay a visit to Vienna's private high school, San Francisco Prep, or for those in the know, simply "Prep." Surely they'd have a collection of old yearbooks in the library or somewhere I could borrow. But not until noon. I couldn't let Dolce down by coming in late today even though she'd told me I could. So I got ready for work at the usual time, dressing carefully in semi-teen style: a stretchy pink top, miniskirt, see-through, classic Bobbie Gray baseball jacket, and canvas wedge sandals.

I wasn't sure the outfit would let me pass as a teen, but after I'd braided my hair in one long braid that I tossed casually over one shoulder, I was more confident. Actually I didn't need to masquerade as a teen, since I was going to the school to get the loan of a yearbook, but I didn't want to stand out either. You never know when you might want to slip in and slip out unnoticed.

But just in case the slipping-in-and-out plan didn't work, I decided to call one of our customers, a fashion-conscious fellow named Harrington Harris, the drama teacher at Prep, who bought an occasional item at the shop. Dolce and I had even attended a sneak preview of one of his plays last fall.

"Harrington," I said after identifying myself, "we haven't seen you at the boutique forever."

"Darling," he said in his deep, resonant voice. "So good to hear from you. Please don't take my absence from Dolce's personally. I'm up to my ears in rehearsals. But I want to hear all about the spring collection. I might drop by on Saturday."

"Here's the thing," I said. "I was hoping to get a tour of your school. One of our customers has a daughter who's looking at Prep and Sacred Heart and Menlo and Saint Francis. She can't decide. She asked us for our opinion, but not being from San Francisco originally, I didn't know what to say except that I knew Prep had a dynamite theatre program."

"So true," he murmured. "If I do say so myself. Why don't you send your customer and her daughter and I'll give them a tour of the facilities. We get points for introducing new students if they actually enroll."

"Really, well what a good idea. I hate to impose, but if you're sure . . ." Of course I was making up the whole thing. Why hadn't I realized that the mythical mother and daughter who didn't exist would get invited on a tour when I was the one who wanted to see the school, the better to get my little hands on those yearbooks?

"The problem is that they're too busy with . . . other things, so what if I took the tour instead?" I suggested. "Or at least dropped by, since I have time today, say around noon? Then I'll pass on my impressions of the school, which I'm sure will be superpositive, and you'll get your bonus." I could only hope Harrington would not hound me about this new student and his bonus. I had to believe he'd eventually forget about it. Or maybe someone would ask my opinion about private schools and I'd be able to say that the excellent teachers, the outstanding activities and Prep's reputation in sports were all worth the astronomical tuition and that he or she should definitely go there.

"Come ahead. We'll have lunch in the cafeteria, which is pretty decent since the overhaul last year. Salads and lots of healthy veggies. At least the teachers like it, while the students sneak out and hit the fast-food places when they can."

"Are you sure I'm not disrupting your schedule?" I asked.

"Not at all," he said. "I have a light class load this semester because of the play. Just have the secretary page me because I'll be in the scene shop supervising the painting of the sets. Kids get assigned to help me instead of having to go to detention, so I have to keep an eye on them. We're doing *Amadeus*. And I'm not sure it was a good idea. I've had my doubts since day one. Sure it's got beautiful music, great parts and of course a spectacular set. But there are too many problems."

"I'm sure you'll work them out," I said. I had no idea what *Amadeus* was about, but I thought it was safe to say that Harrington would solve the problems of putting on the play, or why choose the play in the first place? "Though it is an ambitious choice," I added hopefully.

"Maybe too ambitious," he said. "For starters, the girl playing Mozart's wife comes across as a giggling high school junior instead of a frightened and bitter wife. Sometimes I wish I hadn't tackled a musical again. Or if I had to do a musical, why not pick *Rent*?"

Now there was a musical I'd heard of. "But isn't *Rent* about sex, drugs and criminals?" I asked.

"You've just described high school," he said with a laugh. "Unfortunately, the head of school is a Mozart fan, which is the real reason we're doing *Amadeus*. He insisted his son get the role of Salieri. I'm afraid this kid is going to terrify the audience instead of impress them with his over-the-top performance. His loud outbursts make me wonder if he might really be crazy. If you ask me, he's a bona fide psycho and shouldn't even be here at Prep, but that's how it goes when your father pulls the strings. You'll get a chance to see for yourself if you stay for rehearsal."

"I'd love to," I said, "but I'll have to hurry back to work. In any case, I'll see you at noon."

I couldn't believe all the trouble I had to go to to get those damn yearbooks, and for what? So I could pore over the books hoping something, a picture, a blurb under someone's photo would turn on a lightbulb and there'd be an "aha" moment when all would be clear? Yes, actually, I thought, reassuring myself. Yes, because then I'd know who killed Vienna, and I'd finally get credit for solving the crime. And then we could all go back to work. Faking my way through lunch with Harrington and suffering through a bit of his WIP would be worth it if I walked out with the yearbooks.

When I got to work, Dolce gushed about my party, saying that William had such a good time he'd invited her to take a spin in his Learjet next Sunday to Southern California. It was wonderful to see her back to normal, even better than normal as she seemed to glide smoothly around the shop, wearing a gray, figure-hugging Carolina Herrera dress, which I thought I'd seen in a photo of Carla Bruni, the former model and first lady of France. I was a little surprised by her choice, but this was a new Dolce, one who took chances, one who was dressing for someone besides her customers, and I was glad to see it. I watched her greeting old and new customers with good cheer. I didn't ask her if she'd had to lie about her actions on the night of Vienna's murder. I didn't want to know.

After a morning of helping customers find the right sexy gown or leather jacket or flouncy skirt, I told Dolce I had some errands to do on my lunch hour. She told me to take my time and didn't ask where I was going. Did her laissez-faire attitude have anything to do with her ongoing connection to William? I hoped so. She also surprised me by saying, "I'm thinking of closing the shop on Mondays. We're never that busy, and I think we deserve two days off like everyone else. What do you think?"

A two-day weekend? Closing the shop on Mondays? Maybe she'd gotten the idea when I took Saturday off and left her to cope on her own. What was the world coming to? I couldn't help thinking it had something to do with William. He was retired and probably had weekends and lots of other days off. But Dolce only had Sundays off. That's all she'd ever wanted, but that was before William came into her life. I didn't ask about his divorce.

"I think it's a great idea," I said. As long as I didn't have to take a pay cut. And I could take an occasional Saturday off too when I had a big date that night. Although maybe that was just wishful thinking.

I took the bus to Pacific Heights and walked down the street past the mansions of the rich and powerful to the school where the rich and powerful sent their kids, like Vienna, and the less-than-wealthy sent their scholarship students, like Vienna's poor and needy roommate, Danielle. It was a far cry from my public high school in Ohio with its tired old teachers, its peeling paint and the Friday night football games. The original school building had once been a stately home owned by some gold rush baron, who donated it to the city to educate the youth. It didn't survive the 1906 earthquake, but the rebuilt structure that had stood in its place for over a hundred years was still the school of choice for those who were lucky enough to get in.

Maybe it had always been a school for the city's entitled youth. All I knew was that it was difficult to get admitted even if you had the money for the tuition. You had to be smart too. What I didn't know until today was that the parking lot was full of high-end expensive cars.

Had Lex ever actually given Vienna that car he promised her, and if so, where was it? Or had Bobbi put the kibosh on that plan and Vienna had no car? If she had one, why hadn't she driven it to work? The answer had to be that it was hard to park near Dolce's. Even our customers took taxis or had their chauffeurs drop them off.

Standing at the wide glass front door, I glanced up at the flag flying over the school at half-mast. I frowned. Could it be for Vienna? After I walked in, I followed the signs to the office. There, a stern-looking woman with dark hair and a sort of uniform consisting of a white long-sleeved shirt, a navy vest, a pleated skirt and low-heeled shoes asked if she could help me.

I suddenly realized that the kids wore uniforms at the school and in my teen outfit I wouldn't fit in anyway. Why hadn't I thought this through and dressed like a wealthy matron? Oh well. I *was* expected.

"I'm here to see Harrington Harris," I said. "He's expecting me."

She sighed loudly, as if he had women dropping in every few minutes, which I didn't believe for a minute. Parents might drop in to make sure their kids were given parts in the plays, but did I look like a parent? I hoped not. She finally picked up a phone and spoke into it. "Visitor for Harris," she said. "Harris, visitor in Admin."

While I was waiting, I looked around, wondering if I'd see a Dolce's customer among the teachers—or more likely, a parent here to have a teacher conference. I was desperate to keep my real reason for my visit under my hat.

Some of the students who walked down the hall were wearing regulation skorts, which would be more practical out on the playing field across town in Golden Gate Park. Not enough level ground for a playing field here among the mansions on the hill. Prep was known not only for its academics but also for its soccer team. The boys I saw in the hall wore button-down shirts and green ties, green being the school color, I assumed.

Still waiting, I took a look at the trophies in a glass case. Not only trophies but also artifacts from another era. There was a shovel used to dig for the gold that had ultimately enabled one of the gold barons to endow this school. There was a rough wooden stool that was one of many that the early students of this institution sat on while being instructed in the basics of math and English and manners.

What if I'd gone to school here? Would my life be different? Would I, like other alums, have gone on to an Ivy League college? Would I now be working as a high-end marketing guru for someone like Helmut Lang or Kate Spade instead of selling clothes in a small boutique on the West Coast? Or would I be married to a fellow student who was now making millions in real estate or investment banking?

I might live in this rarified neighborhood, send my kids to this school, shop at Dolce's, have lunch with the other ladies who lunch at the rotunda at Neiman Marcus with its fifteen-dollar cheeseburgers and spectacular view of Union Square. Yes, that sounded like me. Or did it?

One thing I knew I'd love would be to admire the famous stained-glass skylight Neiman Marcus is famous for. But I could do that now. I didn't need a husband or a new job, just a lunch date. I made a mental note to put it on my to-do list along with the classes I was going to take, the ride-along program at the police department, the swim across the Bay and more cooking classes.

"Rita," Harrington said, startling me out of my reverie by kissing me on both cheeks. "Good to see you. You've saved me from a disaster."

"What do you mean?" I couldn't face another disaster.

"It's too awful to talk about," he said. But he did talk about it for at least fifteen minutes while we sat on a bench in the foyer of the high school as my precious lunch hour ticked away and I hadn't had even a glimpse of the yearbooks.

"First my lead, the guy who plays Mozart, is out this week. The official story is he's got the flu, but you know what? He's probably at the family's ski house at Tahoe. Spring skiing. Why not? What does he have to lose? I'm the one whose reputation is on the line. Then the costume department, which consists of volunteer parents, is upset because the girls don't like their costumes. They don't think they're sexy enough. Like they have a say in it?" He paused and shook his head. "Come on, let's have lunch. You don't want to hear any more of my troubles."

He was right, I sure didn't. I tried not to leap up from the bench, but I was anxious to get on with it. Eat lunch and get those yearbooks. I'd already been here for twenty minutes and I hadn't even asked him where they were or if I could have them.

The cafeteria was practically deserted despite the attractive display of healthy choices.

"Too healthy for the kids," Harrington explained once again as he loaded his tray with a turkey sandwich on whole wheat bread, a fruit salad and an iced tea. I followed his lead and got the same things. He waved me on through past the student checker, saying I was his guest so I didn't have to pay.

I ate my sandwich and told myself to get on with it. Ask him about the yearbooks. Why not? Otherwise I could be stumbling around this campus forever and end up being arrested for stealing a yearbook. I could just imagine what Detective Wall would say when he was called to the school after a robbery complaint and had to slap a pair of handcuffs on me.

"I wonder if you know where the old yearbooks are kept and if I could borrow a few to show my friend, the one who's looking for a good high school," I said.

"How old? I've got some in my office."

"Four or five years ago."

"That old? Why not take last year's book?"

"Of course, last year's and a couple of older ones."

"No problem."

"Good, that sounds great." I couldn't believe how simple it was. Why hadn't I just walked in and asked for them? They say there's no such thing as a free lunch, but I'd just gotten one—along with what I really wanted: the yearbook that might unlock the mystery of the murder of Vienna Fairchild.

"By the way," I said as he handed me two yearbooks from a shelf in his office, "how come the flag's at half-mast?"

"Didn't you hear? One of our alums died last week. Finally got what was coming to her—that's what they say anyway."

"You mean she had enemies?" I asked, wide-eyed.

"You didn't hear it from me, but so goes the rumor mill. Yeah, it was one of her classmates who did her in. No big surprise. You know how teenagers are. They never forget. Hold grudges like you wouldn't believe. These girls are long gone from Prep, but once a Preppie, always a Preppie." He sighed dramatically. "I don't suppose you remember the good old days in high school."

I didn't like the sound of that remark. As if I looked like I was too old to remember. Even in my carefully chosen teen-type clothes and hair.

"You mean someone knows who did it?" I asked, holding my breath.

"No names, no names. Just someone who finally confronted her for being a bitch and let her have it. But what do I know? I don't listen to gossip," he said.

I'll bet you don't, I thought.

"I'm not surprised. There are cliques, there are catfights, there's angst and anger, jealousy and hate. Oh, yes, it's a regular TV drama, only it's for real. Never a dull moment," he said with a smile. You might almost think he enjoyed the drama. Why not? Drama was his field.

Fourteen

A scant five minutes later I was walking down the street with two yearbooks under my arm. I was dying to go through them and zero in on Vienna's killer, obviously a girl in her class like Danielle who had a grudge against her, who'd had a run-in with her or whose boyfriend Vienna had stolen. Or a guy Vienna had cheated on. Or someone whom she'd cheated off of. The possibilities were so numerous I was almost skipping down the street, I was so excited.

The downside to my euphoria was that Jack had these same yearbooks and he was poring over them looking for the same clues I was. Of course, what did it matter if he found the killer before I did? Sure, I wanted the credit, but most of all I wanted the cloud of suspicion to be lifted from over my head.

Once on the bus, I leafed rapidly through the pages. I turned to the index where "Fairchild, Vienna" had several references. One was her graduation picture. She was dressed in some kind of drape, which I didn't recognize. It was probably provided by the photographer. She was looking over her shoulder with a provocative smile I did recognize.

I was surprised she wasn't wearing a designer dress, but maybe she wasn't such a fashionista in those days. And under her picture was a quotation she'd chosen: "'One must have a good memory to be able to keep the promises one makes.'—Friedrich Nietzsche."

What did that mean? That Vienna had made promises, but she couldn't remember what they were? Or she remembered but would use her poor memory as an excuse not to keep them?

Under the quotation was a list of her activities. "Spring Fling Princess, Senior Class VP, Cheerleading Squad, Girls' Acapella Chorus, Asian Appreciation Club." Nothing surprising except for that Asian Appreciation Club, one I would have joined if only to appreciate the Asian food I was sure they'd serve at their meetings. But why did Vienna join? Did she have an Asian boyfriend at the time? Did she still have one, and if so, who was he?

I looked to see what others had chosen. Here was her friend, a disgruntled-looking Emery, staring not at the photographer but off into the distance. His quote: "'Nothing is too small to know and nothing too big to attempt,'—William Van Horne." What was he so mad about, or was he just being a cool high school senior afraid to show any emotion other than anger?

I tried to figure that one out, considering Emery was up near the top of my suspects list. Whether he had an alibi or not. I'd watched enough mysteries to know that people faked alibis all the time. Friends lied for them, and they eventually confessed they were lying. Another thing I'd learned was that people can't keep secrets forever. Eventually they have to tell someone. Which made me worried about Dolce. Would she be able to keep her secret about spending the night with William, or would Jack get her to confess she was with him to save her from arrest? In which case William wouldn't be able to get a favorable divorce settlement and he'd lose his private plane, and Dolce too.

As for Emery's quotation, what was the big thing he'd attempted? Winning Vienna's love? Dumping Vienna for not returning his love and getting his revenge in the future? Or none of the above?

Emery's activities were as follows: "Archery Club, Chess Club, Marching Band." If he was an archer and he wanted to kill someone, why not use his bow and arrow? Because it was too obvious, of course. Better to strangle the victim.

Maybe I was out of date, being ten years older than these kids, but in my day marching band was not a cool activity. Neither was chess club or archery. They were definitely for nerds. For such a cool guy as Emery, those were unusual choices. Was he so cool he was not worried about what people thought? If so, I was impressed, and I wondered vaguely what instrument he played.

I moved on to Raold's page. At least he was looking straight at the camera as if he had nothing to hide. He was wearing a turtleneck sweater and a scarf. With his long hair and a name like Raold, he came across as at least part European. An exchange student? Or merely the product of an interesting blend of cultures? Was that what Vienna liked about him until she didn't like him? And then he killed her and took the first plane out of here for Argentina? Was he the one with the European sports car? Here's what he belonged to at Prep: "Mock Trial Club, Outdoor Adventure Club, Surfing Club." His favorite quotation: "'Ask not what your teammates can do for you, ask what you can do for your teammates.'—Magic Johnson."

What had he asked his teammates to do for him? Lie about his whereabouts on the night of Vienna's murder? And how was I supposed to track down these guys and grill them when that was Jack's job—a job he was probably doing while I was riding a bus back to work?

After the initial high of getting what I'd gone to the high school to get, I was falling into a letdown phase upon realizing finding Vienna's killer wasn't quite as easy as I'd thought. But I wasn't finished yet. I still had Geoffrey.

In his graduation photo, Geoffrey Hill looked just the way I'd expected he'd look. Long hair, intense eyes and an "I don't care what anyone thinks of me attitude" visible even to me. He hadn't changed that much. His activities were "Film Club, Earthbound Club, Computer Club." I imagined him after high school, moving past the usual computer-geek activities and experimenting with all kinds of digital painting and drawing tools, which was obviously just what had happened, since he'd ended up as a web designer.

Just as confused as ever, I put the yearbooks back in my bag and got off the bus. Back at Dolce's, I apologized to her for being late, but Dolce was distracted. She had a frown on her face as she took me aside into the Accessories section of the alcove.

"Pam Jennings is in my office," she said. "She said she saw Vienna's necklace in a pawnshop in the Tenderloin."

Shocked, I leaned backward and almost fell over. "What was—"

"What was she doing there?" Dolce said. "She says she was looking for a piece of silver to match her grandmother's service." She shrugged. We were both aware that some of our customers had fallen on hard times during this economic downturn and were reduced to selling off some of their excess belongings from time to time, but we pretended not to know. We pretended that all was well. After all, what is a neighborhood boutique for anyway if not to provide a safe haven for its customers? To make them feel appreciated and welcome whether they bought anything or not. Everyone was treated alike. At least that was our goal.

"I was going to say, 'What was the necklace doing there?'" I said.

"That's what we have to find out. Should we tell Vienna's father or her mother or no one?" Dolce shook her head. "I just don't know. What I want you to do is to go to the pawnshop and check it out. You'll know if it's really Vienna's, won't you?" she asked, clutching my arm.

"Yes, I think so." The image of the necklace hanging around Vienna's neck was so clear in my mind. The way the diamonds sparkled, the depth of the beautiful pink stone. There couldn't be another one in the world like it. There really couldn't be another like it in this city.

"What if it is hers?" I asked.

"Find out who pawned it. Find out how much they want for it."

"Should I buy it?"

"Yes—here, take my credit card," she said, reaching into her purse. "I'll pay for it. Unless . . ." She bit her lip. I wasn't going to buy it without her explicit consent; the necklace looked like it cost millions. Despite what Athena had said. "I know Vienna's family will want it. If they don't . . ." She paused, then continued after catching her breath. "Go. Go now."

After a brief talk with Pam Jennings, I took the credit card Dolce offered and set off in a taxi. By now you'd think I'd be used to the seedy neighborhood where Jack's former police station and my favorite Vietnamese restaurant was, but I still felt a little frisson go up my spine as I got out of the cab in front of Bayview Loan and Jewelry. I hoped no one I knew would see me there. After all, weren't the people who frequented pawnshops most likely to be thieves or addicts, and the guys behind the counter were the ones who took advantage of them?

No wonder Dolce sent me. She didn't want to be seen in a place like this. Neither did I. But I wanted that necklace, and even more, I wanted to know who brought it in here and pawned it. Because then I'd know who killed Vienna. I pressed my nose up against the window with the words "CASH TO GET BY" scrolled on the glass, hoping to see the famous necklace lying on a swatch of black velvet. At least that's how I would have displayed it in all its pink-and-diamond glory. But the window was full of high-end watches, necklaces, earrings and pins, but no stunning necklace. Was I too late?

I walked in. A bell rang. The clerk looked up and gave me a quick scan, then since I must have looked harmless, he went back to his customer, a man leaning over the counter speaking in low tones.

"Look," he said, "I need some quick cash to pay off a debt before my knees get cracked." Then he reached into his pocket and pulled something out. A watch? A necklace? I couldn't see, but I heard it clink against the glass counter. I was just glad I wasn't in danger of having *my* knees cracked. But what if I was? What would I bring in to get some ready cash? All my money was tied up in clothes and accessories.

I wondered what the pawnbroker would say if I offered him a pair of Louboutins or some Zanotti suede boots?

I shifted from one foot to the other. I examined the guns in the locked glass case on the wall. I wanted to butt in. I wanted to ask about the necklace, but it was better to wait because I wanted more than just the necklace. I wanted information. Who brought it in? Who took it out? What if pawnbrokers were sworn to silence? I thought they might be, to protect their customers. That's where Jack had the advantage over me. He could make them talk. I couldn't.

A minute later the bell over the door rang again. I turned around to see Barbie Washburn. We looked at each other for a long moment. She blushed. I just stood there, embarrassed for her. Maybe she was just as embarrassed for me. She probably thought I was there to hock something. Was she? So Pam wasn't the only Dolce customer who was forced to pawn her treasures.

"Hi," I said as if we'd just met at Starbucks. "How are you?"

She gave me a nervous smile. "Good," she said. "Just looking for a necklace for my aunt's birthday. She's crazy about diamonds." She looked around.

"Who isn't?" I said. Especially when they surround a huge pink tourmaline. I bit my lip, stumped for how to explain my presence there.

"What about you?" she asked, eyeing me with curiosity. "Shopping for Dolce?"

I was sure Dolce wouldn't want her to think this was where she got her merchandise.

"Oh, no, I'm on my break. On my own. Just looking for a bargain." I wouldn't want her or anyone to think I was so desperate for funds I would pawn anything I owned.

The bell over the door rang again, and a guy in a wool hat pulled over his ears came in and fixed his gaze on the clerk.

"Show me what guns you got," he said, one hand in his pocket. I froze. This was exactly what I thought went on in pawnshops. Robberies, intimidation, and weapons.

"Now, Al," the clerk said, leaving his customer to come out from behind the counter. "I told you, no guns. You haven't got a permit."

"Don't need one," he said, then he took a gun out of his pocket. I looked anxiously at the door, sorry I'd ever come here. Barbie looked just as sorry as I was. The customer whirled around. "See this? It's no good. He sold it to me, but it don't work good. Gotta get a new one." He waved his gun at the glass case. "One of those."

"Okay, Al," the pawnbroker said calmly. How could he be so calm when confronted with a weapon? Maybe he was used to it. Maybe it happened every day. Maybe he knew the gun was no good and that's why he wasn't afraid.

He reached into his pocket for a ring of keys, and then he unlocked the glass cabinet and told Al to pick out the gun he wanted.

"What do you want it for?" the broker asked. Still sounding as calm as if they were discussing a Swarovski crystal bowl.

"Protection," Al said. "They're coming to get me."

"You still need a permit."

"No, I don't. I told you that. You sold me this one and it don't work." He waved the gun around again. I hoped he was right when he said it didn't work. But it looked like it worked, and I was praying he wouldn't test it in front of us.

Whenever there's a robbery in the movies, the clerk

presses a button behind the counter, which is connected to the police station. Maybe the pawnbroker didn't have one of those buttons. Or maybe this didn't qualify. Maybe it was just a normal sale at a pawnshop. What did I know?

A glance at Barbie's white face told me she didn't know either and she was as worried as I was. I started to back toward the door. Nothing was worth getting shot over, not even finding the famous necklace or a clue to Vienna's murder.

The man in the wool cap caught my eye. "Don't be thinking of leaving," he cautioned, pointing the gun at me.

I managed a shaky smile. "Of course not," I said. "I was just going to put another coin in the meter." Surely that was a good excuse for walking out of a store. "Be right back."

"Don't you go," he said, more forcefully this time. I assured him I wouldn't dream of it. What, and miss all the excitement?

"So you give me the gun, Ray," the man called Al said. "And that other one up there and no one gets hurt."

"Here you go," Ray said, handing him two very nice, shiny-looking guns, one small, one larger. I had no idea if they were really nice or not. Maybe they were for collectors, or maybe they were for shooting up pawnshops.

Al put one in each pocket and then turned toward the door. At that moment a police car pulled up in front of the shop, lights flashing. The cops who got out rushed the store. I dropped to the floor the way they do in the movies, hoping to hit the deck before actual gunshots rang out and the glass shattered. When I looked up a few moments later, I saw poor Barbie was sitting up, straightening her jacket. She appeared unharmed except for her hair, which was standing on end. Maybe mine was too, even with my braid.

The cops were putting handcuffs on Al, who was complaining about police brutality.

Before they left, the policemen took our names and addresses, and I just hoped they wouldn't have to report back to Jack that I was a witness, but since I hadn't seen anything much or done anything wrong, why should I worry?

The pawnbroker acted like it was no big deal, having a customer hauled away. At least he got his guns back. He apologized to us and went back to waiting on the original customer, who appeared to be in a state of shock. Barbie left the shop, and I couldn't wait another minute. This time I interrupted.

"Excuse me," I said to the clerk, trying to sound like I wasn't upset to have witnessed a near robbery. "But do you have a necklace with a big pink stone and some diamonds?"

"Had one," he said.

"What happened to it?"

"It's gone."

"I see. Can you tell me who brought it in?"

"Same lady who bought it. That's what a pawnshop is for, in case you didn't know."

No, I didn't know. Not exactly. What I wanted to know was who she was. Maybe I'd found out as much as I could. Maybe I had to involve Jack even though I didn't want to. It turned out I got a call from him before I could do anything else.

"Hear you witnessed a robbery," he said. "How did that happen?"

"Why don't you ask the perpetrator?" I replied. "I was just an innocent bystander. But now that I've got your attention, I need some help in locating the necklace Vienna was wearing the night she was murdered. Which is why I'm in a pawnshop."

"Stay there, I'm sending someone to get you. I'll need your statement."

I wanted to say, "What will you give me in return?" but I knew better; he'd just say, "Nothing."

A short time later I was back in his station. I called Dolce while riding in the patrol car. "I've had a little delay," I told her.

"What do you mean? Did you get the necklace?"

"It wasn't there, and the pawnbroker said the woman who pawned it returned to buy it back."

"But who was she?" she said. "Was it the murderer? Or just someone who fell in love with it?"

"It belonged to her grandmother—that's what Athena said."

"Then maybe she claimed it."

"Maybe," I said dubiously, recalling Athena's description of her grandmother and trying to envision the addled old woman leaving her retirement home and descending on the pawnshop to retrieve her necklace. I'd like to think the woman had gotten her necklace back, but how were we going to find out who killed Vienna if we didn't find out who pawned her necklace? "But I don't think so."

"Where are you? I'm going to close early. I'm too upset to continue."

"Good idea," I said. "I'm on my way downtown. And I'll go home from there. See you tomorrow." Why was Dolce upset with my story of the robbery? There was nothing she could do about it.

"Come here on your way home. I'll order some food for us. I want to hear all the details."

What could I say? She wanted to see me, and the offer of food was too good to turn down. I agreed to stop by on my way home. Good thing. I'd almost forgotten about the yearbooks, which I wanted to continue looking over tonight.

"I know what you're going to say," I said to Jack when he waved me into his office. "What was I doing in a pawnshop? As far as I know, it's not illegal. I could have been buying or selling something."

"I don't care what you were doing, I'm interested in your description of what happened, and by the way, why do you think this kind of event—and I use the term loosely—seems to follow you wherever you go?" he asked, leaning against his desk while I sat in a chair facing him.

"I have no idea. Okay, I'm in the shop waiting my turn. A guy comes in with something in his pocket, turns out it was a gun. His name is Al—at least that's what Ray, the guy behind the counter, calls him. He knows him. I guess because he's been in before, a regular customer, it seems. Ray doesn't want to sell him a gun because he doesn't have a permit or he doesn't think he should have one, I don't know. Why don't you ask Ray?"

"Don't worry, I am asking Ray," Jack said.

"Then why are you asking me to tell you what happened?" I couldn't help being irritated. "I'm sorry, but I'm tired, upset, hungry, and I want to go home."

"Did you antagonize him? Threaten him in some way?"

"Of course not," I said. "You really think I would threaten a man with a gun or stand in his way? If I was in the way, I didn't mean to be. He wanted a gun. God forbid I should stand in his way. Since when is the victim penalized for being in the middle of a robbery?"

"Fine," he said. "Just sign your statement and you're free to go. I'll have Winston drive you home."

"Thank you," I said, my voice dripping with sarcasm. I

didn't think he noticed. He was flipping pages on his desk and his phone was ringing. "Good luck," I said over my shoulder as I walked out of his office.

Dolce threw open the door when I reached the boutique. It was after five and she was alone.

"What happened? Did you find the necklace? What took you so long?"

"Pawnshops are dangerous places," I said, sinking into the chaise longue in the great room. "I was caught in the middle of an armed robbery."

Dolce covered her mouth with her hand. Her eyes were huge. "Oh no."

"Oh, yes. But I'm fine. Nothing happened except I had to go give a statement at the police station."

"Stay there. You look awful. I just made a pot of tea. Maybe that will help."

I wasn't sure tea had ever made anyone look better, but Dolce's pot of strong Earl Grey did help me feel better, especially when she sent out for dinner from the Mandarin Express.

She found a pair of Norwegian elkskin slippers for me, and when the food came, we pulled up an end table and ate crab Rangoon, spring rolls, bourbon chicken, Chinese string beans and rice, of course.

After what I'd been through, I didn't think I could eat much, but between the two of us we polished off every bite of the food.

"The question is," Dolce said, sipping her tea after she'd cleared the plates. "Who wanted that necklace?" She ticked off the names on her fingers. "Her father, her stepmother, her grandmother, her sister . . . Who am I forgetting?"

Instead of answering, I asked another question. "Who

brought the necklace in? That's what I want to know. Because whoever did was probably her killer, don't you think?"

Dolce nodded.

"Won't Jack have the pawnshop owner come down to the station where he will be forced to violate his confidentiality rules and tell Jack who the seller was and who the buyer was, which, according to the pawnbroker, was the same person, and presto, the case is solved?" I asked Dolce.

Again, she nodded, but she didn't look reassured. "I'll be glad when it's over," she said.

I agreed. We both had very personal reasons for wanting it to be over. I didn't want to be a suspect anymore. and Dolce didn't want to be caught lying about the night of the murder. It must occasionally weigh on her mind, though as far as I knew, Jack hadn't yet caught her.

I picked up the yearbooks from the office, and I took a taxi home. I couldn't possibly face the prospect of a bus tonight. Not after what I'd been through. Everyone I passed on the street looked like a possible gunman. I heard a car horn and I jumped. That's how nervous I was. I locked and bolted my front door and changed into a pair of funky striped Egyptian cotton pajamas. Then I got into bed with the yearbooks, but I couldn't concentrate. My head was full of the sights and sounds I'd experienced today, and every neuron in my brain was shot.

When the phone rang, I practically fell out of bed. It was Jack.

"You work long hours," I said, "or is this a personal call?"

"Did you tell that vampire to call me?" he asked.

I choked on a laugh. "You are referring to Meera, I suppose. I suggested she might be able to help you, since she claims to have special powers, but if not, I am confident you'll know how to discourage her. Maybe you were too nice, too genial at my house the other night when you met her. That's the kind of social behavior that encourages others to confide in you."

"But not you," he said.

"What do you mean? I tell you everything and you tell me nothing, which means I have to figure things out on my own. I don't mind. I enjoy a good murder mystery as much as the next person, maybe even more since I knew the victim and I am thinking I might know the killer too."

"Really."

"Don't deny it. Everyone knows who the killer is likely to be. A friend or a relative. It's hardly ever random. Am I right?"

I knew better than to wait for an answer. He wasn't going to give me the satisfaction. So I followed up with another question he wouldn't answer.

"How did it go with the pawnshop operator? I assume you now know who brought the necklace in. Maybe you've already brought him or her in. Maybe you've already pressed charges. So why are we having this conversation?" I asked.

"We're having it because I am asking you once more to stop interfering. How much clearer can I be? Don't tell people to call me with their off-the-wall suggestions. Don't go to pawnshops. Don't interview suspects. You're getting a name for yourself and that's not good. Not when there's a murderer out there."

"So you haven't found him." I tried not to sound gleeful, but I was. Jack had as good as admitted that he was at a dead end or that I was getting close and he wasn't. Instead of discouraging me, he was having the opposite effect.

"Good night, Rita."

"Wait, what was that you said about my getting a name for myself? What name? Who told you?"

He hung up.

I turned out the light and tried to sleep, but I kept hearing gunshots and seeing flashing lights even with my sleep mask and my headphones on.

Fifteen

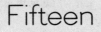

A few days went by with relatively little excitement, and that was fine with me, and with Dolce too. Patti French came by with tickets to the Sports and Boat Show. Dolce bought two. After all, Patti was not just a good customer, she was a fabulous customer, not only spending lots of money at the shop but also sending her friends there to spend freely as well. No one said anything about the event she'd sent us to at the Palace Hotel that was followed by Vienna's demise. It would have been tacky to mention it.

"Wine, cheese, chocolates and yachts," Patti said. "What's not to like? You don't have to buy a yacht, although there are some fantastic bargains these days as some people are forced to sell. It's so sad." She sighed. "Anyway, your ticket is also a raffle ticket. You could go home with a dinghy, an inflatable or a previously owned yacht."

I tried to look excited about the prospect. Maybe I should

take up sailing, I thought. Right after I got my water safety certificate, which I was training for once a week at my health club. The class made it easier for me to stay on schedule. Instead of just recreational swimming, I had a goal.

Dolce left early one evening that week to have drinks with William. She looked her best in a Helmut Lang crepe twist dress in black and white with suede boots, and she carried a pouchy bag.

"You don't mind if I leave you to lock up?" she asked.

I assured her everything was under control.

"I almost forgot. A salesman from Convertible Fashion is coming by to show us his latest thing. Something I saw on Bravo. He sells this sartorial shape-shifter that you twist and wrap and presto, you've got four outfits in one. Kind of intriguing. Tell him I'm sorry I missed him and just reschedule."

I watched from the window as she got into William's BMW. I had my fingers crossed things would go well. With the murder investigation and the loss of Vienna, Dolce needed this distraction, which had come at just the right time.

When the salesman came with his case full of samples, I told him Dolce wasn't here, but he insisted on showing me how the shape-shifter worked. "Everyone's doing it," he said. "Not just our company. You'll see these designs at Target and Victoria's Secret and all over the place. But ours are better. Let me show you how they work."

He lifted a one-piece outfit from his case and held it up. I must have looked unimpressed, because he said, "Okay, so they haven't got much hanger appeal, but they work wonders. Just give me a chance and I know you'll get the picture. In this economy, a garment like this makes even more sense. You can tweak it so you can go from work to the gym and then to cocktails. All without changing clothes. With just a few folds and tucks. Watch."

Then he took the jersey outfit he called "convertible knitwear" and began wrapping himself in the fabric. From a halter dress he made a swingy skirt and then a strapless party dress. Of course, it all looked ridiculous on him, but I could see the possibilities. I had turned down his offer to let him dress me even though I was intrigued. Call me nervous, but after what I'd been through? We were alone in the shop, and though the guy looked harmless, I was not about to undress. I'd wait until he left. Undeterred, he took out another "infinity" dress, which he made into a cap-sleeved sheath and then into a wide-leg discothèque pants outfit. There was also a skirt that converted to a shirt or a culotte. I was definitely interested and anxious to try them out on my own.

"You really think I could do what you're doing by myself?" I asked. "That's the question. Our customers want to be able to dress themselves. They won't want to have to rely on a YouTube video to teach them how to put this thing on. They're busy, active women."

"Of course," he said. "But they're also savvy women, right? They want the kinds of clothes that other women don't have. Tell you what. I'll leave these samples with you. You let me know how it goes. I'm betting you'll be calling me with some big orders. Remember to tell your customers that with a little tweaking, one versatile outfit can go from workplace to gym to cocktails."

I promised to let him know if I was able to take any orders.

"It's not all about the money, you know," he said. "They're

fun to play with. They require creativity. Everyone wants to be a stylist, have you noticed?" he asked.

I agreed and as soon as he left, I slipped into the dressing room to try on the four-in-one outfit I thought might have possibilities. Before I tried to sell it to anyone, I would have to be able to wear it myself in all four ways: baggy pants, cap-sleeve party frock, long-sleeved tunic and outerwear. Imagine how I'd feel when a customer called me up on a Saturday night.

"Rita, I'm stuck in my four-in-one dress. I'm trying to convert it from a rugged parka to a draped Aphrodite gown, and I'm leaving in five minutes for a cocktail party."

I couldn't let that happen.

I tried everything. I hitched it, I tied it, I buttoned it and I draped it, but the so-called versatile outfit just wouldn't do what I wanted it to, which was to look like something I could wear outside on the street. I pulled it up from my ankles, and I pulled it down over my head. At one point my arms were caught in the folds of fabric and my head was covered, which would have been fine if I had to wear a burka. When I heard the door open and a voice call, "Anyone there?" I almost laughed. Finally a customer who'd help me figure this out.

"I'll be right out," I said, struggling to uncover my head. Finally I pushed the curtain to the dressing room open.

"Rita, is that you?" The deep throaty voice was familiar, but I couldn't put a face to it. It would help if I could uncover my own face so I could see, but the harder I tried, the more determined the stretch fabric was to stay where it was in folds over my eyes.

"Sorry," I said. "Dolce's not here, and you've caught me at an awkward time. Just trying on the latest, four pieces in one shape-shifter, can you believe it? Could you come back another time? Or can I help you find something?" Dolce would have been so proud of me, waiting on a customer while I was covered with knitwear and unable to extricate myself. Who was the customer? Someone who could help me out of this mess, I hoped.

The person laughed, but it sounded hollow. Maybe it *was* funny that I, a clothing saleswoman, was caught in a clothing bind. But who was the laugher?

"You're the one I'm looking for," she said. I assumed it was a woman. Our customers were women. Who else would come to Dolce's at closing time for a last-minute purchase?

"Could you give me a hand with this freaking outfit?" I asked.

"Sure." With that, the person approached and pulled the hood down farther over my head.

"Not down, up," I said, a little hysterical at this point. Of course, pulling down instead of up was an easy mistake to make with all that cloth, but still, no help at all.

"How's this?" she said, tying something around my neck. A scarf? A belt?

"No, no," I said to her. If it was a woman, she was very strong. "It's too tight." I gasped. I didn't like the way she'd tied it. And I didn't want to believe I was in danger. Didn't want to believe someone was trying to choke me and leave me here unconscious or worse, but what else could I think with Vienna's unfortunate strangling death so fresh in my mind?

"I don't know who you are, but what do you want?" I asked in a raspy voice as I shook my head to loosen the hood while trying to pry the rope from around my neck with my stiff fingers.

"I want you to stay out of the Vienna investigation," she said harshly. "She wouldn't appreciate your help. She never liked you, you know."

I stiffened. Now I was really worried. "What do you mean?" I said. "It doesn't matter whether she liked me or not. I have nothing to do with her murder. The police—"

"Don't play games with me, Rita Jewel," she said. "I know exactly what you've been doing. You think you can solve this case? You think because you helped the police before they want your help this time?"

"No," I said. "I know they don't. I'm staying out of it. Who are you anyway? Are you a friend of Vienna's? A relative?" I had a vision of her crazy relative Paul, and I remembered our conversation. "Are you her uncle? Did I meet you at her funeral?"

"I was at her funeral, yes," she said in a husky voice. Was it a man after all? "And next I'll be at yours, you meddling bitch."

"You have it all wrong," I said, pawing at the material and trying to stay calm while shaking inside the tent I'd wrapped myself in. "I don't know anything, and I don't want anything to do with it, believe me."

"I've been watching you," she or he said. "You've gone too far. I'm giving you one last warning." With that, she tightened the sash around my neck.

"Stop," I croaked, flailing my arms in what I thought was her direction. But the word died in my throat. I couldn't talk, I couldn't breathe.

Last warning? It was the first warning I'd gotten, and now it was my last. How did that happen? While I was choking and trying to rip off whatever was around my neck, I heard someone call my name. Was it Saint Peter at the gates of heaven? Was it Dolce? Or was it my guardian angel?

"Rita," the faint voice said. "Let me in. Help. It's an emergency. I see your light. I know you're there." Someone out there was calling me and pounding on the door.

Finally I jerked at the rope around my neck and it came loose. I heard my assailant swear, then footsteps, high heels clacking on the floorboards, as whoever it was ran past me toward the rear of the store. And finally the sound of the back door to the shop opening and slamming shut.

With a desperate shake of my head, I finally loosened the hood around my neck. It was not a hanger or rope that choked me, though those would have worked just as well. It was a Hermes silk scarf from our collection. Did that mean the choker was not prepared and simply grabbed the scarf when she saw my face was covered? Did that mean it was a crime of opportunity and not preplanned? As the swatch of fabric fell away from my head, I took a big gulp of air. I ran to the door to see Sarah, a new client, looking desperate.

I was breathing hard, but she didn't notice. "I'm going to the symphony tonight," she said, "and I have nothing to wear."

This from a woman I knew had a walk-in closet full of clothes, and one section for evening wear. What did she mean?

"I'm so glad you're still here," she said, grasping my arm. "You're a lifesaver."

No, I thought, *you're* the lifesaver.

"Symphony," I said thoughtfully as I walked to the rack with the long dresses. Should I tell her I'd just been attacked and now I had to call the police? No, I knew what Jack would say: "Stay out of trouble. Watch your back. You're okay, right? You don't know who attacked you, do you? Call us when you've got some details. Otherwise . . ."

"Rita, you're a jewel," Sarah said, gazing at me with admiration. "What would I do without you?" Then she paused and looked at me. "What's that you're wearing?"

"It's a four-in-one outfit, the latest thing. It's versatile, it's convertible, and it's for the price-conscious. But not for you. Not for tonight."

"I don't have to wear a ball gown and white gloves, do I?" she asked. "You know we're new in town, and Peter refuses to wear a tux. What will people think?"

"Don't worry," I said, as if I was some kind of director of good taste. As if I'd ever even been part of the social scene of this city. "You'll see a little bit of everything there, especially tonight, a week night." What did I know except what I'd heard Dolce say. I'd never been to the symphony or the opera. But I'd love to go, if only to see what people were wearing. Right now I'd give anything to go home and fall into bed. But turn away a customer? Never. On the other hand, my knees were weak, my hands were shaking and I wondered if my stalker-assailant was outside waiting to finish me off.

"Look, Sarah," I said, trying not to sound desperate to close up and get out of there. "Why don't you just wear a little black dress? You've got one or two or three in your closet, don't you? That would be perfect for midweek at the opera." I could imagine what Dolce would say if she heard me. "You said *what*?" she'd ask. "You turned away a customer by telling her to go home and wear an old dress?" Yes, but I was a wreck.

"You mean you don't have anything?" Sarah asked sadly.

"Of course we have." I reached for the first black dress on the rack. It was a spandex and rayon wrap dress with a cutaway collar creating a flattering V-neckline.

"Rita, you're a genius," Sarah said when she came out of the dressing room. I had to agree. By chance I'd found the perfect dress for her. Elegant, sophisticated and understated. It said "I know who I am, I know what to wear and I know I look terrific."

"Honestly, Dolce, should give you a raise," she said. "Here it is almost six o'clock and you're helping me when you should be going home or on a date yourself, right?"

I nodded, took her credit card and, while she was changing back into her street clothes, rang up the sale and wrapped her new dress in a garment bag.

When she came out of the dressing room, she was sneezing. "What's that scent you're wearing?" she asked me.

"I'm not," I said. "Why?"

"Because I'm allergic to perfume. Can't wear anything and can't be around anyone who does. And someone's been wearing a light floral scent. Bluebells, raspberries, ozone, melon and apples, if I'm not mistaken. Who was just here before me?"

"Uh, well, I'm not sure who it was," I said. "I mean there were so many customers today."

"Well, I'm off. If you're ready to go, I'll give you a ride home."

I nodded and grabbed my purse, but before I walked out I closed my eyes and concentrated. A blend of bluebells, raspberries, ozone, melon and apples, she'd said. Yes, now I could smell it. Why hadn't I noticed it before? Because I was overwhelmed with other sensations, like fear. Which proved that my visitor was a woman for sure. That and the

high heels I'd heard when she left. On the other hand, maybe
that was a ploy to confuse me. As for the perfume, so many
fragrances these days were unisex.

"I'm just going to close up," I said. Safety in numbers, I
told myself. At least I hoped it was still true. If not . . . we
were both doomed.

We walked out together, me still in my four-in-one
outfit—currently in baggy pants and long-sleeved tunic
mode—and Sarah in designer jeans with her dress under
her arm. I was terrified of every shadow, ever word that
echoed from the bar across the street. I was extremely grateful for the ride home. Not that I didn't deserve it after what
I'd done for her. I did.

Once at home with the doors locked and bolted, I
removed my outfit and left it on the bedroom floor. My
enthusiasm for convertible knitwear had dampened consid-
erably. I filled my claw-foot tub with hot water and lavender
and acai berry Dead Sea salt to soothe my body and my
nerves.

I lay in the water up to my chin unable to stop thinking
about my close call with the murderous stranger. Only it
wasn't a stranger. She knew me. She had killed Vienna, or
was I just being overly dramatic because of the similarity
in method? Had the woman (assuming it was a woman)
known I was alone? Thinking of someone watching the shop
sent a chill up my spine. Had she known I was caught in a
four-in-one outfit and was temporarily disabled and couldn't
see who she was? Whatever she knew, she'd been frightened
off by the arrival of Sarah.

All the way home in Sarah's car I kept looking over my
shoulder to see if anyone was following us. Who was the
mystery man or woman? Did the person know where I lived?

What should I do next? Who should I tell, Dolce or Jack or no one. Was I exaggerating the threat or was it real? Whatever I'd told the intruder, I was not giving up. I might be scared, but I was more determined than ever.

I decided not to tell Dolce. What could she do about it? Maybe Jack was right. I brought these things upon myself by my actions. Telling Dolce would just cause her to worry more when she was still getting over her shock of Vienna's murder. She had given me the tickets to the Boat Show on Sunday and told me she was instigating the new store hours. From now on the shop would be closed on Mondays. I had a long two days off to fill up. I wasn't sure that was a good thing.

On Sunday about noon I arrived at Fort Mason on San Francisco Bay wearing deliciously soft jeans and Steven Joss boots that could be worn with jeans, as I was doing, or with a motorcycle jacket for a biker look or even with a little black dress. That's how versatile they were and worth every penny they'd cost me. I paired them with a Cacharel oversize printed shirt and a solid-colored jacket, and I carried a vibrant purple handbag. Before I left, I tossed a colorful scarf around my neck. I almost didn't wear the scarf because it reminded me of my near escape earlier in the week. As if I needed reminding. It was hard to keep the episode to myself, but how else was I going to get over my fear of being alone and equally strong fear of the four-in-one shape-shifter?

How else to protect those I cared about or whose opinion of me I cared about except to keep my mouth closed for now? Hopefully, if I stopped my investigation, the person who'd threatened me would relax, realize they'd brought off the perfect murder and, having gotten rid of the woman who'd stolen their boyfriend or badmouthed them or cheated on them, wouldn't try again. I would have to say that I was sufficiently frightened to suspend my efforts and let the police take over. I was sure Jack Wall would be thrilled to hear about my new attitude, but for now I didn't want to talk about Vienna, her family or her friends, or, most especially, her death.

As for the novel garment, I couldn't even bring myself to show it to a single customer. When Dolce asked me about it, I said it was okay for certain occasions, for certain customers.

The boat show, held in the huge pavilion, was full of well-dressed yacht people shopping for a three-hundred-eighty-dollar canoe or a multimillion-dollar luxury yacht or something in between. Some of which were docked outside at the pier just waiting to be experienced by eager prospective buyers. Me, I was just trying to get a new slant on life, a life without a murder case to solve.

I'd taken the warning by my mysterious visitor seriously, and I'd returned the yearbooks this week. Jack was right: it was none of my business. He had the resources, the time and the staff. He didn't need my help. Or want it. And if he never solved this crime, I told myself I didn't care as long as the killer didn't strike again.

I walked past motor boats, yachts, sailboats and rowboats. The salesmen were dressed in white or blue, as if they'd just docked. "Care to take a ride on the Bay today?" one guy asked. "I've got a catamaran out there with your name on it. Easy to sail and easy on the wallet."

"Maybe later," I said. I had to admit it was tempting. The sun was shining, the breeze was cool and the idea of crossing the Bay on a small boat, leaving the land and my troubles behind, was appealing. But I didn't know how to sail or steer or anything.

"Never sailed before?" the guy asked. "No problem. Let me show you how."

I smiled and kept walking. Now the canoe, that was more my speed, but out there on the waves? Maybe not.

"Take it to the Russian River," the canoe salesman suggested. "Strap it on your car and off you go, only two hours away."

I didn't tell him I didn't have a car and I couldn't afford a canoe.

"Rita, good to see you. Where's Dolce?" Patti French greeted me at the concessionaires' stands, a glass of wine in one hand.

"She had plans for today," I said.

"I'm glad you could make it. Sit down, I'll get you a glass of wine. They're having a demo with that chef Ida who shows you how to cook gourmet food on your yacht."

"That's handy," I murmured, taking a seat at a small table as Patti went to get the wine. She came back with a tray loaded with samples that Ida the Galloping Gourmet had made.

"Saffron seafood soup, chili-lime prawns, scallop linguini," Patti said, handing me a fork.

"Ida can make all this on board a boat?" I asked. Pretty impressive. I had a hard enough time putting together a small dinner in my apartment. Cooking in a tiny galley aboard a boat rocking from side to side? No way.

"She says she can. When you get your yacht, you can hire her and see if she's right."

After trying a prawn and a bite of linguini, I vowed I wouldn't set sail without Ida.

"Lots of Dolce customers here today," Patti said, turning her head and waving at someone in the crowd while I dug into the spicy seafood soup. "No big surprise there. If you have a boat of any kind or you hang with the yacht-club crowd, you shop at Dolce's. By the way, I love your bag," she said. "Gucci?"

I nodded, not mentioning that it was a knockoff.

"Oh look, there's Lex and Bobbi. Poor guy. He'll never get over losing Vienna. Don't tell me he needs a new yacht. He competed in the San Francisco Yacht Race last spring and almost won. Maybe 'almost' wasn't good enough and he needs a faster model. You know Bobbi, don't you?"

"Actually I've never met her," I said. "Though we've spoken on the phone, and I did see her at the funeral."

"Who could miss her in that red dress she wore?" Patti said. "I never understood that. You didn't sell it to her, did you?"

I shook my head.

"She's headed this way. I'm going to duck out of sight. Sorry, Rita, but you know how it is."

I wasn't sure I did know how it was. All I knew was that Bobbi, dressed in white wide-leg pants, a striped T-shirt and a casual denim blazer, was headed toward me. Why me? I hardly knew her. I didn't know her.

"You're Rita," she said, setting her wineglass on my table. "I'm Bobbi."

"How are you?" I asked politely.

"Still looking for that moto jacket," she said.

"I could order one for you and if it doesn't work out, no problem," I said. "Size ten?"

She nodded. "Why not? I deserve it after what I've been through."

I knew I should ask what she'd been through, but I really didn't want to hear about it. Was she referring to Vienna's death?

"My husband is having trouble coping with, you know . . ."

I said I did know.

"I thought I'd buy him something here to take his mind off of . . ."

"I thought he had a boat," I said.

"He does, but it's not a family craft, if you know what I mean. It's for racing and that's all. I was thinking of something we could both enjoy. Just because I don't like racing doesn't mean I don't like boats. I grew up on boats. My family belonged to the yacht club. That's where I met Lex. Right after his divorce. He was a wreck. I cheered him up."

"What about a catamaran?" I asked. Wasn't that what one of those salesmen was trying to get me to take a ride in?

"Too slow," she said. "Even for me. Do you have a minute? I'd like your opinion on a little motorboat."

That's what I did for a living: give my opinion on what was suitable for a customer. I thought maybe that was how Bobbi saw the purchase of a boat, something she'd look good in.

She glanced around. "I don't want Lex to see me going out on a boat. This has to be a surprise."

"Going out?" I said.

"Otherwise how do you know if it's what you want? Don't be afraid, I know my way around boats, at least small ones."

I followed her out of the building to the pier, where it was obvious she was expected. I wasn't sure why I went with her except it was a beautiful day and what else did I come to a boat show for if not to have a boat experience? I couldn't hide in my apartment just because some crazy had threatened me. I had to get back to the old Rita, the one who took chances. Who took cooking lessons, and who was the star student in her water safety class.

"Can you swim?" Bobbi asked me suddenly.

"Yes, can you?"

I didn't hear her answer because the salesman was telling us that a small powerboat was just what we wanted. For the whole family to enjoy. "Water skiing, fishing, trolling." I heard the words "fiberglass hull" and "three-year warranty."

The salesman wanted to take us out, but Bobbi told him she had to get the feel of the motor, the waves, the current.

"I know what I'm talking about," she told the salesman. "I've had boats before. But don't tell my husband I'm going out on the water in this boat. It's a surprise for his birthday."

The salesman pressed his lips together and took a vow of silence. But he still didn't want us to go out by ourselves.

"If anything happens, it's my fault," Bobbi said. "I'll sign a waiver if it makes you feel any better."

He said it would and went to get the waiver. But Bobbi didn't want to wait. She looked at her Cartier watch with the wide band. "I don't want him to come looking for me," she said. I assumed she meant Lex. "Get in. We're going for the ride of our lives."

Her enthusiasm was contagious. I stepped in the boat and sat at the far end. She grabbed the rope, untied it from the post and jumped aboard. I had to say she moved well and had me convinced she knew what she was doing. She even patiently explained the function of the drive lever, which included the clutch that engages the propeller, the throttle that controls the speed, and the reverse gear.

"Fascinating," I said politely.

We'd gone about one hundred yards out into the Bay when I saw the salesman standing on the pier waving frantically to us. Bobbi waved back and laughed. The boat hit the waves head-on and bounced over them, sending saltwater spray all over me.

"Shouldn't we be wearing life jackets?" I shouted over the noise of the engine.

"I think they're under the seats," she said. "We'll get them out when we get to the island."

I didn't know which island she meant, Alcatraz or Angel Island or Treasure Island. She looked ecstatic; her face lit up as she sent us at top speed out into the Bay, leaving behind other pleasure boats. Her hair was streaming out behind her, one hand on the steering wheel, the other on the throttle. Her eyes were huge, a big smile on her face.

"Having fun?" she shouted.

I nodded, although the wind was coming up and I felt a chill, especially since my shirt was wet. "Maybe we should head back," I suggested.

She laughed so hard I thought she was going to fall over. "We just left," she yelled. Then she stood and the boat swerved.

"Bobbi," I shouted, "what are you doing?"

"I'm giving you what you wanted. An exciting ride."

"It's a little too exciting," I said, inching my way toward her.

She grabbed me by the shoulders and shook me. The boat stalled. "You think you know who killed Vienna?"

"No," I said. Because until that moment I didn't know. But suddenly the smell of bluebells, raspberries, melons and apples filled my nostrils; even there in the fresh air I could smell it. It was her. "I don't even know what happened to her necklace," I said calmly.

"Really. I pawned it."

"You? Why?"

"For the money, stupid. Why else do people pawn necklaces? So I could buy the Rolls Royce Lex wouldn't give me."

"But he's a car salesman."

"It doesn't matter. Not to him. The cobbler's wife has no shoes, ever hear that? So now you know why I took it from her. But not just for the money. Because I didn't want her to have it. I was furious that she wore it that night. It wasn't hers."

"It was her grandmother's," I said. This whole thing was a misunderstanding, I told myself.

"That's where you're wrong," Bobbi said, shoving me back down onto my seat. "It belonged to Lex's mother. He gave it to Noreen years ago, and she never gave it back when they got divorced. She gave it to her mother for safekeeping, but didn't dare wear it. Of course not. When I saw Vienna had it on that night . . . I was furious. I thought Lex gave it to her. He gave her money, presents, a car. And now the necklace."

"Yes, but—"

"You had to get into it, didn't you?" she demanded. "You had to tell the cops it was me. They came to see me yesterday. But I got rid of them."

"I didn't . . . It's not my . . . Who told you that?"

"Nobody told me you'd figured things out. Nobody had to tell me. San Francisco is a small town. Everything you did got back to me. Like your going to the pawnshop to get my necklace."

"But it was gone."

"Of course it was gone. I bought it back when Lex said he'd buy me a Rolls of my own. Get it?" she asked, leaning toward me with a maniacal smile on her face.

"Yes, I get it," I told her, eyeing the steering wheel and the throttle. If only I could overpower her and get back to shore. But she was at least three inches taller than me and heavier.

"Bobbi," I said, "why did you . . . ?"

"To get the necklace. Are you dense? Don't you see?"

I shook my head.

"I wanted the necklace back. It was mine."

"But it belonged to Vienna's grandmother." I don't know why I said that, I just knew I had to stall for time. Think, I told myself, think of how to convince Bobbi you don't know anything. Pretend you still don't get it. How hard can it be to act clueless?

"I just told you, that's a lie," Bobbi said, her face mottled with pink splotches, her hair whipping around her face in the wind. "That was not her necklace. When I saw it on Vienna that night at the die auction, I saw red. I demanded it. Told her it belonged to my family, not her mother's. She refused to hand it over. I followed her to the shop, and she still wouldn't listen to reason even after I told her how it was stolen from my mother years ago. I can show you pictures of it from the family album. I think I know what's mine and what's not. I didn't mean to kill her. I just wanted the damn necklace back. If she had handed it over, if she hadn't struggled, she'd still be alive."

I stood and stared at Bobbi openmouthed while the boat rocked beneath us. What part of her story was true? That she took back the necklace when Lex gave her her own Rolls? That it had belonged to her mother, and not Lex's? It

didn't matter. All that mattered was that she'd killed Vienna.
I knew it and she knew I knew it.

"So where is it now?"

"I don't know. I don't know," she screamed. "Somebody
bought it."

Why she bothered to lie when she intended to do me in
I'll never know. She was not making sense, and I wasn't
either. Under the circumstances, who would?

I only had a moment to ponder all this conflicting information before she shoved me backward. I fell down but got
up on my knees and lunged forward. I grabbed her by the
ankles. She toppled over like a tall stone statue. She
screamed and got back up. We shoved and pushed each
other. I was desperate. I knew she wouldn't want me to live
to tell her convoluted story. Whether she'd meant to kill
Vienna or not, she'd done it.

"You used the hanger, didn't you?" I demanded, breathing hard. "And you almost strangled me the other night."

"I wouldn't have killed you then. I needed to wait until
now, when there are no witnesses."

I looked around. We were on the other side of the island.
No boats, nobody around. I couldn't let her get away with
it. Maybe she wouldn't. Maybe the salesman would say,
What ever happened to that attractive young woman you
left with? Then would Bobbi tell him I'd fallen overboard?
Or gone for a swim and disappeared? But I'd be dead and
Bobbi would get off Scott free.

"Bobbi, I won't tell anyone," I said earnestly. "Your secret
is safe with me. Let's go back to the boat show. We'll forget
this ever happened." I knew I was being naïve, but I was
desperate too.

Her answer was to grab me by the hair and yank me

forward and back like the doll Vienna and Athena fought over. Would I lose my arm too? Or would I lose my life?

She pushed me hard one last time, and I toppled overboard. I hit the cold water with a painful thud, and I knew I'd be dead from the elements in minutes. Bobbi walked to the front of the boat just as a rogue wave hit. She fell over and hit her head on the side of the boat before tumbling into the water. I screamed at her. She didn't hear me. She sank like a stone.

I swam the few strokes back to the boat, pulled myself up and into the boat with my arms aching and the adrenaline pumping. Otherwise I could never have done it. I knew I should dive back in and try to find her, but I was shaking with the cold. I had to get back and get warm or I'd die too. And that wasn't fair. I hadn't killed anyone.

Fortunately the engine was still running. I plopped myself in front of the steering wheel and pushed the drive lever forward the way I'd seen Bobbi do. The engine roared and the boat surged forward. I turned the steering wheel and headed back to the boat show. My teeth chattered, my body ached, but I was alive.

There was a crowd waiting for me on the pier, including Detective Wall, Lex Fairchild, the boat salesman and many of our customers, as well as quite a few curious strangers. I didn't really know what I was doing as I banged the boat against the pier before it came to a shuddering halt. Detective Wall jumped in the boat, threw a blanket around my shoulders and said, "What happened?"

"Bobbi killed Vienna," I mumbled, my lips cold and stiff.

"I mean what happened out there?" he said.

"She tried to kill me."

"So what did you do, kill her first?" he asked as he led me inside.

I shook my head. "We fought. She tried to throw me over,
but she fell instead. I couldn't save her."

He looked disappointed I hadn't tried to save her, but not
surprised. I wasn't sure what he felt. What I felt was weak
and empty. I sat on a bench and kicked off my boots. When
I turned them upside down, gallons of water gushed out.

Jack directed the police boats to go out on a search immediately in case Bobbi had resurfaced. Then he insisted that
I change into dry clothes immediately, a pair of jeans and a
sweatshirt in my size he had in his car. Don't ask me where
he got them. I didn't want to know about other women in
his life who'd left a set of clothes with him. I just went into
the bathroom and stuffed my wet clothes in a plastic bag. A
glance in the mirror told me I looked like I'd been ship-
wrecked, hair hanging in strings, face pale. Then we went
to the hospital so I could be checked out.

I told Jack I was fine, and I just wanted to go home. He
nodded, but he was on the phone to the Coast Guard telling
them about the accident. I knew he wouldn't let me leave
right away. I'd have to go make a statement somewhere,
probably at his station. He said having a medical checkup
was police procedure. While he stayed in the Urgent
Care waiting area, I went into a small examining room
wearing a paper gown. On my way in I looked up and down
the hall just in case Jonathan was on duty, but he probably
still worked nights. The room I was in had a list of do's
and don'ts on the wall, like "Don't Drink and Drive." It
might have been the same room where I was treated for a
concussion and sprained ankle last year after falling off a
ladder.

This time, I was diagnosed with shock and hypothermia.
They could tell because my temperature was hovering

around ninety-five and I was still shivering despite a heat blanket they'd wrapped around me.

"Where were you?" the young doctor asked. A man with none of the bedside manner of my favorite MD.

"In the Bay," I said, my lips still stiff.

"Without thermal protection, swimming in the Bay is not advised," he said sternly.

"I know," I said.

"Without a life jacket, drowning is inevitable."

"Then I'm very lucky to be alive, since I didn't have a life jacket or protection against the cold."

He gave me a pamphlet on the causes of hypothermia, which I glanced at. Then I added, just to see if he'd stop lecturing me, "Besides, someone wanted to kill me."

"They did? Why?" He looked mildly curious. Maybe he heard that a lot in the ER.

"It's a long story. Can I go home now?"

After he told me to drink hot liquids, keep warm and get plenty of rest, he added, "No alcohol. No caffeine. You may seem irrational, but you'll get over it."

"I doubt it," I murmured.

I got dressed and then took one more look around for Jonathan, but it was just as well he wasn't on duty. I couldn't imagine recounting my unbelievable story of survival in the San Francisco Bay again. Maybe later, after I'd recovered.

"You think you can live through a brief session at the station before I take you home?" Jack asked. "I can promise you some hot soup and the use of my Forty-niners football blanket to wrap around you."

I sighed. "I guess so." Even though I was feeling a little better, especially knowing he was doing his best to keep me comfortable, I wanted him to think I was doing him a big favor after all the times he'd told me to butt out of this investigation. Besides, there were a few things I wanted to know in exchange for my cooperation.

One was, what was he doing at the boat show?

"Believe it or not, I *was* not, I *am* not on duty today. I was thinking of buying a boat. In fact, I made an offer on a small sailboat. Then I heard someone yelling. A guy who said his wife had disappeared and he was afraid she'd gone out in a boat by herself."

"Lex."

"Yes. He didn't know she wasn't alone. Why the hell did you go out in a boat with a murderer?" he demanded as he drove down the street toward the Central Police Station.

"I didn't know Bobbi was the murderer."

"Then why did she try to kill you?"

"It was all a misunderstanding. She thought I was after her."

"Who were you after?"

"Anyone and everyone. But not her. I suspected Vienna's old boyfriends, her roommate, her family, and yes, Bobbi too. But I didn't know it was her until she told me. How did you know?" I asked him.

"The prints on Vienna's clothes and her skin and even the hanger used to kill her just came back from the crime lab in Sacramento. I'd gone to arrest her this morning, but she wasn't there. There was an all-points bulletin, and I had a deputy and a crew watching her house."

"But she was at the boat show."

"Yeah. And now . . ."

"She's at the bottom of the Bay. You don't have to find her body, do you?"

"We have to make sure she didn't survive. The boats are out there now searching the area."

"I learned today that nobody could survive more than fifteen minutes in that water. Untreated hypothermia leads to heart failure, respiratory failure and death."

"Did Bobbi tell you how she killed Vienna?" he asked

"Just like she tried to kill me, by strangling her. Only she used the hanger on Vienna, and a Hermes scarf on me."

"I wasn't aware you reported an attempted murder," he said, raising his eyebrows.

"No, but I will next time, I promise. Shall I go on?" I asked impatiently. "After the benefit Bobbi followed Vienna to the shop, where I assume she was going to change out of her gown, and when Vienna refused to give up the necklace, she killed her."

"But how did the necklace end up at the pawnshop then?

"Bobbi took it there to get money for it so she could buy herself a Rolls that Lex wouldn't buy for her. But he did, so she decided to keep the necklace. Only she didn't get it back until the night she killed Vienna. Then she took it back to the pawn shop for safekeeping, knowing it would be a damaging piece of evidence if it was found anywhere near her."

I sipped the hot soup Jack had brought from a vending machine, while he went behind his desk and unlocked a drawer. He pulled out the famous necklace and held it in the palm of his hand.

I gasped.

"Is this it?"

I nodded. "*You* got it from the pawnshop."

"Just dumb luck. I happened to be passing by while in my old neighborhood and I saw it in the window, but I didn't want to make the purchase myself where they know me, so I sent my assistant in to buy it."

"But the pawnshop guy said the same woman who dropped it off bought it back."

"Not true," he said. "He was confused."

"But you'd never seen the necklace. So how did you know . . ."

"I'd heard a lot about it."

"Who gets it now?" I said, admiring the way the diamonds sparkled around the deep pink stone.

"I'll let you know," he said and locked it up again.

Jack drove me home and made sure I was warm and safely ensconced in my small bedroom. "You going to be okay?" he asked when he saw my eyelids drooping.

"I'll be fine. When I wake up later, I'll call Meera at the pizza place and have something delivered."

"What time would that be?"

"I can't believe you'd cadge another dinner invitation from me. Have you no shame?" I asked. Then I drifted off into a deliciously warm slumber, knowing I'd solved another crime and the streets were safe for well-dressed honest citizens again.

Style Tips

Rita's Underwear Rules

1. If you're worried about telltale underwear lines, you're ready for a thong. Look for something simple and comfortable. Avoid lace; it looks sexy, but it's uncomfortable and itchy. Buy something in cotton or seamless microfiber.

2. If your bra is riding up, it's too big (in number, not letter). Exchange your 36B for a 34B.

3. Don't buy underwear that has to be hand-washed. Who has time for hand-washing? Besides, eventually you'll throw it in the washing machine by mistake, so check the labels or ask the sales staff at the lingerie department to be sure you can machine wash whatever you buy.

4. Bra straps can show, so be sure and choose your bra with that in mind. Some call it tacky, others call it high fashion. Check out the celebs who show their straps on purpose. How about a yellow tank top with red bra straps? Red is a power color, after all. Or a white top with black straps that match your black, color-intense lipstick?

Rita's Hair Tips

1. Long hair set in loose waves is always sexy.
2. After shampooing your hair, be sure to make the final rinse in cold water—this will make your hair shinier.
3. Don't make the mistake of not rinsing the shampoo completely out of your hair. Rinse and rinse again, using a ton of water. If you don't, your hair will be dull and listless.
4. For maximum volume, blow-dry to the side rather than upside down.
5. Braids or one single braid is a cute and sexy style. At night wash your hair and braid it. In the morning, take out the braid and voila—you've got waves!
6. You wear your haircut every day, so don't be afraid to spend a bundle on a good cut. If a great cut cost more than your shoes, it would still be reasonable.
7. If your hairstylist trashes the beautician who last cut your hair, dump her or him! The best stylists concentrate on doing a good job for you no matter what shape your hair is in. It's not their job to tell you what's wrong with you.
8. Stick with something that's closest to your natural hair texture. If you have natural waves, don't hide them by straightening your hair. If you have long straight hair, iron it and make sure it's clean, shiny and swingy. For a change, put it up in a bun or tuck it into your hat.
9. A bad haircut? It's not the end of the world. In a year you won't even remember this disastrous cut. In the meantime, first you cry. Sure you feel ugly and maybe even stupid for going to the wrong place. Then write it down. Where you went, how much you paid and your vow never to make that mistake again. Finally, accept what happened. Your hair will grow and it will look great once again.

10. Round face? Try a layered haircut with fullness on top, but keep it close to your face at the sides. Go either short or longer than chin length. A rounded style that ends at your chin will make your face look rounder, just what you don't want. Oval face? Lucky you, you can wear your hair any length or style you want.

11. Color your hair? Don't do a wild color like blue no matter how crazy you feel. You'll be sorry in the morning. But deliberate messiness is okay. After all, Jennifer Aniston gets away with it, why not you? Perfumed hair? A great idea unless your hair is dry, in which case spray your nape instead because the alcohol in most fragrances sucks out moisture.

Rita's Wardrobe Must-Haves

1. A fluffy sweater. Even in the summer you must have one to go with your jeans, your shorts or your miniskirt. Especially if you live in San Francisco where summer can be really chilly. Sweaters are cozy and sexy at the same time, whether they're slouchy or fitted, alpaca blend or mohair, scoop-neck or turtleneck.

2. Colorful booties. You can go solid or print with these. In a bright color, they stand out and make a statement. If you decide on printed booties, it's because they're whimsical, bold and attention-grabbing. Choose polka dots or jewel-toned velvet. Wear with slouchy socks or jeans or, for a stunning contrast, a lacy party dress.

3. A tuxedo shirt. The look you want is that you just borrowed the shirt from a guy who's almost the same size as you. Keep the neck exposed by unbuttoning at least three buttons and adding jewelry. Try wide-cuff bracelets at your

wrists and metallic wedges on your feet, and carry a vintage silk clutch. Then top it off with a black satin blazer,
which is subtle and understated. Finally, a bright short silk
skirt with—what else?—black tights, of course.

4. The gown. You may say, as Rita did, that you have no place
   to wear a formal gown, but you never know. When you do
   and you don't want to look so formal, go with a pattern and
   a wild color. How about a temporary tattoo? So fun and so
   much attitude. With your gown, wear a tough leather jacket
   and a pair of colorful sequined pumps.

5. The party skirt (and what to wear with it even if you're not
   going to a party). The skirt is a nylon-blend flouncy skirt.
   When Rita is in her preppie mood, she wears it with a blazer,
   a turtleneck shirt, black tights and a pair of faux-suede
   shoes. When she's feeling European, she wears her fitted
   shrunken-tweed jacket, a leather bag, mulberry tights and
   high-heeled booties. There are days when Rita wants to look
   more girlie. That's when she goes to her closet for a thin,
   lightweight wool cardigan, a silk chiffon blouse, rhinestone
   earrings and, of course, her best black tights with classic
   black pumps.

6. An all-black outfit. Some days Rita likes to wear black. Even
   in spring. It feels clean and strong to her. When the mood
   strikes, she opts for black J Brand zipper jeans with a black
   Lainey Keogh cashmere sweater, bold wire-rim Ray-Ban
   sunglasses and a pair of black sneakers. In this outfit she
   can go anywhere from work to dinner and even fit in a little
   sleuthing, since everyone knows that black is great for
   sneaking around at night.

7. Hot pants and boy shorts. Rita convinced Dolce to place a
   big order for these items, sure she could sell them. So of
   course what better way than to wear them to work? This is

a shorter-than-short style and admittedly is not for every-one. But for those who want to wear them, a gym member-ship is a must to tone the muscles. That's why Rita will be seen pedaling around Golden Gate Park on her rented bicy-cle, in her boy shorts, naturally. Sometimes she'll wear her knee-high or over-the-knee socks with them.

8. A day-off look. Even though Rita had had only one day off a week, she needed a special look. First a pair of lean and sexy chinos, which form the neutral base for a khaki-'n'-color combo. Then she added an anorak in a bright color in case of wind or rain. Or she liked a sequined vest to jazz up her basics or add a fashionable touch to a tank and khakis. Wedges are very spring. When it's her day off, she likes to wear a bra top under blouses or oversize shirts. They're great with something sheer.

Recipes

Meera's Romanian *Mamaliga* Balls

These delicious appetizers are an excellent example of the Eastern Europeans' love of one food tucked inside of another. In this case, begin with cornmeal porridge (*mamaliga*) and cook until thick; then form into balls with your hands, stuff with meat such as smoked sausage, and finally, fry the balls until crisp and hot. Serve hot with sliced tomatoes, sour cream or—if you don't care about being traditional—a marinara sauce. *Mamaliga* is a wonderful appetizer, snack or addition to any meal. You can substitute the sausage stuffing with chunks of ham or feta cheese.

Notice that cornmeal porridge is the equivalent of Italian polenta, which can be substituted for cornmeal.

This recipe makes 6 to 8 servings.

2 cups yellow cornmeal or polenta
2½ cups water
¾ teaspoon salt
1 tablespoon butter
Vegetable oil for frying
1 cup roughly chopped salami or cooked smoked sausage

Stir together cornmeal, water and salt in a heavy saucepan. Bring to a boil, reduce heat and cook 12 minutes, stirring frequently, until thick enough to be scooped. Stir in butter; taste and season to your liking.

Heat oil in a heavy-bottomed pot or deep fryer to 350°F. Using a cookie scoop or your hands, portion the cornmeal mixture into balls. Flatten the *mamaliga* in your hand, add a chunk of meat to the center, seal and reroll into a ball.

Fry balls 2–3 minutes until golden brown. Drain on paper towels.

William's Recipe for
Steak Diane

Steak Diane was traditionally cooked tableside at fine restaurants like Delmonico's. The headwaiter would roll a food trolley to your table, and as you watched wide-eyed, he would slice, dice, debone and flambé. The excitement came when he'd set fire to the cognac in the sauce. It's hard to find a restaurant that will actually do a traditional flambé these days. Maybe it's because they fear an accident followed by a lawsuit, or perhaps it's just that the waitstaff is not trained in the art of flambé.

It's too bad because flambéing is not just for show. Igniting the cognac or brandy in the recipe intensifies the flavor of the sauce by caramelizing the sugars. During caramelization, the sauce develops its mouthwatering flavor.

5 Secrets to a Stunning Flambé

1. Start with a dry piece of meat.
2. Use high heat.
3. Use a heavy skillet.
4. Use a skillet large enough to accommodate the steaks without overcrowding.
5. Use high-quality cognac, brandy or rum

Steak Diane

4 3-ounce filet mignon medallions
½ teaspoon salt
¼ teaspoon fresh black pepper
1 tablespoons unsalted butter
4 teaspoons minced shallots
1 teaspoon minced garlic
1 cup sliced mushroom caps
¼ cup cognac or brandy
2 teaspoons Dijon mustard
¼ cup heavy cream
¼ cup reduced veal or beef or chicken stock
2 teaspoons Worcestershire sauce
2 drops hot red pepper sauce
1 tablespoon chopped green onions
1 teaspoon minced parsley

Season beef medallions on both sides with the salt and pepper.
Melt the butter in a large skillet. Add meat and cook for 45 seconds on first side. Turn over and cook for 30 seconds on second side. Add shallots and garlic and cook 20 seconds. Add

mushrooms and cook until soft. Place meat on a plate and cover to keep warm.

Tilt pan toward you and add the brandy. Tip the pan away from you and ignite the brandy with a match, or remove pan from heat to ignite and then return to the heat. When the flame is burned out, add the mustard and cream, mix thoroughly and cook, stirring, for 1 minute. Add veal stock and simmer for 1 minute. Add the Worcestershire and hot sauce and keep stirring until smooth. Return the meat and juices to pan and turn the meat to coat with the sauce. Remove from the heat and stir in green onions and parsley. Serve immediately.

Rita's Slow-Cooked Pork Roast
(A Slight Variation to the One She Actually Made)

A note about slow cooking: if you, like Rita, don't have a slow cooker, you can also make this in a Dutch oven or other heavy covered pot. Cook at 250° for about 4 hours.

This recipe makes 8 to 10 servings.

3–4 pound pork roast
Kosher salt
Fresh black pepper
1 cup white wine
¼ cup fresh sage leaves
8 cloves garlic
1 teaspoon allspice berries (optional)
Red pepper flakes (optional)

METHOD 1

Rub the pork roast all over with salt and pepper. Bruise the sage leaves (Rita didn't know what that meant, so she skipped it), and mince or slice the garlic—anything quick—it doesn't need to be pretty. Put the roast, white wine, sage, garlic, all-spice berries and red pepper flakes (if desired) in the slow cooker and cook for 10 hours on low or 5–6 hours on high. If desired, add small potatoes and/or small baby carrots during the last hour of cooking.

METHOD 2

This method takes some preplanning and a slow cooker. The day before, rub the meat lightly with kosher salt and black pepper. Wrap in plastic and refrigerate. On the day you are going to cook the roast, heat a little olive oil in a large skillet and fry the garlic until golden, then remove it from the pan. Turn the heat up to medium high and when the pan is very hot, add the pork roast and brown until it's very dark on all sides. It helps if you cut the pork into pieces first. Don't worry about the meat drying out—it will reabsorb all its moisture and more. Crack the allspice and fry it, along with the red pepper, with the pork just as it's finishing browning. Add everything to the slow cooker and cook for 10 hours on low or 5–6 hours on high.

Turn the page for a preview of
Grace Carroll's next Accessory Mystery . . .

24-Karat Killer

Coming soon from Berkley Prime Crime!

I'm not a native, but I do know one thing about San Francisco: the weather is as unpredictable as the people. Take that warm, cloudless September day when I was on my way to work wearing a pair of Bruno Magli Italian leather sandals. They were all the rage that spring and summer, and I still loved them because they worked with either a pair of jeans or a skirt. No matter what else you were wearing, it looked like you made an effort because of those shoes. And believe me, I always made an effort. Not just because my job was selling clothes and accessories in a boutique, but just because that's the way I was, and still am.

I was on the Thirty Stockton bus in a bright jade blue flowy dress by Cladiana that could go from work to cocktails and a cream-colored Nicole Farhi linen blazer that gave it a daywear look, and was reading a depressing article in the *San Francisco Chronicle*, "Changing Weather Patterns

Spell Doom for Humanity." Suddenly the sky clouded over, and just as I got off the bus it started to rain, dampening my clothes and the chic fedora perched jauntily on my head. Talk about doom. Rain in September in everyone's favorite city? Not going to happen. But there it was.

When my boss, Dolce, saw me come through the door of the historic Victorian house she'd converted to a stylish shop, she said, "Rita, get out of those wet clothes. You'll catch your death. What were you thinking?" She shook her head. It wasn't really a lecture, not from Dolce. She was simply showing her concern and sympathy for me, the daughter she never had.

"Isn't it true," I asked, "that September, October and November are the best months in San Francisco weather-wise? 'Fall days are warm and sunny, nights are cool and clear.' That's what I heard before I moved here. What happened?" I asked, with a shiver as I tossed my damp hat toward a rack on the wall. "Can't be global warming."

Dolce shook her head but said nothing about the weather changes indicating the end for humanity. Maybe she hadn't read the paper (which I wished I hadn't) or she was in denial, which wasn't a bad place to be.

"Go put on something warm. You'll feel better." She waved an arm at the racks of fall clothes in earth tones and basic black hanging on racks in the large show room that used to be the salon of the grand old Victorian residence. Once upon a time in the mid-1800s, this Hayes Valley neighborhood was filled with even more of these beautiful homes, along with smaller houses for the craftsmen hired to build the mansions. Thankfully, the area was spared the fire that burned much of the city after the 1906 earthquake. But old houses are not always taken care of like this one; Dolce's

aunt who'd willed her this house had saved it from demoli-
tion, and Dolce had restored it to a bit of its former grandeur.
Her small well-appointed upstairs apartment above the shop
might have once been the servants' quarters.

I wondered if those old-timers wore black and earth tones
too? Or did they get tired of the same-old, same-old and
long for some warm fall days to break out the satin slippers
and their bright flirty Victorian dresses, if there were such
things? I sighed and went to pick out something that said
"fall" in the strict sense of the word, but the only word I
could think of was "dull."

Pawing through a shelf full of cashmere sweaters in
shades of eggshell, eggplant and ochre, I just couldn't get
excited about wearing such *blah* colors. I refused to let the
rain dampen my spirits the way it had my clothes. I had to
deal with the unpredictable nature of the weather and
the populace. Wearing a bright dress lifted my mood, but
was I pushing my luck by pushing my fashion sense to the
brink?

"Remember to mix it up," Dolce called from the jewelry
section where she was arranging a display of chains, huge
chunky rings, cuffs and leather bracelets. "Add some mohair
with brocade or popcorn knits. And tweeds with flat wool.
Instead of linen, why not try a tailored wool blazer with
padded shoulders?"

Why not? Because my shoulders didn't need any pad-
ding, but Dolce was my boss and she was usually right when
it came to fashion. That's what made things interesting, I
told myself. Different styles, different people, different sea-
sons and different weather.

It was so typical of Dolce to offer me anything in the shop
even though I couldn't really afford the haute couture she

sold. Either she gave me a huge employee discount or she just gave me things that were left over from the last season.

Dolce must have seen me dawdling indecisively because she said, "If you want to, you can just add leggings or a straight leg pant under the Alexander Wang botanical print dress on the rack. It offsets the graphic element, don't you think? And add a belt. Belts are in and very figure-flattering."

I guess everyone needs some figure-flattering, so I didn't take her suggestion personally. I chose a sand leather belt from Yves St. Laurent that went with the dress, a pair of dark leggings and Hunter Champray wedge boots and went to the dressing room to change my look from spring to fall. I hated to ditch my sandals, but I did keep my linen blazer.

Dolce gave me an approving thumbs-up when I came out. "That's better," she said. "I think we'll have a big crowd in today. Especially with this rain. It reminds everyone that they need to update their wardrobe for fall."

Which is just what she'd done for me. Updated my wardrobe with a new dress and a few special additions. I was warm and dry and even more stylish than when I'd arrived. Someday maybe I'd be the saleswoman Dolce was. Until then I'd work at it with her as my example and enjoy the ambience in the shop.

It was not only the ambience but the gossip I enjoyed. Usually. But today the conversation seemed a little less than stimulating. It went like this.

"Guess who was with Brianna LaRue at the Edwardian Ball? I'll give you a hint. It wasn't her husband," Tracy Livingston said to a small group of her "bffs" who were gathered at the accessory counter looking through a stack of our latest shipment of scarves in silk, chiffon and wool.

"They're done, over, kaput," Angela Boursin said, rubbing her hands together. "Everyone knows that."

"Does everyone know why?" Maxine Anderson asked eagerly.

The others stared at her Missoni sweater set she wore with pearls as if she had come from a different era. It was partly her dated outfit from last year's collection and partly her naiveté that earned her pitying looks and made her stand out from the in-crowd. And made me feel sorry for her. But what could I do to help her fit in except what I'd always done: make tactful suggestions. After that, customers had to make up their own minds. Not that I'm an advocate of "the customer is always right." Far from it. But all I can do is to give advice and fashion tips.

As a rule, our customers don't have jobs. Most of them spend their days doing charity work and having lunch and shopping, which is good for business. But Dolce wouldn't be the success she was if she didn't have a philosophy of treating everyone with respect, whether they're super rich or only extremely well-off. Whether their taste is impeccable or downright terrible, Dolce never misses a beat.

"Of course we know why they're breaking up," the ladies chorused.

Maxine was afraid to ask why, I could tell. She didn't have to. They told her anyway.

"She's having an affair with her Pilates coach."

I tried to look shocked, but I felt like I'd heard it all before. Socialites having affairs with their yoga guru or the swimming pool guy. And frankly I didn't care what they did after they left our shop.

For a moment I was afraid I was going crazy. Here I was folding sweaters, some chunky, some bulky and some belted while I shamelessly listened to empty gossip. Was this really what I should be doing with my life?

What was wrong with me? I had the world's greatest job and the world's greatest boss. I was wearing a dynamite outfit that everyone had noticed but . . . something was wrong. All I'd ever wanted was a dream job and some cutting-edge clothes to wear, but all of a sudden I wanted more. I wanted somewhere to go after work. And someone to go there with. In other words, I wanted a life.

I needed a place to wear the clothes besides to work and I needed a purpose and I needed a man in my life. I was spoiled. Since I'd come to San Francisco over a year ago I'd met three eligible men who'd taken me to all kinds of fun events. But I hadn't heard from any of them for months. That didn't help my outlook.

Instead of brooding about my sudden onset of angst, I took Maxine aside and asked her if I could help her find anything. I hoped she'd take my interest as it was intended and not as a knock on her personal lack of style. I was trying to make up for the others being so snarky.

She gave me a grateful little smile and said she was looking for a pair of wide-leg pants. It was a good sign that she was trying something new and trendy and I pulled out a few for her to try on.

"Do you like your job here?" she asked when she'd chosen a pair of MaxMara palazzo pants in a herringbone tweed that had a relaxed kind of cool and gave off a super casual vibe that I told her was new and different. I folded and wrapped them in tissue paper at the front desk.

"Oh, yes," I said. "We've got the latest in clothes, jewelry, hats and stockings all under one roof. What's not to like? I love fashion. But I also love to eat. I'm not much of a cook, so tonight after work I'm going to sign up for another class at Tante Yvette's Cooking School." I didn't usually confide in new customers about my other life, such as it was, but I wanted to say something to Maxine besides the usual. I sensed she didn't have many friends here. Not that I would ever be her friend. None of the customers were my friends. We came from different worlds. They were all older and richer and married and better connected than I was.

"I've heard of it," she said. "Someone recommended it to me. I've been meaning to go sign up for lessons from the celebrity chef, Guido Torcelli. He's only doing one class as a favor to the owner. As you probably know, he's Diana Van Sloat's personal chef. When she's in town, that is, and not filming commercials in Hollywood. She buys her clothes here, doesn't she?"

"Yes, she does," I said. "She's been Dolce's best client since forever. That's why he's usually too busy to do the classes. Diana has him on retainer," I explained. I'd never met the rich and gorgeous Diana Van Sloat, but I'd heard plenty about her during my time as Dolce's salesgirl.

"Well, have fun," she said.

At the end of the day I spoke to Dolce about my lack of a social life before I left. I didn't plan on it, it just slipped out. I didn't complain, I didn't whine. I just mentioned my single status with what I hoped was a rueful smile. But being the sensitive person she is, she picked up on my anxiety. She frowned, carefully knotted a Ballantyne print scarf around her neck and waved me into her office, once a former closet. I sat down opposite her desk and she rested her elbows on her desk and looked at me.

"The last I heard you were seeing three different men. One was a doctor," she said. "What happened?"

"Good question," I said. "Dr. Jonathan works nights in the ER, and when he's not working, he's surfing, which doesn't leave much time for dates. Unless he's seeing one of those attractive nurses at the hospital. Which I couldn't blame him for. They have so much in common and there's the proximity of course." I tried to sound like I was understanding of his professional responsibilities and okay with them, but it hurt to think of him out on the town without me. Naturally I wanted the best for him—a fulfilling and rewarding job healing the sick and wounded, and a lively social life as well. But why couldn't his social life include me? Wasn't I lively enough? Compared to a kind, caring and selfless nurse, maybe a clerk in a boutique didn't measure up.

"Isn't there a way you could run into him the way you first did when you fell off that ladder and had to be taken to the hospital?"

"You mean like have another accident or come down with some rare disease? It's possible but it would have to be something severe and sudden because that's the kind of cases he sees in the ER. I just can't count on that happening again." I gnawed on a fingernail while I tried to think of some plausible reason to drop in at the hospital. "When I had the accident with the ladder, I was only unconscious for a short time, and when I came to in the hospital, there was Jonathan. Talk about luck."

Dolce nodded and moved on to candidate number two. "What about Nick the Romanian gymnast you met on the plane, the one with the crazy aunt?"

"The last I heard he was recovering from a sprain he incurred at work. He's probably training some students on the uneven bars for the Olympics. As for his Aunt Meera, she scares me. I know she's not really a vampire as she claims, but she's definitely weird."

"And that very attractive cop whom you helped solve the murder of our dear Vienna?"

"You mean Detective Wall. I don't think he'd appreciate your framing our relationship that way."

"However he frames it, he can't deny you risked your life on the high seas to trap that murderer into confessing."

"I only did what anyone would have done," I said modestly. Though it was possible that no one else but me would have plunged into the cold waters of the Bay just to solve a murder.

"It's a shame Bobbi couldn't have been brought to justice before she drowned out there," Dolce said.

"On the other hand, it saved the city a lot of money from a big murder trial," I said. "I have to say that Detective Wall finally reluctantly agreed that I'd tried to help him, but not that I'd succeeded. He got assigned to the Central Station, so he doesn't hang out in our neighborhood anymore except when there's a major crime. I certainly wouldn't mind running into him, but he disapproves when I butt into his cases. It seems the only time he wants to see me is when I'm involved in a murder as a suspect. That's when he calls and comes by and tries to get me to confess, especially if he thinks I'm guilty. What are the chances of that happening again? I mean really." I laughed lightly, although I'm aware that murder is no laughing matter, especially when the victim is someone you know.

"So that's what we need to do, stir up some excitement, shake things up a little," Dolce said, her eyes gleaming with anticipation. "Think up a reason to see the doctor and/or the gymnast and then we have to encourage our friend the detective to come around too."

I wasn't sure if she meant we should try to have another murder occur on the premises or just a minor infraction like a parking ticket so I could get another chance to romance an officer of the law. Surely that's not what she meant. I couldn't believe she'd even suggest such a thing. Maybe I shouldn't have confided in her about my ridiculously small problems. Now she felt she had to do something about them. Something I might not want to be a part of. Like getting sick or breaking the law. On the other hand, if I got desperate . . .

Not long ago she'd had to cope with the death of Vienna, her treasured employee. Dolce seemed to have finally bounced back to normal while I was moping around complaining about a trivial matter like no men in my life. Of course I said nothing about being bored at work or that I was irritated by the shallow nature of the customers.

I wondered if Dolce meant that of the three men who passed in and out of my life, she preferred the doctor, since he was the first one she'd asked about. If she did prefer him, she wouldn't say. Just in case I ended up with one of the others. At the moment it looked like I'd end up alone. But enough of this gloom and doom.

"Any plans for tonight?" Dolce asked hopefully.

I couldn't bear to say no, so I told her I was going back to my former cooking school.

"I plan to sign up for another class from Guido if he's still teaching. He's the celebrity chef at the school and a dynamite teacher. The thing is I really need to learn my way around the kitchen." Even though my kitchen was so tiny I could stand in the center and reach the stove and the fridge, as well as the sink, telling Dolce my plan made it more likely that I'd follow through with it. Because the next day she was sure to ask how it went. I couldn't say I'd flaked out and hadn't gone. She'd be disappointed in me, and I needed to have a little pressure on me or I'd slip back into my old lazy ways.

I could have said I was going swimming at my health club or shopping at the Marina Safeway, where the produce department was a well-known hook-up spot, or attending a speed-dating party, but I'd save those activities for another night.

"I'm looking forward to another delicious dinner at your house," she said.

"As soon as I get a few more lessons under my belt I'll have you and William over to dinner again," I promised. I was good at promising things and then panicking when it came down to the wire. But how do you try something new if you don't step out of your comfort zone? Easy for me to say, but harder to do.

I didn't know if Dolce was still seeing William Hemlock, a dashing retired airline pilot she'd met at a society benefit. I sincerely hoped she still was, though she hadn't said anything about him lately. We had a few unwritten rules, my boss and I. One was that we didn't criticize the men in the other person's life, and two was that we never said "I told you so" when things went wrong. Even though Dolce felt comfortable asking about my social life, I didn't want to ask her about William in case the news was bad or there just wasn't any news at all.

Before I left, Dolce took a look outside the bay windows of the Great Room and said I should keep the clothes I was wearing, seeing that the weather appeared to be cool and gusty out there, but no rain. Then she hugged me and told me to have a good time at cooking school.

"You too," I said. "Have a nice evening." I waited for her to say something like, "I'm going to William's house for a cozy cheese fondue dinner," or "I'm going to meet his overly possessive grown children at last to see if they approve of me," but she didn't say anything about herself. Instead she turned to me.

"I'm worried about you, Rita," she said, holding me by the shoulders and looking at me with a concerned frown.

"Who me?" I said raising my eyebrows. As if that was a crazy idea. I was fine. Really I was.

"You didn't seem yourself today, even Frieda Young noticed it when you showed her a bow blouse when she wanted a sweater. She thought you seemed distracted."

I almost said "Who me?" again but I bit my tongue. "I'm sorry about that. I got off to a bad start today, you know, with the rain and all, and I never readjusted. I'll be fine tomorrow." I tried to smile, but my mouth just wouldn't cooperate.

"It's clear to me what's wrong with you," she said.

"Oh?" I said. Dolce is very perceptive, and I was afraid she had cottoned to how I was feeling disillusioned about my job, the customers and life in general.

"No murders, no mysteries for you to solve. No police cars outside, no yellow tape around the place. No investigations and no handsome detective hanging around either. This is what you've gotten hooked on. Without the excitement of a puzzle to solve, you're bored, Rita. I knew there was something wrong. I could tell."

"Me bored? Not at all," I insisted. I shook my head to

indicate what an absurd idea that was. As if I wanted someone else I knew to be murdered here at the shop or at their
home. As if I enjoyed being hauled down to the police station to answer questions no matter how sexy the detective
was. I always thought that Dolce was always right. But not
this time. If I secretly longed for another murder on our
doorstep, I'd know it, wouldn't I?

Truth can be deadlier than fiction . . .

ELLERY ADAMS

The Last Word

A BOOKS BY THE BAY MYSTERY

Olivia Limoges and the Bayside Book Writers are excited about Oyster Bay's newest resident: bestselling novelist Nick Plumley, who's come to work on his next book. But when Olivia stops by Plumley's rental she finds that he's been strangled to death. Her instincts tell her that something from the past came back to haunt him, but she never expects that the investigation could spell doom for one of her dearest friends . . .

**"Visit Oyster Bay and you'll long
to return again and again."**
—Lorna Barrett, *New York Times* bestselling author

facebook.com/TheCrimeSceneBooks
penguin.com